Omen Operation

The Isolation Series, Book One

By Taylor Brooke

Omen Operation

Limitless Publishing, LLC
Kailua, HI 96734
www.limitlesspublishing.com

Formatting: Limitless Publishing

ISBN-13: 978-1-68058-465-3
ISBN-10: 1-68058-465-0

Dedications

To my parents, thank you for nurturing my creativity and embracing my peculiarities, for teaching me to jump if I want to fly and being there to catch me if I fall.

To Matt, my best friend and brother, thank you for believing in what this book could be, for taking the time to read it first, and for encouraging me to believe in it too.

Chapter One

Flames chewed on a pile of logs in the middle of a large fire pit. Five faces sat around it, huddled together for warmth. Brooklyn always sat closest, palms outstretched and glowing against the flames. Somehow, the idea of burning wood made things feel more temporary—even if every night it reminded her of making s'mores on the beach back home and how the air tasted like salt in San Diego.

Home seemed so distant now.

The grounds had an array of fire pits scattered between the housing cabins that coaxed the fifteen inhabitants of ISO Recovery Camp Number Eleven to spread out amongst themselves and unwind.

"Hey, is your hand okay?" Gabriel's soft voice purred up at her.

Brooklyn turned her gaze to Gabriel, who was lying in her lap. Her eyes reminded Brooklyn of something out of a comic book. They were green like jungle canopies, sharp and defined by dark lashes and thick brows. The day the tall blonde had been dropped off at the camp had been the first day

Brooklyn hadn't felt alone. That day, a year and seven months ago, she'd found it a little easier to be brave.

"It's fine," Brooklyn answered. She lifted one shoulder into a shrug. "I just tweaked it when we were training."

The plush of Gabriel's bottom lip was shadowed by a small scar on the right side of her smile. It was hardly noticeable, a tiny defect on a face that could grace the cover of magazines. Maybe in another life, Brooklyn thought.

Black combat boots shifted on the other side of the circle. Dawson, a boy with a hard jawline, tilted his head to the side. He wore bitterness like some kind of badge and lifted his chin to peer over the fire at Gabriel. "You're too strong for your own good, girly."

Brooklyn sighed.

Gabriel grinned. "Well, wouldn't you know? I had you tapped out in under a minute yesterday, didn't I Dawson?"

His lips twitched upright. Smiling suited him.

"You did…" He held his hands against his chest in mock surrender. "Maybe you should take it easy on us."

Two others sat beside them on either side; one was a boy with black tunnels set snugly in the stretched lobes of his ears and a stud buried in the middle of his tongue. His smile was wide and contagious, set neatly on a narrow face with high cheek bones. His name was Julian; he had been the first to introduce himself to Brooklyn when she had arrived.

It was easy to remember. He had had the sun in his eyes, and the first thing he had said to her was "I don't know where the hell we are, but apparently we're not gonna die." He laughed through his words, showed her around, and didn't pretend to have any answers. His uncertainty was refreshing.

Brooklyn swayed when the last of their small pack nudged his head against her shoulder.

"You should let me wrap it up for you in case it's sprained," Porter said.

"I'm fine," Brooklyn stressed.

Porter leered at her over the black rimmed glasses that rested on the tip of his nose. "Suit yourself," he muttered playfully, reaching under his beanie to scratch the back of his head.

The stars were abundant and utterly uncomplicated against the black sheet of night. They glowed, shining bright and commanding attention. The sky, vast and constant, seemed so much more alive compared to back home. Brooklyn rolled her lips together, her gaze settled on the constellations resting low behind the trees that lined the outskirts of the camp and curved over the peak of a distant mountain. If there was one thing the occupants of Cabin A could all agree on, it was the beauty of this place.

The shrill squeal of a whistle coaxed them to their feet and into their cabin, a rural excuse for a home away from home. It reminded Brooklyn of the science camp she had been shipped off to during sixth grade. Three sets of bunks made up their living quarters. To the right through a doorway was an adjoined bathroom. To the left was a closet filled with boots and coats. The scratch of cheap sheets and a heavy comforter kept the cold at bay.

They said goodnight to each other in hushed whispers that accompanied the click of each lamp on their nightstands. Brooklyn fell asleep to the sound of the bed squeaking above her under the weight of Gabriel's hips and the hum of Julian's soft snores from across the room.

When she closed her eyes, she hoped for peacefulness. For nothing.

But the same memories played like an old reel of film when Brooklyn slept.

It happened on the day of Winter Formal. Senior year.

"Honey, I really think you should go with the black shoes." Her mother, a woman with dark chestnut hair and loving eyes, pushed a bobby pin into the tight bun on the top of Brooklyn's head.

"Aw, Mom, you don't like the red?" Brooklyn whined and kicked her foot up over her leg to show the glittered firetruck red pumps wrapped around her ankles.

Her mother's hands brushed down the sides of her neck and rested on her shoulders. *"They're a little flashy—that's all—but..."* She paused, adjusting the dainty silver chain around Brooklyn's neck. *"Let's get a good look at you."*

Brooklyn gazed in the mirror and felt the rush of that evening pass by. Her mother telling her how beautiful she was echoed like something long forgotten being washed ashore on an unfamiliar beach. Her father's smile when he had pleaded for *one last photograph was a stain on the inside of her eyelids. One hand on the window, she looked over her shoulder after climbing into the car with the rest of her friends. She glanced back as the view of her parents standing in the driveway shrank in the distance.*

They were on their way to dinner. Brooklyn's hands swayed above her head as she sang along to a song on the radio. The music couldn't muffle the sound that cut her short.

The scream was ear-splitting, something she never thought she would be subjected to hearing. A terrifying, shrill, broken sound. The kind that rattled the nerve endings on the back of her neck and made goose-bumps rise over her forearms. Brooklyn held her breath.

Someone said, "what was that?" and no one knew how to answer.

The girl sitting next to Brooklyn told them to keep driving. Told them to ignore it.

Another horrible wail. A scream for help. The sound of something heavy hitting the ground.

"Pull over," Brooklyn breathed, sitting up to look at the driver. Her hands shook. "Pull over!" The tires screeched when they stopped along the sidewalk.

The driver, a boy with shaggy brown hair, reached for her arm when she hopped out of the black Jeep.

What happened after that was blurry. Jagged. The sounds melted into a soundtrack. Her friends, their voices a constant loop overlapping the click of her heels against the concrete, of her lungs expanding around a gasp.

The woman screaming for help was on the ground. What stood over her was something Brooklyn still didn't completely understand. It was long and lean with dark hair that hung in a matted mess to its elbows, wearing all black with no shoes. It was a woman, she thought, whose hands visibly shook, eyes bulging from its skull. Something was wrong, terribly wrong.

"Are you okay?" Brooklyn asked.

The creature twitched, jaw snapping shut, teeth chattering together. Long fingers stretched out, knuckles clenching and popping.

Liquid ran out of its nose, dark and thick. Brooklyn thought it was blood, but she couldn't get any closer.

The sound that thing made when it hunched over and opened its mouth was something Brooklyn would never forget. A guttural howl. A desperate, high-pitched, angry scream that sounded as insane and rabid as the look in the wide protrusion of its eyes.

Brooklyn ran. She ran as fast as she could into the neighborhood at the opposite end of the street. She swatted at the tears that sprung past her eyes. Footsteps behind her beat hard against the asphalt.

A house with a dark copper door had their garage open. She didn't hesitate to run inside, hoping her feet could carry her fast enough.

It was hard to make decisions, to think clearly. Emotions spiraled around her. Everything she'd been taught, every emergency drill in school, all of it hurled toward her like an oncoming train. One *moment, she was reaching for her phone to call for help—the next, she was dialing her mom's cell. She tripped, skidded against the tile, found herself in a stranger's kitchen, and sank down behind the marble island in front of the sink. One of her hands shuffled through the drawers to her left and right until she found something sharp and cold. It was a serrated knife used for cutting bread.*

The sound of her heartbeat was the only thing she could focus on. She held a trembling hand over her mouth to muffle her breathing.

She heard the press of feet against the ground on the other side of the breakfast bar and labored breathing that sounded like it was being funneled through liquid, soupy and drowned. She swore she could even hear teeth being smashed together. She could hear it hum. She could hear it laugh.

"Babbling brook, babbling brook, babbling brook," it stuttered loudly, tongue crisp against the words, spat and hissed like something vile.

Brooklyn wanted to cover her ears. She wanted to close her eyes.

The creature turned quickly on its heels, a pot clattered against the floor. Brooklyn yelped a nervous hiccup and panicked. She thrashed against the sudden grip of sweat-slicked hands around her ankles and black, crusted fingernails scraping her skin.

Brooklyn thought she'd been mistaken, but up close, it still resembled a woman. Same bone structure. Pale skin. Flared nostrils. A wide open mouth revealing rows of blunt human teeth. But something oozed out of the corner of its eye, black like tar, and it stained the sunken space between its cheek and jaw. It dripped from its nose, painted the inside of cracked lips, and bled from its gums. The veins on its neck and shoulders were like splintered charcoal spider webs, bruised and broken shadows pressed under its skin.

Its teeth snapped together, jaw clenching and unclenching as it reached forward with one hand, gangly arm flailing and prominent bones cracking as it twisted around, possessed, unreal...sick.

Brooklyn didn't comprehend her reaction, but something inside her was convinced it was her only option. Fight or flight. Live or die. Kill or be killed. She didn't know what drove her to do it, but Brooklyn gripped the handle of the knife and shoved the blade through the creature's mandible into the roof of its mouth. A disgusting crunch was heard, followed by the slick slide of metal slicing through skin. Bile filled the back of Brooklyn's throat.

Coagulated blood and black secretion stained the low neck of her strapless cream dress. Her phone was smashed, the glass front shattered on the tile floor. She shoved the heavy body of whatever that thing was off of herself.

Brooklyn tried to stand, but her knees buckled. She crawled away, kicking back against the limp body slumped in the corner of the kitchen while her satin dress slid against the ground.

It hurt, the tight constriction of her chest trying to gather each breath in. She was confused, battling shock and fear. She wanted to lift herself up and run, to carry herself back home so she could dive under the protection of her father's arms and her mother's reassurance.

It repeated itself, the same memory from start to finish.

While the sound of shouting droned numbly in her ears from the doorway of the garage, Brooklyn could still hear the song that was playing in her friend's car, her mother's voice as she fiddled with the necklace that was now in shambles on the kitchen floor, and her father's gentle "be careful" as he slid the baby pink lily corsage onto her wrist.

Hands wrapped in blue rubber gripped her shoulders. Brooklyn felt her legs buck and kick.

Don't touch me. Don't touch me. Don't touch me.

The words never left her lips, but they bounced off the walls of her mind in different octaves.

"Have you been hurt? What is your name? There has been an emergency isolation operation set in place. We are taking you somewhere safe. What is your name?"

"Don't touch me!" Brooklyn gasped.

"Brooklyn!"

Wide eyes stared down at her. Calloused palms held her shoulders against the bed.

"It's me." Porter swallowed uncomfortably. His hands drifted away as he craned his neck, shying from the small blade pressed against the middle of his throat. "You were dreaming. It's all right. It's me."

Brooklyn's heart raced. Her fingers trembled around the handle of the small pocket knife.

Porter's eyes were gentle and soft in the

darkness. He carefully reached up, touching the inside of her wrist. "Come on, put that down. You're okay."

The nightmares came and went. They had happened every night for the first few months and still snuck up on her when she closed her eyes. Once a week at least. Sometimes twice.

"I'm sorry," Brooklyn croaked as her fingers went slack. She allowed Porter to take the knife and set it down on the nightstand. "I didn't mean to…"

"Don't apologize," he said, voice just above a whisper. "Just go back to sleep. I'm right here." He pointed to the lower bunk a few feet away. "Open your eyes if you're scared, and throw something at me. I'll come right over."

She swatted him when he grinned.

Porter moved back to his own bed. Brooklyn inhaled a long, drawn-out breath, easing her heart into a regular rhythm.

A slender arm hung down over the edge of the bed above her, and Gabriel snapped her fingers, lavender nail polish shining in the darkness.

Brooklyn reached out and took her hand.

"You okay, Brookie?" Gabriel's voice was raw with sleep.

Brooklyn squeezed Gabriel's hand and closed her eyes.

Chapter Two

The door of the cabin swung open, and sunlight poured in over the floor boards straight onto Brooklyn's face. She scrunched her nose and smashed her cheek against the pillow, groaning as heavy hiking boots kicked the side of her bunk.

"Come on, sleeping beauties. I let you have an extra twenty minutes. Now it's time to get up," a woman with short platinum hair said as she stomped around the cabin.

Brooklyn's eyes cracked open. Her lips parted into a wide yawn. It was still surreal waking up in a world without the daily news or an up-to-date magazine to read. No celebrity gossip to catch up on. No Super Bowl halftime show to watch. Life seemed incredibly empty when it lacked the option to focus on the things going on around the world. Brooklyn even yearned for school, and a structured education was one of the major things most of them never thought they would miss.

The people in the camp were all fairly young. Most had been going to college when the outbreak

11

happened. Some, like Brooklyn and Gabriel, were in their last years of high school.

Terry was the camp supervisor, the eyes and ears of the outside. She'd been a nurse before the government had recruited her to help with the recovery lodges set up around the country. Whenever someone asked where exactly they were, what was happening, or why, she answered with vague, scripted lines.

You're safe, and you'll be back with your families soon.

The virus is contained but has to burn itself out before we can return to a life of normalcy.

You have everything you need.

I am here to keep you safe.

Terry curled her fingers into a fist and knocked on the edge of Brooklyn's bed.

"Up," Terry shouted, "and running in ten minutes. Don't be late for breakfast."

Strands of dusty brown hair fell in front of Brooklyn's eyes. She huffed, toes curling when she stretched her legs out and lifted her arms up over her head. She rolled both her wrists and then her ankles, flexed her hands, and sighed. Another morning in remote nowhere. Another day waiting to be notified of their clearance to dispatch. Another day waiting to go home.

Home was different for everyone besides Gabriel and Brooklyn, seeing as they happened to live in the same city.

Gabriel had been on pep squad, while Brooklyn had preferred soccer, and though they'd crossed paths a handful of times, neither one had ever

12

introduced themselves to the other. Gabriel had been a junior when Brooklyn had been a senior. They were like ghosts haunting different parts of the school, sharing brief nods and a friendly "hello" on occasion.

It had been four weeks after the initial outbreak in southern California when a gunmetal truck had dropped Gabriel off. Three days after Brooklyn had arrived. The younger looked scared, lost, and just like everyone else, she had raked her gaze across the grounds in search of anything relatively familiar. Brooklyn, shy and reclusive, had waved. Gabriel's eyes had widened.

"Hey, I know you, right?" was all Gabriel had said, and halfway through the question, she had linked her arm around Brooklyn's elbow.

It seemed so long ago.

"Mornin'," Porter said, clearing his throat.

Brooklyn turned over on her side to face him, glancing briefly at the knife on the night stand. "Morning…"

Porter had been going to med school before he'd landed himself in the camp. Lucky for them, he had ways to pull strings and get certain luxuries that other camps didn't. He had an *in*; someone in his family apparently was a main supervisor for the program, and he did his best to appeal to his comrades in Cabin A. Nail polish, literature, snacks, and sometimes a beer or two were thrown their way from the stock that Terry got off the provisions truck every month.

Small things like a book and a bag of Skittles made life a little more manageable.

"How's that hand?" he asked, nudging his jaw forward before he sat up and slid his glasses on.

"Seems fine." Brooklyn shrugged and stretched out all her fingers, quirked her wrist to one side and then to the other.

Porter nodded as he ran his fingers through the front of his short, dark locks, askew from restless sleep.

Julian pawed at his eyes with the back of his hands and stumbled toward the communal wash room at the end of the cabin.

"It's guys' turn to shower first. You might wanna wake her up," Julian said to Brooklyn, waving lazily at Gabriel, who was hiding under her comforter.

It took a couple shoves, a few aggravated shouts, and finally a promise of her choice of juice at breakfast for Brooklyn to coax Gabriel out of her nightly hibernation. Once awake, they brushed their teeth.

Brooklyn looked at herself in the mirror as she washed the foam of the standard mint toothpaste out of the sink and tied her shoulder length hair into a ponytail. Her face was smooth, tanned from being outside even if the sun hardly made an appearance. She rolled her small, thin lips, and stared at the flecks of gold hidden inside raindrop shaped eyes. *You've got Saturn's rings in your eyes.* That's what her mother always said. She didn't like looking at her own reflection anymore. Even though training in the camp had made her body stronger, Brooklyn missed her makeup bag and soccer cleats.

Gabriel shouted for her from the front of the

cabin, prompting her to strap on her running shoes, throw on sweatpants, and then run out the door.

The dew on long strands of wild grass slid against Brooklyn's ankles, and the sun tried its best to break through the heavy mist settled over the ravine where the camp resided. One of the fire pits still smoldered on the back side of the smallest cabin, and they watched a few other campers complete their morning runs around the edge of the territory. There weren't any serious markers, just the outline of trees on all sides of them besides a dirt road that led out to a highway. They were secluded and, as Terry always liked to remind them, *safe*.

The cushion of Gabriel's hip bumped into Brooklyn's as they ran. "You think I should move to L.A. after all this? I mean, that's probably where all the best cosmetology schools are, huh?"

Brooklyn nodded. "Yeah, that's where I would start if I were you. You still sure about doing the hair and makeup thing? It's a pretty cutthroat business."

Pretty green eyes rolled, and Gabriel swung her head back to laugh, long golden pony tail tapping her lower back as she trotted ahead.

Sometimes Brooklyn forgot that cutthroat was Gabriel's middle name.

The morning went by like any other. The dining hall smelled like egg whites and protein pancakes, tangy grapefruits, and sugar-free maple syrup. They took the time during meals to make bets on which of them would hit their target first at mid-day firing practice. Then they chatted about the outside world, camp gossip, so on. At the end of breakfast, Julian popped the traditional question that they all took turns answering:

"If you could be anywhere else, doing anything else, where would you be, and what would you be doing?"

Dawson shrugged. "Probably eating real food." He wrinkled his nose at the scraps on his plate. "Somewhere warm with someone pretty."

Gabriel smiled down at the table. "I'd be on a plane, drinking champagne, on my way to Paris for fashion week."

"Oh, that's a good one," Julian said.

Porter hummed and drummed his fingers against a glass of guava juice. "In Aspen, snowboarding with my dad, drinking Irish coffee."

Everyone's eyes turned to Brooklyn, and she rolled her bottom lip between her teeth.

It was hard to focus on one place when so many were calling her name. The city streets of New York, the white sand beaches of Fiji, the distant Indonesian temples of Bali, they swarmed her thoughts and lit up like a fluorescent string of Christmas lights deep behind the rest of her thoughts.

"I, uh, I mean, I don't know," she stammered. "I guess…" The tip of her tongue darted out to wet her lips.

"Oh, come on, something has to sound good!" Gabriel said.

Brooklyn sighed, shoulders slumping as she closed her eyes. "*Sushi*," she moaned through a small laugh. "I want to be eating fresh sushi at a little bar in Tokyo."

Julian smiled wide and nodded in agreement. "Well, if you can't make it to Japan, you're always welcome at my mom's place." He leaned on the back legs of his chair. "She's the best sushi chef in the city of angels, if you ask me."

"I always forget you live in L.A.," Gabriel said. "I'll have to find you and crash on your couch when I finally get up there for school."

"You're more than welcome," Julian said. "But only if you use me as your canvas and teach me how to make my own fake elf ears and shit."

Gabriel arched a brow. "Deal."

They practiced shooting after that, which Terry said was for their collective safety.

"Everyone should know how to shoot a gun," Brooklyn mocked, irritated and tired of the snap, thrust, and pull every time she tapped the trigger on the handgun that was assigned to her.

Two hands pressed against her wrists and strong arms bracketed over her shoulders. "Like this."

Porter had constellations of moles dusted along his clavicle and up over his neck, little splatter marks that stained him from the sun. Brooklyn had a strange habit of trying to count them when he was close to her.

"It's a big gun," he said, angling her hands and squeezing the top of her knuckles. "So it has a kick. That's why you have to adjust your grip."

"Why'd she give me the Judge? I asked for the .22," Brooklyn said, ignoring the press of Porter's chest against her back.

"I don't know. But it's not like you need a gun

17

anyways."

Brooklyn could feel him smiling and pulled the trigger.

The sound splintered the sky. Porter winced, bouncing on one foot as he pointed with his thumb toward the other side of the field where Gabriel stood with her shoulders squared, a desert eagle clutched between her hands.

"See! Better! Now let's see if blondie's as good with that as she is with an AR," Porter said.

They walked together toward the other targets. Brooklyn smiled, watching Gabriel adjust her stance. "How's it going over here?"

Gabriel sighed, one eye closed as she tilted her head, staring at the target. "Shitty. I feel off balance."

"Both eyes open," Dawson said, standing a few feet away.

"They always close one eye in the movies. I never understood why." She turned to look at him, gaze traveling down where his arms were folded across his chest.

"It's more dramatic," he answered with a shrug. "Now hurry up and shoot."

Pale pink lips curved up. "At breakfast, you said you wanted to be somewhere warm with someone pretty." She focused on the vibrant color of his eyes, glacier blue like the syrup at the bottom of a snow cone. "Do you think I'm pretty?"

Julian watched as he sat on a large log and tugged one of his ear plugs out so he could properly eavesdrop. Brooklyn took a seat next to him, and he smirked, eyes drifting back to where Dawson was currently put under the stress of a very tricky question from a very tricky girl.

"I think you're dangerous," Dawson said quietly, almost too quiet for the rest of them to hear.

Gabriel grinned, her gaze still wrapped around the smug expression Dawson wore. She lifted the gun with one hand. "I'm flattered."

She pulled the trigger, and Porter winced, covering his ears from the blast.

"Damn." Julian craned his neck to see the target at the base line of the trees now split down the middle. "Gabriel wins."

Whoever won in firearms had the privilege of picking dessert.

Terry's whistle was their queue to take a break. Hydrate. Stretch. Relax.

The rest of the afternoon was spent doing endurance drills and combat simulations.

Brooklyn was quick and ruthless when it came to hand to hand. She was always ready to engage, and her unpredictability gave her an upper hand in most cases.

Julian was the first to spar with her. After she dodged two fast jabs and a roundhouse kick, she swiped his legs out from underneath him, pressing her foot down across his chest.

"Down one," she breathed, yelping when he knocked her back with his knee.

He was quick to rise and twisted her arm back. He bent her forward until she hissed for him to release.

"Up one," Julian corrected. "Try to slow down."

Brooklyn nodded and stood, rubbing her index

finger and thumb together before launching forward again. She slid down around his knees as Julian aimed another jab at her and knocked him to the ground, snatching his wrist and folding it up behind his back.

"Down two," Brooklyn said.

It was Dawson and Porter after that. They switched partners, one right after the other until the score was tallied.

"It's a tie," Gabriel said. "Porter and Brooklyn."

"Tiebreaker for the side dish?" Dawson asked.

The sun was starting to set, and Terry's whistle sounded from the dining hall.

"No time, but I do want mashed potatoes tonight." Porter shrugged, glancing at Brooklyn.

Brooklyn grinned. "Good, me too."

"See? We don't even need a tiebreaker," Porter said, shoulder bumping into Brooklyn's as he walked by. "She gets me."

Gabriel appeared at her side, cat eyes narrowed playfully from under her lashes.

Brooklyn told her to be quiet before she had a chance to say anything.

Julian glanced over his shoulder as they all trudged through the grass toward the dining hall. She followed his stare and found what he'd caught sight of, Dawson's muscular frame slinking around Terry's small, secluded lodge near the front of the grounds.

"What's he doing?" Julian mumbled. He linked his arm through Brooklyn's as they walked.

Brooklyn glanced over her shoulder again, watching closely. "I don't know," she said softly.

Dawson's silhouette disappeared behind the cabin's front door, and Brooklyn looked away.

Something didn't feel right.

But nothing ever felt right anymore.

Chapter Three

Brooklyn held her breath as she curled further under her bed sheets. The floorboards dipped under the weight of footsteps. The five of them knew where to step in the night, the quiet paths to take so they didn't disturb the others.

Brooklyn knew that whoever was awake didn't want to be alone.

The first thing Brooklyn saw when she opened her eyes was Porter staring back at her from his bed a few feet away. His jaw was set hard, lips pursed into a tight line.

He glanced up, and Brooklyn followed the tiny flick of his lashes until she noticed that the bunk above him was empty.

She heard laces being tied and pants being tucked into the top of a pair of boots. A jacket, the slide of it against bare skin. A zipper.

"What're ya doin?" Gabriel slurred.

Brooklyn started to sit up when Gabriel swung her legs over the side of their bunk and let them dangle there. The shine of shell-pink polish glittered off her toenails.

"D," Gabriel whined, "what the hell are you doing?"

Dawson rolled the sleeves of his black jacket up and crouched down to pull a heavy duffle bag out from under their bed. Brooklyn held her breath when he looked over his shoulder and said, "We're leaving."

Julian was on his feet, reaching for the lights. Dawson snatched his arm. "Don't," he hissed. "Do not turn on the lights. Just get your stuff."

The thoughts that circulated through Brooklyn's mind were a mess of memories and warnings. They swarmed around Dawson's words, *we're leaving*, and she felt tightness in her chest that reminded her of what it was like to be vulnerable. To be scared. Because people like Dawson didn't make empty statements like *we're leaving* without reason. People like Dawson didn't run.

Gabriel said his name, "Dawson," like tires skidding to a stop on the asphalt, like an emergency break being pulled. "We can't just leave…there's nowhere for us to go."

"We can just leave, and we're going to. Tonight."

"We can't." Gabriel slid off the bed and took a couple quick steps toward him. "Everything's contaminated. Everything's gone. We can't…"

Dawson thrust a magazine against Gabriel's chest, which she fumbled to catch. Brooklyn watched as she analyzed the cover then the back, soft fingertips peeled open page after page. It was one of those glossy beauty magazines. A picture of a woman smiled on the cover and block words spelled out the headlines **"what makes her sexy"** and **"please your man this fall"**.

Dawson reached forward and pinched the spine of the magazine. Gabriel let him take it, and he shook it until a folded piece of paper fell at Gabriel's feet. She didn't move. She didn't breathe. Just stood, swaying slightly with her eyebrows pulled down toward the bridge of her nose.

"What…" Brooklyn picked it up off the ground. She glanced at Julian who was in front of the door with his arms crossed over his bare chest, silently asking for guidance. She didn't know how to do this; she didn't know how to keep Dawson from exploding.

"Read it," Dawson interrupted her mental plea for help. "Out loud."

Brooklyn wanted to snap at him, to tell him to calm down and not to bark at her, but the way his eyes moved, careful and nervous, made her reconsider scolding him.

It was a handwritten letter with a smudged signature decorating the bottom of lined notebook paper.

"We miss you," Brooklyn sighed out the words, eyes drifting over the first line before she continued. "Marly did well on her science project…" Her voice dropped lower, eyebrows pulled together as confusion started to spread like frostbite under her skin. "But she wishes you were here to help pick out her homecoming dress. She keeps asking where you are. This is getting too hard, Theresa…"

Brooklyn's hands started to tremble.

"My parents asked about you. They want us to fly out to Chicago for Christmas this year; will you be home by then? I love you." Brooklyn's voice trailed off. "Marly loves you. Please ask for some time off."

She paused before clearing her throat. "P.S they published my article in The Times. Hope you like the magazine. Marly picked it out."

The piece of crinkled paper felt unbelievably heavy in her hands. Her eyes followed the swoop of the curved "S" on the sender's name at the bottom of the page.

Gabriel's breath was shaky. Julian stared down at his feet.

Dawson kicked an empty duffle bag toward Porter. "There's a truck behind Terry's cabin, and the transport bus is on the other side of the field. The surplus trucks brought supplies and food yesterday that we'll stock up on before we take off." Stern blue eyes darted around from one person to the next.

"I don't..." Brooklyn heaved a sigh. "I don't think we should jump to conclusions."

"That letter," Dawson said, pointing down where Brooklyn had it clasped in her hand, "was sent from Seattle. Not from a 'recovery camp,' from *Seattle*."

Gabriel tossed the magazine on to the bed and shook her head, turning to stand next to Dawson. "It was published this month," she said bitterly.

That wasn't possible.

"They're lying to us," Dawson said, teeth grinding together as he spoke. "Terry and whoever brought us here."

25

"You sound paranoid and insane," Brooklyn said, eyes narrowed as she stood and waved her hand between them. "They've done nothing but take care of us!"

"Take care of us," Julian repeated. He turned his gaze from the floor and looked at her sadly, an unspoken apology for not taking her side. "By training us how to use military grade weapons?"

"You saw what the virus does to people," Brooklyn said, heart beating fast against her ribcage. "They have to train us so we can defend ourselves if there's ever another outbreak. It's standard."

Dawson shrugged and pointed toward the door. "Go on then. If you have so much faith in her, then go and ask Terry, I mean *Theresa*, if you can call your parents."

He challenged her with his eyes, jaw clenched. He gave a slow nod when she looked away.

"Yeah," he growled under his breath. "That's what I thought. Miss Theresa is allowed to hear from her family, but we're completely cut off from ours. It's been almost two years, but I bet it's just *standard*."

Brooklyn shoved past Gabriel and was busting through the door of their cabin before Dawson could finish the last sarcastic word. She couldn't defend something when everything he was saying made sense. She couldn't keep her friends under the safety of this camp if she didn't have some kind of leverage.

Brooklyn was scared, scared of the idea that perhaps Dawson was right and scared of the reality that something else was going on. The unknown had been so far away, a flicker of noise through the trees. Now it knocked feather-light and enticing against their lives. Against her life.

Julian stood in the doorway, his voice a hushed whisper calling her name as she barreled through cold wet grass and misty air toward the small lodge.

The fire pit was still smoldering.

The stars shone bright.

But the moon was hidden and cowered behind thick clouds.

Hesitation wasn't an option. When she reached the large wooden door, Brooklyn twisted the handle and tried to push forward. It was locked.

"Terry!" She didn't expect to sound so desperate. "It's Brooklyn!" Her knuckles rapped against the door. "Can you open the door please? I really…"

Brooklyn paused. Her neck craned forward to press against the splintered wooden panels. She wasn't one to lose her words in a fit of rage or to have them punched out of her by fear. But that sound, the click, click, roll, click was so familiar. The faint slow clicking pieced together an image stored away in Brooklyn's mind.

The image of a gun.

It sounded like wind when the bullet was fired, like a dart cutting through the air. It sliced right through the door, inches from the lock, and sank into the soft flesh stretched over Brooklyn's abdomen.

The pain came after the sound, after the sight of blood and the bewilderment. It came in slow waves. An ache and then a burn, lapping like the tide, pulled in and out with every breath she took.

Dawson was right.

One hand pressed hard over the small hole torn just shy of her belly button. Brooklyn took a step back, readied herself, and winced as she slammed her foot against the door. It swung open on its hinges. There on the other side of it was Terry with her gun, a long black silencer screwed on to the barrel.

"Stay where you are, Miss Harper," Terry said. She sounded different, guarded and controlled.

"What's going on?" Brooklyn gasped. She stumbled forward, her trembling hand slick with blood where she held it over her stomach.

"You were almost ready. They were making plans to have you transferred; you didn't even have two weeks left. But they'll find you, you know." Terry shook her head, a wry smile crossing over her face. "No matter what, they'll find you."

Brooklyn winced when a pair of hands gripped her hips, hauling her backward. She squirmed and yelped until a hand smashed over her mouth.

Porter pressed his lips against her ear. "Keep pressure on it."

"She shot me," Brooklyn breathed when Porter's hand slid away. "That bitch shot me…"

"I can see that," he sang matter-of-factly. She could practically hear him rolling his eyes.

Another bullet ricocheted off the edge of the doorway. Brooklyn huddled back against Porter's chest as they crouched down just a few inches away.

The sound of running matched the uneven

rhythm of Brooklyn's heartbeat. She closed her eyes until Gabriel's voice, shrill and filled with rage, cut through the heavy air around them.

"You shot her?" Gabriel squealed, leaping forward past Porter and Brooklyn through the open door of Terry's cabin. "*You shot her?*"

Brooklyn could make out the sound of Gabriel's foot, the thud of it connecting with the side of Terry's head, and the skip of the gun as it clattered against the ground.

Dawson followed behind her, offering a sympathetic glance down to Brooklyn as he stepped around them into the cabin. "Hold her," he said calmly.

Brooklyn wiggled in Porter's arms until he let her go. She crawled forward and held her breath, pain surging into her lower back. Her father had always said that it was impossible to look away from a train wreck. It was the truth. Because as she peered around the edge of the door, she saw Gabriel with her foot smashed between Terry's collarbones, and Dawson's hand wrapped around their camp supervisor's jaw, pushing her head back.

"They'll find you," Terry choked.

Brooklyn didn't look away when Dawson dragged the knife in a perfect line across Terry's throat.

Chapter Four

"I need to get the bullet out." Porter adjusted his glasses, leaving a smear of Brooklyn's blood on the bridge of his nose.

Julian nodded as he struggled to prop Brooklyn's arm over his shoulder so they could get her inside the cabin.

It felt like a hot piece of coal was charring her insides. Her entire abdomen ached, and pain shot down her legs, up her chest. Brooklyn gasped, whimpering when the two boys hauled her up and helped her walk through the doorway.

Terry's lifeless body was on the living room floor, a wide puddle of blood leaking out around her shoulders from the deep slash below her chin. Brooklyn was bitter that she hadn't been the one who'd killed her.

Gabriel turned on the lights. Dawson laid a blanket out on a small coffee table where they helped Brooklyn lie on her back.

Brooklyn kicked when Porter pressed his hand over her abdomen. "That h-hurts!"

Nimble fingers lifted the edge of her shirt up to expose the mangled, torn hole. Brooklyn tensed, constricting the wound, and went pale as she watched it cough out globs of dark blood.

"Okay," Porter breathed, unfastening his belt and handing it to Julian. "Put this in her mouth."

Julian winced, shifting nervously on his feet. He reached out and took the leather belt from Porter's hands. His eyes batted down to Brooklyn, who was glancing around like an animal looking for somewhere to hide.

Julian swallowed nervously. "You want me to..."

"Yep. That or you can let her bite your hand," Porter said, glaring at Julian, whose cheeks were frosted a deep red.

Brooklyn stammered, fighting with the words that all seemed to come out at once, "What are you doing? I...I'm fine, just—n-no, no, seriously Porter, is it that bad?"

"I need you to trust me." Eyes the color of whiskey watched her from behind the lenses of his glasses, and Porter nodded.

Gabriel's hands clenched down over her wrists. Brooklyn surged against them while her ankles were held tight by Dawson, who knelt down by her feet.

Julian whispered, "I'm sorry," before he slid the folded belt between her teeth.

Brooklyn trembled as she tried to avert her eyes, to find anything else to look at. Sweat beaded up on her temple. She couldn't tell if it was adrenaline or anxiety that leaked into her veins and burst out from her pores. None of that mattered when Porter's fingers dipped into the small open pocket on her hip. It felt like she was being gutted—like a rabbit being skinned for a pack of hungry wolves. The muscles below the surface of her skin clenched. Her back bowed off the cherry wood table.

Gabriel's grip tightened. Brooklyn could feel the sensation of her friend's thumb rubbing back and forth along the side of her wrist.

Tears burst from Brooklyn's eyes. She whined, loud gritted puffs of air tinged with sobs and muffled curses.

"Got it, got it, I got it," Porter rambled as he withdrew his fingers. He let the bullet drop to the floor.

Brooklyn's entire body was wracked with violent shakes. She tried to breathe, but the pain was a constant throb. The wound itself had a burning, fiery heartbeat that sent ripples of heat down into her left leg.

"Okay, hey." Porter hovered over Brooklyn, touching her tear-drenched cheek with his clean hand. "I'm almost done. It was shallow, so it'll heal up quickly, but, hey, c'mon, eyes open."

Three fingers tapped against her cheek. Brooklyn bit down hard on the belt still shoved between her top and bottom jaw. She jolted forward, forehead wrinkled as she snarled at him. If there was anything she didn't want, it was to have her eyes open. She didn't want to face the reality of the situation. She felt betrayed, used, bamboozled. Her eyes being open meant she had to feel something other than the pain in her hip.

Porter sighed. "You don't have to like me right now, but you have to listen to me."

"Are we cauterizing it?" Dawson asked.

Brooklyn snapped one of her legs loose, and swung a hard kick to Dawson's jaw.

Gabriel tightened her grip, seething down at Dawson. "Nice way to keep her calm, asshole."

"I was just asking!" Dawson blurted.

"No," Porter said quickly to Brooklyn. He gripped her cheek. "I'm not gonna cauterize it, I'm not gonna burn you. But I need to close it. You understand that? We're almost done, okay?"

Regret sank down into the pit of her stomach, and Brooklyn nodded quickly, craning her neck to look at Dawson who was rubbing his chin.

"I'm sorry," she slurred around the belt, shifting her leg to rest against his arm as he continued to hold her down. "I'm so sorry."

It was clear that she wasn't apologizing for kicking Dawson but rather for not listening to him in the first place.

Porter disappeared momentarily. He returned with a slender glass bottle and a small portable first-aid kit.

"If you continue to lose blood, you'll just get weaker," Porter said as he twisted the top off the bottle. "This will have to do."

"What about the medical unit in Cabin D?" Gabriel asked.

Porter shook his head. "That would be an option if we had the time."

Brooklyn arched her back and cried when the liquid cascaded down over the bullet hole. It stung worse than any burn, any cut, any injury had ever burned. The inside was the worst, where her flesh was raw and new. It screamed out through the rest of her body as it was drowned in top-shelf vodka.

The gentle stroke of Porter's palm along the curve of Brooklyn's side made her turn away and hide her face in the inked skin of Julian's bicep. She knew what a touch like that meant; it was an apology in advance. But being stitched up wasn't as bad as she anticipated.

Julian let the belt go and knelt down around her shoulders so he could cradle her head. She hid against his chest, closing her eyes. She squirmed every time Porter would scrape the needle against the burnt peaks of her injury. Gabriel released her hands and cooed ridiculous loving things at her while she brushed her hands along Brooklyn's face, removed the spit, sweat, and tears that Brooklyn couldn't help but be ashamed of.

Two hands gripped her ankles. Dawson rubbed his hands soothingly against her calves.

She didn't deserve to be cared for so efficiently after running headfirst into a dangerous situation. She should have trusted them. She should have listened.

"I'm done," Porter said quietly.

A piece of light gauze was taped over the now tightly stitched skin.

Brooklyn didn't want to move, but Julian stood up, which forced her to look at Porter, who leaned over her. He tried to smile, but it was broken and timid.

"Thank you," Brooklyn whispered.

Porter nodded.

The even rise and fall of her chest was enough to remind Brooklyn of their vulnerability. They were no longer safe.

They'd never been safe.

The heavy bounce of a shattered phone hit the ground next to the table.

"She wiped it," Dawson said as he ran his hand through his hair.

"Terry must have done it when she noticed that the letter was gone," Gabriel said.

Brooklyn laid her hand over the white patch on her stomach and wrinkled her nose. She lifted off the table, leaning into Portland's shoulder. The ache was dull and monotonous, but the injury would heal. Everything always healed. However, the bone-chilling impact of Terry's words, the pain from them would linger.

They'll find you

"Guys..." Julian's voice was crisp. It pulled the attention of the group toward the door, where he stood with his eyes focused on the outlines of bodies in the dark. "I think we need to explain."

A girl with long curly red hair stood in sweats and a baggy t-shirt next to a large group of other campers. Aquamarine eyes took in the scene in Terry's cabin. Stephanie tried to catch her breath, to suppress a scream.

"What...?" Stephanie swallowed, stepping forward. She had her hand outstretched behind her, signaling for the others to wait. "What happened?"

Dawson sighed through his nose and shook his head. "We don't know, Steph. But we're getting out of here."

Chapter Five

Julian found Terry's laptop in her bedroom. The screen blinked to life, revealing a picture of a man wearing a wide smile with a little girl climbing over his shoulders. Julian wanted to look away, but when he did, his gaze moved to Terry's body growing cold on the floor.

"We didn't have to kill her," he said to Porter who stood by his side.

"She shot Brooklyn," Porter said under his breath. "She would've killed all of us."

"How do you know that?"

"Just do."

"Don't you have a way to get a hold of your uncle or dad or whoever it is that always sent us shit? Shouldn't they know what's going on…?"

Porter tensed. "Terry was my bridge; she didn't like what I was doing, but she couldn't necessarily say no. I have no way of getting a hold of him unless you magically find a phone that isn't bricked."

Julian bit the inside of his cheek as he clicked

around the screen only to find that the laptop was just as useless as the phone. Terry was smart. Trained. She hadn't left them a scrap of information besides the notion that Seattle wasn't contaminated.

Brooklyn was propped against the wall. She watched Julian walk back into the living room, followed by Porter.

"No good," Julian said as he glanced over at Stephanie, who held her breath and stared down at the dead body in the middle of the floor.

Dawson cursed. "Well, then we head toward the highway and follow the signs toward Washington."

"Washington?" Gabriel asked.

"Seattle," Dawson clarified. "It's where the letter came from, which means it's where we need to go. If the city is clear, then we have a shot at getting answers."

Gabriel shook her head. "No," she said. "I wanna go home. I'm going back to California."

Dawson's irritation was prevalent. "We all want to go home, but we have to understand what's going on first."

"Whatever we do, we need to stay together," Porter chimed in.

"I'm. Going. Home." Gabriel dragged out each word. "We're all going home."

"I'm not going anywhere, actually," Stephanie blurted, shifting her weight back and forth on her heels. "I'm going to wait right here in this camp for the next recovery team to get here and transport us to a safe zone."

"There's no safe zone!" Dawson yelled. His voice boomed through the cabin, hands clenched into angry fists. Brooklyn looked down at the ground.

Dawson was probably right. In the end, they had to choose which risk they were willing to take. Should they take the risk that left them isolated in the camp, or should they head for the road? Should they run?

"There's no safe zone," Brooklyn repeated and felt all eyes turn toward her. "There's no one good coming for us. We have to go."

"*Home*," Gabriel added, "right Brookie? We're going back to San Diego. We're going…"

"We're going to worry about that when we find out if there is a home to go back to," Brooklyn said. "For now, we're with Dawson."

Dawson's cold, blue eyes darted around Brooklyn's face, and he gave a curt nod, stroking his short, sandy hair.

"Come with us," Julian said to Stephanie, who was looking over her shoulder at the group of people just outside the cabin. A few had peeked inside, but none followed her lead. Most were scared. All were confused.

Brooklyn just wanted to leave.

"We can't run away," Stephanie said.

"We are." Dawson gestured to the group from Cabin A.

A gentle voice cut through the darkness outside the door. "So are we."

A boy walked into the cabin. He was tall, with light eyes that darted around from face to face, completely bypassing Terry's body. A few others were behind him, young men and women that were willing to face the unknown.

"Rayce…" Stephanie rolled her eyes. "You're not going anywhere. You're staying here with me, and so is the rest of the camp. They're just trying to run because they're scared. There's nothing to be afraid of here."

"I'm not afraid." Rayce chuckled. "I'm just ready is all."

You were almost ready.

They'll find you.

Brooklyn winced at the fresh memory. She felt a hand on her arm and opened her eyes.

"You okay?" Gabriel asked, giving her arm a short squeeze.

"I'm fine," Brooklyn said.

Rayce was built like Dawson, muscular with broad shoulders. His face was all sharp angles with a chiseled jaw, deep, kind eyes, and rich, dark skin. He shot Brooklyn a sympathetic smile before he stepped forward and picked up the broken phone.

"So, the laptop is no good either? No internet, no files, nothing?" Rayce asked.

Julian nodded. "She ran a full wipe on both. The laptop just has a few family photos and a spreadsheet, but there's no data."

"Does it have a name?"

"Yeah, the document itself was labeled ECHO."

Porter inhaled a sharp breath, and his jaw clenched.

Dawson was nodding, thinking to himself while he rubbed his hand up over his mouth. His forehead creased, foot tapped against the floor.

"You're with us?" he asked.

40

"All the way," Rayce answered, holding his hand out for Dawson to clasp tightly.

All Brooklyn could think about was the outside. The world beyond the arms of their little forest and the trees that had kept them secluded. She thought of her parents, of her friends. She wondered if they would recognize her now, if they would remember the girl who left.

"Amber—" Dawson brushed past Stephanie, whose lips hung open in silent offense "—go raid Cabin D. Fill a bag with medical supplies. Take as much as you can."

A girl with cropped black hair nodded.

"Gabriel—" he looked over his shoulder "—can you help Brooklyn get dressed and finish packing our cabin?"

Gabriel nodded. She slipped her hand into Brooklyn's, where their fingers interlaced.

"What can we do?" Porter asked.

"Find the keys to the bus and the car while Rayce and I get the guns."

"Whoa, you aren't taking guns!" Stephanie shouted.

Dawson's lips pulled up into a smug grin. "Yes, we are. Actually."

"I'll…" Stephanie huffed and puffed with wide eyes as she searched her surroundings. The redhead grunted and she dove to snatch up Terry's gun. "I'll stop you! Those guns are staying, and so are all of you because someone is going to come relocate us!"

Dawson tilted his head to the side, analyzing the gun trembling in Stephanie's hands.

Before he could open his mouth to say anything,

Stephanie's back was slammed against the near wall, and the gun was once again clattering on the ground. Gabriel kicked it away, her hand wrapped tight around Stephanie's throat. She squeezed hard, lips pulled back into a snarl.

Stephanie choked and kicked her feet while blood rushed to her face.

"Point a gun at him again," Gabriel seethed, "and you'll wake up without the use of your legs."

Stephanie gagged and choked. Gabriel let her go. Stephanie's thin body slumped into a heap.

"I could've handled it, ya know?" Dawson said playfully as Gabriel returned to Brooklyn's side.

"Or you could just say thank you," she quipped as her lips spread up into a smile.

Dawson rolled his eyes and stepped over Stephanie's legs to look outside at the rest of their peers.

"For those of you who want to come with us, get your things. We leave in an hour." He looked back at Stephanie, who smacked away the tears trailing over her cheeks. "For those of you who don't want to come with us, stay out of the way."

They dispersed.

Dawson and Rayce jogged toward the weapons shed. Amber gathered a couple of people to get the medical supplies. Porter stayed with Julian to look for the keys, and Gabriel guided Brooklyn back to the cabin.

***

When everyone was ready, they met in front of

42

the long white bus with black windows. It'd been parked behind Terry's cabin since the very beginning. A way out in case they needed to evacuate, in case there was a breach.

Brooklyn stood on her tiptoes so she could look around the other side of the cabin, where a tough-looking four door black truck slept in the grass. That was theirs.

"We'll follow behind you. Keep your walkie on, yeah? Our best bet is communication at this point." Rayce slid his half of the pair of walkie-talkies they'd found onto his belt.

Dawson nodded. "You guys have enough food and water in there?"

"We'll be good," Amber said from her place beside Rayce.

Brooklyn watched the small group disappear into the bus and listened to it roar to life.

Gabriel had to physically pull Brooklyn to get her to move—every hair on her body stood on end.

They were leaving.

Brooklyn's face crinkled into a grimace when she lifted herself into the back seat of the truck. Her hip ached, but the adrenaline coursing through her veins made it easy to ignore. Excitement. Terror. Curiosity. It was hard to focus. It was hard to breathe.

The vibration of the truck made her sink further into her seat.

Porter rode in the front while Dawson drove.

No one said anything. No words of encouragement. No late protests.

The back seat was spacious. Brooklyn glanced

over her shoulder and looked out the window. Julian sat on one side and Gabriel on the other.

They turned the corner down the long dirt road toward whatever paved highway was waiting for them. The camp disappeared into the darkness, and the trees swallowed the image of it whole.

Chapter Six

A dark wooden sign sat on the base of light grey boulders at the end of the dirt road. Letters curved and swirled in an inviting display, white and vibrant against the darkness.

"Mt. Hood National Forest." Dawson leaned over the steering wheel as he read off the name.

"Oregon," Julian said. "We've been in Oregon."

"We need to head north, then," Dawson said.

The wheels gripped the asphalt. That sound—the crunch of thick rubber smashing pebbles into concrete—it was so strange to hear again.

"It's almost morning; it'll take us until noon to get there." Brooklyn yawned.

Porter glanced in the rearview mirror, catching Brooklyn's eye. "I'll need to change out your bandages in a few hours. Let me know if it starts to itch or if you feel any sharp pain."

Brooklyn looked down at her stomach and wrinkled her nose, annoyed by the tiny circle of red in the middle of the thick white bandage. She found his eyes reflecting back at her again in the mirror.

"It seems okay, just sore," she said.

Porter nodded, leaning his head back against the seat. "Lemme know when you get tired so we can switch," he said to Dawson.

Brooklyn watched Dawson's eyes flash in the rearview mirror as the bright blink of the bus's headlights appeared behind them.

Rayce's scratchy voice came over the speaker of the walkie-talkie on the dash. "A couple hundred miles to go?"

Dawson pressed his thumb down on the green button and said, "We'll be there in half a day."

The road was wide and dark with the exception of the lights that cast a dim glow on the traffic barriers.

Julian stretched his arm over Brooklyn's seat, and Brooklyn leaned into the warmth of his chest. He laid his chin on the top of her head while Gabriel shifted so that Brooklyn's legs were draped over her lap. Long fingertips danced lazily over Brooklyn's shins until Gabriel reached out and grabbed Brooklyn's hand.

It was easier to fall asleep than she imagined.

***

Brooklyn woke to the sound of Gabriel's loud laugh and the tap of her nails against the window.

"Apparently people are still driving to and from work," Gabriel said.

Brooklyn's eyelids pulled apart, and she hissed at the overwhelming brightness from the sun. It was hidden behind a sheet of thin grey mist that only helped amplify the morning light.

Gabriel was right, though. People were driving next to them on the freeway. A woman was eating an apple while she drove to their left, and a man with an SUV full of kids sipped a cup of coffee on the right.

Normalcy.

Blatant, surreal normalcy.

"We're coming up on Portland," Dawson said. "We'll make a stop there, eat something, try to get some cash for gas, and then keep going."

Brooklyn pawed at her eyes with the back of her hand.

Julian shifted underneath Brooklyn. "You're all soft and warm like a kitten," he cooed playfully.

Brooklyn smirked and sat up. She rolled her neck from side to side and flexed her torso until a sudden prang of pain reminded her that she'd been shot less than five hours ago.

Gabriel kicked her bare foot across Brooklyn's knee and let it rest on the center console while she busied herself with the magazine that belonged to their late camp supervisor. That damn magazine was the start of it all.

"You brought that?" Brooklyn snorted, eyebrows pulled together as she leaned over to try to get a look at what Gabriel was reading.

"Yeah, I figure if we're going home soon, I should probably catch up on the latest trends." Gabriel's voice was stale and deflated.

Brooklyn pulled at the edge of the page she was reading. It was about nail polish, what colors to wear with what outfits, and the statements they

47

would make. Nothing about it was important to Brooklyn, not that she didn't enjoy her fair share of beauty products—she most certainly did—but keeping up with the trends and the ins and outs of fashion was exhausting.

"That's pretty," Brooklyn murmured. She pointed at a nail polish ad featuring a beautifully airbrushed model caught mid-laugh with her hand covering her mouth.

Gabriel shook her head. "Canary yellow? Looks more like a cry for help if you ask me."

She smiled at Brooklyn, and they pushed their shoulders together to share the magazine. It was the sliver of a tiny materialistic portal out of the camp and into whatever the real world was. The cars that whizzed beside them, the signs they continuously left behind as they drove through town after town, all of it was so foreign. The high-gloss, mass-produced, cosmopolitan beauty bible had been their lure. Now they were on their way to find answers to questions they didn't even know how to ask. It was nerve-racking.

"Everything seems normal," Julian said as he looked out the window.

He was right. Everything did seem so surreally normal.

"It could just be a clean area," Brooklyn offered. "I mean, there was no cure for the virus, but they said they had it contained. I don't know how…exactly, but this could be one of the better areas. Maybe Oregon didn't get hit so badly."

"Did they ever end up giving that shit a name? I've been calling whatever it was 'the virus' for way too long now," Julian said, emphasizing with air quotes.

"Mutation of rabies," Gabriel mumbled, licking her index finger so she could turn the page of the magazine. "Apparently an infected possum bit a woman at an animal clinic who had been recently vaccinated with the yearly flu shot. She started seizing, foaming at the mouth, the works. When they got her to the hospital she'd already spread it to the EMT's and one of her coworkers."

"We all know that story," Dawson said.

Brooklyn looked down at her lap.

"Anyways, I don't know its name. I don't call it anything," Gabriel added.

Gabriel was good at a lot of things. She was good at gymnastics, hand-to-hand combat, beauty rituals, and she was a master of deflection. If there was something she could ignore, something unpleasant that she could pretend wasn't there—then by god whatever it was wouldn't have a place in her world.

The virus was one of those things she washed away. She covered the stain of it with something expensive. The spritz off a black bottle of Chanel perfume usually did the trick or even the wet smack of her lips after she coated them thoroughly with red lipstick.

Brooklyn followed in her footsteps because giving it name was like inflating it with power. Giving it a name gave it purpose. Whatever that virus was and whatever it did to people, it had no place in their world. There was no room for its name.

The road swooped down. Brooklyn saw vines crawling up the bricks on the barriers lining the freeway. The bridges overhead were decorated with old graffiti. Deep green leaves sprouted from the cracks in the cement.

Portland emerged all at once. The sudden view of tall buildings made Brooklyn lean over the center console so that she could stare into the vastness of concrete and earth. Trees still loomed overhead; they shared the space with apartment buildings and stacked parking structures. It was a city hidden in the sanctuary of deep forest and constant rain, a metropolis inside a snow globe full of ferns.

"Wow," Brooklyn whispered.

Porter's knuckles brushed against her hand. "Yeah, everyone says this is where young people go to retire."

"I can see why."

People on scooters whizzed by, followed by bicycles and joggers paired with canine companions.

Dawson parked in the Rose Quarter, a bridge away from the meat of the city in an empty parking lot behind a grocery store.

The white bus pulled up behind them. Dante stepped out followed by Amber and the rest of the larger group.

Julian and Gabriel exited on either side of the truck. Brooklyn was slow, scooting herself toward the edge of her seat so her feet would dangle out of the open door.

"C'mon, let's take a look," Porter said.

He adjusted his glasses. Brooklyn felt her cheeks

heat when he stepped in between her legs and poked her chest. "Lie down."

"Bossy," Brooklyn laughed around the word.

He hummed in response. She just barely caught the glimpse of a crooked smirk before he took off his gloves and reached for the zipper on her jacket.

She swatted him away. "I can undress myself, thank you."

Porter's mouth turned upwards into a grin. Brooklyn prided herself with the ability to make him blush.

He held his hands up so she could see his palms and arched a brow. "Go for it. I'll watch."

They laughed like they were free for the first time in two years. Brooklyn giggled like she was actually twenty-one, young and ready for a life that didn't include being taught how to shoot a gun or throw a knife properly. Porter covered his wide smile with his hand and shook his head. He didn't look like a doctor, but his hands felt like they could heal, and his laughter felt a little healing too.

She pulled the black jacket aside after unzipping it and lifted the thin tan shirt up so he could get to the bandage.

He was gentle, and it helped, even when he pressed his fingers down on the edge of the sewn-up hole. "Tell me when it starts to hurt."

He walked the tips of his fingers in until they brushed against the stitches.

Brooklyn hissed, "There, ow. Yep, right there."

"Hold on, I'm gonna grab some alcohol swabs and Neosporin."

She heard chatting between the two vehicles.

Rayce's deep voice was easy to pick out, followed by Gabriel's sultry charm.

"What're they talking about?" Brooklyn asked when Porter walked back over.

"Gabriel wants to go in the city to look around. Dawson thinks we should try to get some money from the gas station across the street. Rayce is hungry. Amber has to pee."

"Oh, thrilling...cold, cold! Cold hands, damn!" She squirmed when the wet swab licked around the stitches and his icy fingertips rested on her stomach again.

"Sorry," Porter said. "You're healing fast though, really fast."

"I've always been that way." She shrugged, sitting up on her elbows as he dabbed the jelly antiseptic over the wound and covered it with a fresh piece of gauze. "My parents just said I have a high immune system."

Porter taped her up and stepped back so she could slide out of the truck.

"Thank you for taking care of all this." Brooklyn gestured in a circle to her hip as she zipped her jacket back up.

"Anytime."

She thought she felt his hand on her lower back, but it vanished when he stepped away and walked toward the rest of the group huddled beside the bus. Gabriel had her arms folded across her chest and frowned.

"Everything is fine! We can just go into the city for an hour, look around, ask some questions, and then we can go. I don't know what the big deal is."

Gabriel tapped her foot.

"We've been held hostage in a camp for two years without the ability to contact anyone. That's the big deal," Dawson said.

Gabriel rolled her eyes. "Shouldn't we be immersing ourselves? Shouldn't we be trying to blend in?"

"Terry said something to me," Brooklyn interrupted. "She said 'they'll find you.'"

"Who's 'they'?" Rayce asked.

"I don't know, but she seemed pretty confident they would come looking for us." Brooklyn leaned against the door of the bus. "I think Gabriel might be right. We can at least get a feel for what's been going on."

"We shouldn't split up," Porter said.

"We can kill two birds with one stone if we do, though."

"I just don't think it's a good idea, Brooklyn."

"I don't think it's a bad idea," Gabriel chimed in.

"Fine," Dawson sighed loudly, "what do you think, Rayce?"

"I think your girls got a point…"

"I'm no one's girl," Gabriel snapped.

Rayce pursed his lips. "Sorry. She…" he pointed at Gabriel "—has a point."

Concentration boiled over Dawson's features as he stared at the ground. "Fine. Go." He said quietly. "Do not make any phone calls; do not tell anyone your name. Rayce and the rest of us will stay here and try to get some money. Be back in two hours." He held up two fingers, asserting the words again. "Two. Hours."

Gabriel bounced on her feet and turned toward Brooklyn, a toothy grin stretched between her dimples.

Porter's gaze stayed glued to the concrete, fists clenched at his side.

They grabbed a few things. Julian carried a backpack, and Porter pulled a beanie on.

Dawson snatched Gabriel's arm before they left and pulled her aside while Brooklyn re-laced her boots.

"Be careful," he said tenderly.

Mossy eyes sparked, and she smirked. "You worried about me?"

"Yes," Dawson answered far too quickly.

Gabriel smiled and tapped his nose with her index finger. "I'll be fine, D. Two hours."

"Two hours," he said again.

Brooklyn turned and walked beside her as they headed toward the sidewalk. The bridge was just around the corner past the freeway entrance.

A city, hustling and bustling with people who didn't know their names, their faces, or their stories, was waiting for them across the Willamette River.

Chapter Seven

"Do you smell that? I haven't smelt that in so long!" Gabriel's eyes closed. She lifted her head, nostrils flaring as she inhaled a deep breath.

Brooklyn looked through the frosted windows of the little coffee shop to their right. A couple tables were set up outside, where Portland natives sat huddled in coats and scarves. A yellow Labrador whimpered at them from his place beside an older gentleman who was reading on a tablet.

"Oh, hi," Brooklyn cooed and knelt down. The pain in her abdomen had lessened, but it was still uncomfortable. She resisted the urge to grimace. She held out the back of her hand and received a sloppy wet kiss from the dog. "What's your name?"

"That's Miss Sunshine." The man smiled, his eyes crinkling up around the edges. "I overheard your friend say that y'all haven't enjoyed the smell of a good cup of coffee in quite some time. I don't know where you've been, but if you haven't been smellin' coffee, then you haven't been in Portland."

"We've been camping for a while," Julian was

hesitant, but he continued. "We've been out of the loop. Do you remember what happened with that virus scare?"

The man looked confused, but after a moment, his eyes lit up, and he lifted a wrinkled pale index finger. "Oh, you mean that whole bird flu pandemic from way back when?"

Brooklyn scratched behind Sunshine's ears. Julian shot a worried look to Porter, who leaned against the window.

"Yeah," Julian said slowly. "Yeah, that must have been it."

"Well, that got cleared up years ago. You young people been campin' that long?"

"We wander," Porter said.

Brooklyn feigned a smile. They waved as they continued to walk down the sidewalk past a long alleyway riddled with bright pink tables and a shop whose icon was a pastry in the shape of a voodoo doll.

Gabriel rolled her lips together as they crossed the street. "That guy…he probably just…" She searched for excuses, for reasons, "J-just forgot or something. He was elderly."

"I don't think so," Julian said.

They walked past a large fountain and found themselves trapped in a thrift store, playing dress-up with old coats and hats. A three-story bookstore across the street caught their attention. They walked from room to room, flipping through science fiction novels and cookbooks. Julian buried himself in an aisle labeled "history of music." They all had to pester him for close to fifteen minutes before he finally put away the three books he was skimming and followed them out.

"We should get back." Porter bumped his shoulder against Brooklyn's as they walked.

"We're fine," Gabriel assured crisply. "Let's go in here."

A one-story building with two black doors loomed on its own at the end of the street next to a pizza parlor.

"What is it?" Brooklyn asked, tilting her head to the side.

"I think it's a theater. Just c'mon, let's look." Gabriel swung one of the heavy doors open and disappeared inside without a second thought.

"We need to go." Porter said. He grabbed Brooklyn's arm when she turned to follow. "Please, trust me."

"Porter, it's not a big deal. She's just excited to be somewhere new. We'll be here for five minutes, she'll get bored, and then we'll head back to the truck," Brooklyn said, glancing down at her arm before she pulled it away.

Julian said nothing; he simply shook his head and held the door as they walked inside.

The carpet was dark red, stained with years of being trampled on by muddy shoes. A concession stand stood in the back, next to the small empty box office window. Popcorn popped in an old machine, a freezer with an ice cream display was taped shut, and only three out of the seven sodas on the dispenser were available.

Gabriel stood with a cell phone perched in her hand. It hovered away from her ear, shook from the tremors that pulsed through her arm. Her mouth hung open in silent disbelief. Confusion was an emotion she didn't wear often, one she kept hidden behind her air of confidence. But in that moment as her eyes welled with tears, Gabriel blinked at the ground and her lips twitched into a defeated frown.

"Shit," Porter growled. "We need to go. We need to go now."

Brooklyn stomped forward just as Gabriel was handing the phone back to the cashier behind the counter.

"Who did you call?" she asked as she reached out to touch Gabriel's shoulder.

"My parents," Gabriel's said meekly. "My mom she...she just sat on the line, and then—" she paused and raked her hands nervously through her hair "—she started to cry."

Porter kept glancing over his shoulder. He paced in front of them. "We have to go," he repeated.

"It's like she thought I was dead," Gabriel whimpered.

It wasn't the sound of the back door slamming that jostled Brooklyn into backtracking toward the door. It wasn't the scuffling of the cashier's feet on the dirty tiles behind the counter or his escalated breathing as he locked himself in the storage room. It wasn't even Porter's voice when he yelled to Julian.

When he shouted, "Get the gun!"

It was the sick, deteriorated scream that was torn from the throat of a tall, thin, infected creature that skidded into the front of the lobby and bared its teeth like an animal.

It was masculine, skin dry and pale, peeling up on its forehead where its eyes protruded out of its skull. Black blood dripped from its nose in a thick line over trembling cracked lips. The blood continued down the expanse of its throat to a bare chest. Dark charcoal lines fanned out over its torso like broken glass, mimicking the image of veins.

The creature was bruised. Its jaw clattered and clanked together, grinded back and forth.

Julian fished around inside the backpack and tossed Porter a gun. Gabriel jumped forward and almost tripped to get in front of Brooklyn.

There were two more. They came running in behind the first, howling and screeching. They cackled like a pack of hyenas, blood-thirsty and crazed.

"Angel," one of the creatures spat as they took a step toward Gabriel, "angel, the angel, the angel."

"If we run, they'll follow us," Porter said and took aim.

"We only brought one gun!" Brooklyn heaved in breath after breath as they all took quick steps backward toward the double doors at the front of the theater.

"You don't need a gun!" Porter yelled.

Brooklyn's eyes were wide. She stared over her shoulder at Porter who ducked down and fired a shot at the one in the middle.

The creature looked confused as the bullet tore a hole through its stomach. The thing didn't bother looking down at its wound, but instead staggered forward, eyes pointed accusingly at Porter.

"What do you mean I don't need a gun?"

Brooklyn screeched.

Porter shouted, "Fight them! You're stronger! *Fight!*"

She was frozen. The three beings in front of them moved like they were broken, quick and sharp. Their legs snapped forward. The one to the left, focused on Julian, opened its mouth, jaw sliding back and forth as tar-like saliva coated its lips. It looked like a woman. All Brooklyn could think about was the evening of her winter dance. How petrified she had been. How brave she had been.

"Get behind Porter," Gabriel huffed, shoving Brooklyn backward with her arm.

Brooklyn didn't have time to protest. Gabriel launched forward and cocked her leg back, kicking the oncoming creature in the chest.

Julian was scrambling to dodge the flailing arms of the one on the left as it tried to grab him.

Porter fired another shot.

Brooklyn shrank back until she felt a hand latch over her shoulder. Warm, putrid breath dampened her cheek. The bony hand on her jacket was moist with sweat. She gasped when it gripped harder; swinging a clenched fist, Brooklyn knocked the tall, bulky creature back. Its whole body shook. The sound of its teeth gnashing together made her want to wretch.

"Move!" Porter yelled. "Brooklyn, move to the right!"

It was hard to focus on his words when she was falling to the ground, trying to kick the creature's legs out from underneath it. The gun went off, and the creature turned. Its eyes, soaked in the same onyx liquid that they all seemed to share, stared at Porter. That creature, whoever or whatever it was, looked completely taken aback.

Seconds later, Gabriel's lean figure ran by in a blur. Her palms hit the ground; she vaulted herself into the air, legs wrapped tight around the creature's face. She twisted and the sound of a strangled growl was followed by a loud snap.

There was only one left. Its hands were around Gabriel's throat before she could regain her footing.

It was the same feeling from the kitchen that swelled inside Brooklyn—the same instinct that drove her to kill, to shove a knife under that woman's chin all those months ago. That primal urge was what made Brooklyn place her hands against either side of the creature's head and twist.

Its body hit the ground. Brooklyn looked across from her, and was staring into Gabriel's wide green eyes.

Gabriel clawed at her throat to make sure everything was intact.

Brooklyn turned in a quick circle and found Julian slumped against the wall beside Porter, trying to catch his breath.

Three dead bodies littered the floor of the old movie theater lobby. The smell of their blood was rotten and sour.

Chapter Eight

Porter's hands were on Brooklyn's hips. He turned her to face him.

"Brooklyn." His voice was calm and direct. "I need to check your stitches. Are you hurt?"

She shook her head, focusing on Gabriel, who stared at the crumpled bodies on the ground.

"We killed them," Brooklyn whispered. "H-how did we…? And why…" Her words trailed off, dropped lower and lower until they vanished. Her gaze drifted back to Porter, who was kneeling in front of her. He lifted her shirt and sighed.

"They're fine," he said softly.

"Why didn't they attack you?"

Porter looked at the ground. His shoulders flexed, muscles clenched. Brooklyn heard the tiny inhale, the sudden shakiness of his breath. He stayed where he was, resting on his knees at her feet while her fingers curled into fists.

Julian coughed. His hand fell heavy on Gabriel's shoulder as he pulled her into his chest. "You're something, you know that?"

"Yeah, I guess I am," Gabriel said as she looked from one body to the other and back again.

"We need to get out of here." Porter stood, watching Brooklyn carefully.

"You need to tell me…"

"I will explain," he hissed under his breath, tugging at her hips as he lowered his mouth next to her ear. "I will explain everything when we're back with the others and you're safe, all right?"

Brooklyn glared at him. Her lips pursed as she smacked his hands away.

Porter looked more relieved than he did hurt by her actions. He nudged his head toward the emergency exit near the back of the theater next to the restrooms. They were quick to shuffle around the bodies. Gabriel made a point to step over them, kicking one as she walked by.

They didn't speak. Not to each other and not to anyone else as they hurried toward the bridge. Brooklyn's stitches stung in protest as she took long strides down the rain-dampened sidewalk. They kept looking over their shoulders like clockwork. First Julian would look, followed by Brooklyn and lastly Gabriel. Porter kept his eyes ahead. They were narrowed behind his glasses, shoulders squared, body tight with anxiety. Brooklyn could feel the emotion pouring off him. It felt like heat. Like distress.

All she could think about was the way those things looked at him, like they knew him.

"Shouldn't we be finding a place to hide?" Gabriel asked. She huddled closer to Brooklyn as they walked.

Porter was in front of them with his hands shoved deep in the front pocket of his jeans. "No," he threw the word over his shoulder and shook his head. "We need to stay in the open, in public areas."

"I think he's right," Julian said.

The road curved up toward the bridge above the train station. The roar of an approaching train echoed off the buildings. Brooklyn looked down over the chipped maroon railing and stared down the Willamette River, eyes trailing over the train tracks nestled up beside the river banks and the apartments across the way. She wondered how easy it would be to sneak into a train car and get off on the last stop. To erase the familiarity of her name and adopt a different personality, cut her hair, get a tattoo. Let go of the questions and the lies and the past. She wondered if it would ever be possible for her to let go of it all.

The chill of a cold hand swept down, soft fingertips lacing around Brooklyn's own. Gabriel latched onto her hand and held on.

Brooklyn couldn't let go.

***

Amber was the first person to see them walking up the sidewalk toward the gas station. She called to Rayce and shoved a mouthful of mixed nuts into her mouth.

Porter touched Brooklyn's arm, but she pulled it away.

"Hey!" Gabriel called to Dawson, who was digging through one of the bags in the back of the truck. "Is everyone ready? We need to get out of here."

"What happened?" Dawson said. His hands moved to the sides of her arms, and Gabriel leaned into them. His eyes were wide, his gaze moved down her neck to her shoulders, continuing on. He analyzed her for injuries. A gentle pull told her to turn, and she did so, allowing him to be sure she was unscathed. He noticed a black stain on the top of her beige hiking boots.

It was strange how the human mind worked. How something as simple as a black smudge, a tiny splatter, could jostle Dawson into holding his breath. Thick eyebrows were pulled tight, drawn down into a worried expression.

Brooklyn had never seen him look so fretful. She watched as Gabriel gasped when he nearly crushed her. His arms flew around her body and he nestled his face down against the pale skin exposed on her neck. She could feel him breathing, could feel his chest expand as he inhaled the smell of her hair. His thumb was under the hem of her shirt, rubbing circles on her side.

"I'm fine..." Gabriel didn't mind being held, but her hands were unsure as they smoothed over his shoulders. "I'm fine, D...really, there were three of them and..."

"I told you!" He pulled away and held her at arms distance. "It wasn't safe, and something worse could have happened. You should have listened to me!"

"I killed them," Gabriel spat. "I killed two of them. One was attacking me and Julian, and the other went after Brookie. She killed the one that tried to rip my head off."

"You killed them?" Dawson asked. His eyebrows shot up, and his forehead wrinkled.

Gabriel's hands were set hard on her hips. She gave a curt nod. "I *slaughtered* them."

Dawson's gaze darted over to Brooklyn, who was standing awkwardly next to Porter.

Brooklyn nodded. "We killed them. We need to go."

"What happened? How did they find you?" Dawson asked. He waved his hand toward the group huddled by the bus and pointed at the door. They were quick to follow direction and scrambled to gather the bags and supplies so they could repack everything.

Gabriel's jaw clenched as she looked at the ground.

"Gabriel used some kid's cell phone to call her parents while we were in an old theater off Burnside," Porter said. He sighed, and when his fingertips brushed against the top of Brooklyn's hand, she tugged it away and shuffled closer to Amber.

There was so much Brooklyn wanted to say. So many questions she wanted to shout at Porter. Answers she wanted to beat out of him with her fists, but there was something squirming inside her that kept her quiet. That, along with the rallied confusion and anger, had her mind and heart digging for clues. For anything that would make sense of what went on in the lobby of that dusty movie theater.

"You used a phone?" Dawson gritted the words out at Gabriel, who turned her head, refusing to look at him. "I told you. I explicitly told you not to make any goddamn phone calls—"

"I get it!" Gabriel shouted. "What do you want, D? I'm sorry. You're right—now let's go. We need to go."

Brooklyn wanted to reach for her, but Gabriel was already storming off toward the bus to help the others load up the supplies.

Gabriel was right; they needed to get on the road.

Brooklyn looked around until she found Julian. He was leaning against the side of the truck, picking at his nails. She watched and listened as Rayce stepped directly in front of him.

Rayce tilted his head to the side, "You all right?"

"Me?" Julian glanced over his shoulder to make sure he was the one being spoken to.

"You."

"Yeah…?" he tested. "I'm fine, I think. I really don't know due to the three black-spitting flesh suits that just tried to maul us to death."

"But you're all right?" Rayce smiled.

"Yeah, I'm all right." Julian's eyes narrowed. "Have we like…" he gestured with long, spidery fingers between the two of them "—ever spoken before? I'm pretty sure we haven't."

Rayce chuckled. "I've seen you, though."

"Oh, you've seen me?"

"I've seen you." Rayce grinned and shook his head. He tapped the bottom of Julian's chin before he turned on his heels, walking toward Dawson who was pacing back and forth on the other side of the black truck.

"Why's your mouth open?" Brooklyn asked. She rounded the side of the truck and opened the door to get to the dark brown bag in the back seat.

Julian shook his head. "Well, I think I'm still trying to catch up with the fact that we killed three people."

"People?" she snorted.

"Yeah, people. Sick people."

Brooklyn huffed. "I don't consider them people."

She lifted up the bottom of her shirt and held it up with her mouth. A short wince pulled her lips into a glower when she peeled off the bandage and poked her stitches. They seemed to be healing, but were sore from the hurried walk from downtown.

"Hey!" Porter rushed around the car when he saw Brooklyn prodding at her bare skin. "What the hell are you doing? You're just asking for infection. Let me…"

"Do not touch me," Brooklyn snapped.

Julian's eyes went wide when he heard the venom in Brooklyn's voice. He glanced at Porter, shrugged, and walked toward Dawson and the others.

"Brooklyn, c'mon, I'm a doctor."

"I'm just putting some antiseptic on it because it stings," she mumbled.

He took another step forward. She turned away from him.

"Please, let me help you."

Brooklyn continued by herself and flinched when the tip of her finger dabbed the jelly antiseptic over the ridge of stitches sewn through her skin. It hurt, but what hurt worse was the way Porter hovered just behind her. He didn't breach the space she'd set between them but stood on his tip toes so he could be sure she wasn't doing any harm to her already sore injury.

"They'll kill you," Brooklyn breathed suddenly. The words weren't supposed to come out cold, hard and brittle, but they did. They fell into the space between them as she struggled not to lash out at Porter for making this so hard, for being so good for so long.

"I'll kill you," she emphasized, turning to stare at him as she smoothed out her shirt.

Porter didn't move. His lips were loose and parted, but his eyes were the same constant warmth she'd grown fond of over the last two years.

"I need you to know that," Brooklyn said. "If you're a part of this. If you're a part of them, whoever they are. I'll kill you myself."

It was hard to look at him, so she walked away. Distance. That was what her mind kept saying would be best.

But Porter was at her heels, grasping her shoulder.

"There isn't a virus," Porter blurted.

He was shaking.

"Those people, they aren't sick. They were just unsuccessful cases. They call them Surros."

Brooklyn didn't turn around. Her eyes were straight ahead, and her heart was hammering against her chest.

"And they call you Omens."

69

Chapter Nine

Static energy shot into the tip of Brooklyn's fingers. Her chest lurched forward, her stomach twisted into a ball, and her lungs burned with the urge to scream. But she didn't move—she didn't say a word. She stared wide-eyed past the far traffic light down the street and focused on Porter's uneven breathing as her silence took its toll.

She expected him to ramble on. She expected him to cave.

But Porter stood at her heels, unmoving. The stillness was an eerie shadow cast over the two of them.

"Omens," her voice came out weak and breathless as she finally spoke, repeating what he'd said.

He still didn't move, but his hand kept its place curved over her shoulder, and his grip was tight.

"Don't touch me," the words came stumbling out of her mouth, loud and piercing. Brooklyn felt a few pairs of eyes shift over to where they stood.

Porter withdrew his hand.

"How much do you know?" Brooklyn asked.

"Enough."

"You'll tell them everything," she snapped. Her hair whisked around her shoulders when she finally spun to face him, eyes stone cold. The bridge of her nose was pinched. Her lips shook. Adrenaline and anxiety made homes out of the holes in her heart that Porter had blown open with only a few words.

Every fleck of anger that sparked inside her was accompanied by a memory of the last two years. Of the way Porter's head fell heavy on her shoulder by the fire. Of the exhaustion that coated his voice in the middle of the night, and how even the tiniest stir from her bunk would have him at the edge of her bed, sharing whispered words of comfort that chased the nightmares away. She looked at him, and he looked back. Porter's eyes seemed younger than ever under the grey Oregon sky.

Brooklyn wanted to wrap her arms around him almost as much as she wanted to crush her fist into his cheek. The whirlwind of different emotions had her heart galloping in her chest.

His lips were chapped. It looked painful when he tried to catch his breath.

"I will tell them everything," he whispered.

"You..." Brooklyn almost choked, but she swallowed down the lump in her throat. "You—" she shoved her index finger against his chest "—are an asset. Once we stop to make camp, you will sit down and explain. That's the only reason *I'm* not killing you."

"The only reason?" Porter leaned in against her hand and reached up to clasp it firmly in his own. "I don't think that's the only reason."

Brooklyn's heart sputtered, her throat closed, and she felt the blood drain from her face. The back of her hand struck his cheek before Porter noticed the crack in her already worn reserve.

Julian's head peeked over the top of the truck to see what was going on.

Brooklyn walked away, almost stumbling to escape the situation. She left Porter there, standing on his own, staring at the concrete with a patch of deep red blooming over the left side of his face. She hoped his pride felt the sting just as much as his cheek did.

Julian reached for her and she shrank against him. "What happened?"

"I don't wanna talk about it yet," she mumbled.

"We're getting ready to go. Are you gonna be all right?" Julian was testing, edging forward as he opened the back door of the truck and watched her slide in. "I've never seen you hit anyone outside of training before."

Brooklyn bristled and turned her head away to look at Gabriel through the window.

"I've never had a reason," she said.

She readied herself for an onslaught of questions, but none came. Julian leaned his arm against the top of the door and rested his forehead against his wrist. He sighed. She thought maybe she heard him start a sentence, but it faded away when Dawson called out to everyone.

"We're on the edge of Washington." Dawson's voice boomed between the bus and the truck. "We'll set up some of the emergency tents in a campsite just outside Seattle."

Rayce stood on the step stool on the driver's side of the bus. He nodded to Dawson before he climbed in.

Gabriel squeezed in beside Brooklyn, and Julian followed.

"Can you drive?" Dawson asked when Porter walked up to the truck. "My head's pounding."

The sound of her teeth grinding down against each other echoed between her ears. Brooklyn stared long and hard at Porter until he cleared his throat, shaking his head.

"You know, maybe Julian should drive. I'm still…" Porter held up his hand which gave a slight tremble. "I'm still, ah, a bit shaky from earlier. Go ahead and ride in the back with the girls. I'll stay up here."

"You up for it?" Dawson shrugged as he held the keys out to Julian.

"Yeah." Julian nodded, crawling over the center console.

Dawson slid in next to Gabriel and kicked one of his feet up on the center console.

Gabriel smoldered at him with her nose in the air.

With everyone in place, they left. The lights of Portland fell dark behind the winding freeway and the wall of trees that kept it sheltered. The chill of the glass window felt nice on Brooklyn's cheek. She counted the lights on the barricades as they passed them. One. Two. Three. Four. One right after the other. The only thing that distracted her was the reflection in the side mirror, the shine of

Porter's glasses. His eyes gazed somewhere far away, tracing the outline of comets that lingered in the night sky.

"Come on," Dawson huffed under his breath, glaring at Gabriel. "You're exhausted. Lie down."

He moved over, bundled up a jacket, and put it in his lap for her to lay her head on. Gabriel gave a dismissive glance out of the corner of her eye. She blinked, looked from his lap to his chest and then to his face.

A slender finger poked Brooklyn's hand. "How's your tummy?"

"It's fine, Gabriel," Brooklyn smiled fondly and shifted, lifting her arm so that the other girl could curl up against her chest.

Gabriel rubbed her warm cheek against Brooklyn's shoulder. Green eyes narrowed at Dawson, who huffed in return. Her legs lifted and draped over his lap. She dug her heels into the side of his thigh until he scooted in closer to her.

"I don't like being away from you," Dawson mumbled.

Gabriel didn't say anything in return. She just looked at him with her face resting on Brooklyn's collar bone and reached out to touch his hand.

Brooklyn could feel how tight his hold was on Gabriel. How his hands smoothed up Gabriel's legs and held them against his chest. Brooklyn didn't move, she didn't say a word, just stroked Gabriel's hair and listened to the rain begin to pelt against the windshield.

***

"Hey."

Porter's voice was a cool breath on the back of her neck. Brooklyn felt something pull in her abdomen. A startling jolt. An electrifying pulse. She swung around too quickly for her own good and jumped back when she realized how close he'd been.

It was the first time she'd seen him.

Her hand was in front of her, fingers stretched out like she was trying to woo a wild animal.

"I'm in your cabin," Porter clarified. He lowered his head, and his glasses slid down to rest on the tip of his nose.

Brooklyn still hadn't said a word.

He'd been wearing one of those long sleeved flannels, the soft ones that reminded her of Christmas. The black beanie he was so attached to clung to the back of his head.

His eyes looked like the honey that she used to pour into the bottom of her cup before she filled it with tea. The bundles of moles that crawled down his body started on his jaw. He was a little taller than her, shifting back and forth in his boots. His smile was nice, curving up more on one side than the other.

"I'm Porter." He reached out and opened his hand. "Porter Malloy."

His hands were soft. Softer than she'd expected.

"My name's Brooklyn."

Julian yawned loudly from the front seat. The scene dispersed behind Brooklyn's eyelids as she woke from the short nap.

Gabriel was up, leaning over the center console.

"It stopped raining. We should set up here for the night," Julian said as the truck entered a vacant campsite equipped with a rusty barbeque and a tiny fire pit.

Dawson nodded sheepishly as he pawed at his eyes.

The campsite was quiet and unenclosed. A couple long logs served as seats on either side of the rain-soaked fire pit and a large patch of dirt was a few feet behind the barbeque where they could hoist up the tents. Trees stood tall overhead, and some bushes were lined prettily along the dirt road where they parked the bus.

It was hard to concentrate on getting things done, on mundane but necessary tasks, when Porter was in her line of sight. He beat the dust out of one of the tents while Rayce hammered posts into the dirt. Brooklyn hated how hard it was for her to align the words just right in her head. They didn't seem to fit. Even as she placed them one right after the other in perfect synchronism, as soon as she went to whisper them to herself, they vanished.

"You should have Porter check on your stitches when we're done," Gabriel said.

They unrolled sleeping bags from the compartments beneath the windows on the passenger's side of the bus.

"They're fine," Brooklyn lied. Her stomach was itchy and tight.

"Still—" Gabriel shrugged "—just to be sure."

"Yeah, okay," she mumbled and tucked a strand of hair behind her ear. It was easier to pacify

Gabriel than to argue with her.

"Can you believe all this?" Gabriel sighed. "I mean, I just don't get it. Do you think it's the whole fight-or-flight thing? I've read about mothers who lift entire cars up to get to their babies and people who can crush concrete with their fists, but what we did was kind of crazy...kind of scary."

Kind of was an understatement.

"We're all primitive at our core. I think we just did what we had to do."

Gabriel's lips were parted, and she scoffed. "Do you know how much torque it takes to snap a human neck?"

Brooklyn chewed on her lip.

"A thousand pounds, Brookie." Gabriel narrowed her eyes and slid one of the sleeping bags over her shoulder. "And you did it like it was nothing."

They walked together toward the three tents that were now fully upright, ready to be occupied. Some of the group opted to sleep in the bus, which was probably a bit warmer, but Brooklyn didn't mind the tent as long as she would be sharing it with Gabriel.

They spread out their sleeping bags, topping them with thick quilts.

"Hey, Julian? Rayce was looking for you and..." Porter's voice fell away when he peeked inside the tent and saw the two girls sitting down next to their duffle bags.

"Oh, hey!" Gabriel flashed a wide grin. "We were just about to come looking for you. Brookie needs her stitches looked at."

Brooklyn shook her head and stammered, "I-I'm fine, actually. I'm good. They're just kind of sore, a little. It's fine. I'm fine."

"They're sore?" he asked as he leaned further into their tent.

"She was limping a little," Gabriel chirped.

Brooklyn scoffed. "I wasn't limping."

"You were, actually. I'll go help Amber start the fire."

Gabriel was up and out of the tent before Brooklyn could continue protesting. That left her alone with Porter, which was the one thing she'd been trying to avoid since they fled Portland.

"Can I please help you?" he asked.

"No."

"C'mon, Brooklyn, the stitches probably just need to be taken out."

"It's too soon," she croaked, glancing down at her stomach. "There's no way it can be done healing by now."

Porter took a step toward her, and she shimmied away from him.

"I'm fine!"

"I know you are, but if you don't let me clip those stitches, the pinching is only going to get worse. The skin will tear back open, and it'll be a mess. If you would just listen to me—" he paused and took a minute to catch his breath "—I can make you more comfortable."

"I doubt it," Brooklyn gritted.

"I would doubt me too if I were you, but I'm still a doctor. You're healing at an accelerated rate; I'm assuming you're used to that, aren't you?"

78

He held his hand out to her and took the opportunity to kneel down so he could look at her eye to eye. He sat back with his shoulders hunched and sighed, heavy and tired. His question took her by surprise. Brooklyn froze in place. All the muscles in her legs tensed. The hair on the back of her neck stood up. He wasn't wrong. She bit down on the inside of her cheek and decided to stay quiet.

"Bruises? Bumps? Scrapes? They all seemed to disappear after a night or two, didn't they? You told me about a time on the soccer field when you swore you heard your own ankle break, but by the time they'd gotten you to the hospital the doctor only saw a small fracture? And then training at camp, all that fighting and conditioning, yet none of you ever had an injury that took longer than a day or so to heal. It's not a coincidence."

"I'm resilient." She bit down on the word and rolled her eyes.

"You're evolved."

"Evolved?"

"Yes," Porter said under his breath. "Now please, lay down so I can take those out."

"You don't just get to say things like that and then not explain them."

"I will explain while I take those stitches out of your stomach."

Brooklyn lunged forward, nearly knocking him backward. Her hand clenched around his neck and squeezed.

He braced himself with his arm outstretched behind him. Brooklyn fisted her free hand in his shirt. Her lips drew back into a snarl. She narrowed her eyes when she felt his arm loop around her waist. It astonished her how confident he could be.

"Are you *evolved*, Porter? Are you like me?"

The rasp that wrapped around her words when she said them made her throat start to close. She wanted to cry. She wanted to yell. She wanted her hand to squeeze. Just *squeeze* the life out of him until there was nothing left. Until the betrayal, the lies, and the truth all drifted away with his last breath. But she couldn't do it. She knew she couldn't do it, and so did he.

Porter leaned into her, and she could feel the warmth of his torso against her own. Her grip loosened. He lifted his chin just enough to brush his nose against her jaw.

"No," he whispered. "I'm just a doctor."

A few strands of her hair fell from behind her ear. Even though she no longer had a tight grip around his throat, she let her hand stay there for a moment. His body was warm, and it felt good to be held. For his arm to soothe up her spine and cup the back of her head, for him to trace the bony ridge of each of Brooklyn's knuckles as her fingers uncurled from around his neck.

"You're going to take the stitches out," Brooklyn said softly, "and then you're going to tell us everything."

The pitter-patter of his pulse sped up and knocked steadily against her index finger.

"Everything," he repeated.

His eyes were forlorn and fogged behind his glasses.

"I'll tell you everything I know."

Chapter Ten

It was tense when Dawson walked into the tent followed by Rayce and Julian.

Brooklyn sat with her hand over her stomach where Porter had been poking only minutes before. Her palm was sealed over the wound, and she held her breath. Those words, the perfectly synchronized sentence, just couldn't roll over her tongue and out of her mouth. It stayed put, repeating again and again behind her lips.

"Gabriel and Amber are working on getting a fire going, but the logs are all pretty damp." Rayce nudged his chin toward Brooklyn. "What's this all about?"

Say something

Brooklyn swallowed dryly.

Say everything

Her throat closed when she opened her mouth and her lungs burnt.

She was trying to breathe, desperate to speak, and completely one-hundred percent not ready for what was about to happen. She inhaled a tiny breath, glanced at Porter, and then lifted up her shirt.

Smooth skin was revealed, obscured only by miniscule pin pricks from the stitches. The nasty bullet hole that they all had all seen only hours before had been replaced by brand new silky flesh.

Dawson's mouth went slack. His eyes narrowed when he leaned forward to get a better look.

Julian shook his head. His hand rubbed over his mouth and chin. "That's not possible," he said.

"Yes, it is," Porter said gravely.

The color drained from Julian's face. Brooklyn squirmed at the sudden tightness in her chest.

"How exactly is it possible for her to already be healed after being shot less than fourteen hours ago?" Julian asked.

"Same way it was possible for her to be up and walking so quickly. She heals faster than the typical person would—" he looked from Julian to rest of them "—and so do all of you."

Brooklyn heard Dawson's breath catch, and she heard the whispered protest from Julian when everything started to come together. Rayce loomed behind Dawson, his eyes stayed focused on Porter, who nodded slowly.

"My father is Juneau Malloy, head biologist and development coordinator for the Omen project. I was recruited by him and then placed in ISO Recovery Camp Eleven. My job was to obtain information and analyze the progress of each individual in the camp."

Brooklyn wanted to close her eyes, but she couldn't look away from him.

Dawson's nostrils flared. His fingers curled into tight fists.

"Us?" Dawson asked. "When you say each individual you mean *us*, don't you?"

"Yes," Porter breathed. "That's exactly what I mean."

"Why?"

Porter didn't flinch when Dawson barked at him. He just looked at his lap and tried to mask the pained look on his face by gesturing loosely to Brooklyn.

"Because each of you were given a flu shot when you were between the ages of twelve months and seven years old. Instead of your standard vaccine, what you were dosed with was a concentrated form of two extremely powerful viruses."

A breathy laugh flew out of Julian's mouth. "This is a joke right? Like, you're joking? You have to be, because what you just said is completely insane."

"He's not joking," Brooklyn interrupted.

Four pairs of eyes beamed toward her.

"Keep going," she said.

Porter glanced at her from under his lashes and licked his lips. "Merging two viruses isn't easy; it took years of trial and error before they got it right. It was a problem with stability; the cells either died on contact or destroyed the human tissue immediately after introduction. Everything changed when my dad started experimenting with microbes. He hollowed out the cells of proteins and filled them with the conjoined viruses, but it still didn't work, not until they started reprogramming the genome."

Dawson wasn't moving, but it was clear that he was absorbing and processing each detail as Porter spoke.

"They used the microbes to get things done. They're cells that are grown and programmed by computers, harvested and manifested with code rather than genes. It's a whole new level of science that we're just starting to understand. I never got why my dad and his associates were playing with something so fucked-up until he told me what they'd accomplished."

Porter paused and exhaled a shaky breath. "I didn't know what it meant. He'd been working on all this shit for years. When he told me they were ready to start human trials, I didn't know how to react. I was on a plane out of San Francisco, on my way to Denver that afternoon. My father's always had his home life and his work life separate. I never questioned it until that day. I never really cared. But the Surrogates…they were the first thing I saw when he took me to the lab."

Julian growled, "Get to the point."

"What my dear old dad left out was that when he said he was ready to start human trials, he really meant he was ready to find them by using the failed test subjects as bloodhounds. Those subjects are the creatures that hunted each and every one of you down two years ago. The ones you thought were infected."

Brooklyn pressed her tongue against the roof of her mouth to keep from screaming. She picked at the edge of her nails.

"Surrogates, or Surros for short, are your predecessors. Strong, flexible, fast, but extremely frail in the mind. They can be given a task to retrieve or to kill but not much else. They're lacking due to the microbes not reversing the aspects of the viruses completely once the proteins were released into the bloodstream. It was apparent that the viruses needed more time to bond and coexist in one host before evolving. They needed to age, to manifest naturally so…a handful of practitioners around the country were given the responsibility of choosing the hosts when their bodies were still young and malleable."

Dawson's eyebrows pulled together, and his bottom lip quivered.

Brooklyn felt faint.

"Once you reached the appropriate age, they collected you and started to test your abilities," Porter concluded.

"And you…" Julian whispered, jabbing his index finger at Porter. "Took notes on us like lab rats and sent them back to daddy? You pretended to care. You…you let us believe that there was a virus out there. You let us suffer—"

Porter interrupted. "It was my job. I didn't have a choice."

"You always have a choice!" Julian shouted.

Brooklyn thought it was a twig snapping at first. The click, snap, click. But it dawned on her when she tore her gaze away from Porter and saw Gabriel standing at the front of the tent that what she'd heard wasn't the sound of something breaking. It was the hammer being pulled back on the pistol in

85

Gabriel's hand, pointed directly at Porter.

Dawson stopped Rayce from jolting forward. He shot his hand out toward her. "Gabes, put that down," Dawson eased.

"You knew?" Gabriel whimpered.

Tears dripped down the curve of her cheek, and her voice cracked. "This was all some charade, and you just let us go along with it? What is going on? What the hell am I?"

Her arm straightened, and the gun trembled in her hand.

"Don't," Brooklyn gasped suddenly. Her legs dipped when she lurched forward in front of Porter. "Gabriel, don't shoot him."

"Tell me what it is," Gabriel spat. "What are the two viruses?"

Porter's eyes were wide. He tried to nudge Brooklyn away, but she wouldn't budge.

"Tell me!" Gabriel yelled.

"Polio," Porter blurted quickly.

Gabriel's expression fell flat.

"It's polio and CJD."

Gabriel's eyes crinkled at the edges when she started to cry, which gave Dawson just enough time to knock her wrist toward the ground and gather his arms around her midsection. The gun went off, leaving a hole in the bottom of the tent a few feet away from Porter's leg.

Rayce snatched the gun once it was wrestled out of her grasp, but Gabriel continued to thrash and kick as Dawson pulled her out of the tent.

Gabriel's voice was shrill and angry. "You lied to us, you son of a bitch! You *lied*! I should kill you!"

It would have been easy for Gabriel to get out of Dawson's grip, but she let him carry her off even as she bucked and writhed against him, spitting profanities back toward the tent.

Porter's face was pale and sickly. He didn't look up when Brooklyn turned to face him. He didn't say a word when Rayce let out a long tired sigh.

"What else do you know?" Rayce asked. His voice held a tenderness that made Brooklyn impossibly angry. How could someone be soft with Porter after such a confession? How could strong and noble Rayce talk to Porter like he was someone worthy of coddling?

"I was briefed on the project and the desired outcome," Porter said. He smashed a hand over his ear and rubbed.

"Can you explain why someone would ever choose to infect a group of children with polio?" Rayce asked, staying calm.

"Like I said before, it wasn't just the virus that you guys were dosed with. It was more than that. The microbes actually changed the identity of both viruses. Polio in its entirety rarely causes any symptoms, but when it does, it's because the cells enter the central nervous system and destroy certain neurons. When they reprogrammed the genome, they reversed the natural purpose of the virus, so instead of weakening the muscle tissue, it went to work enhancing it."

"And the other?" Rayce asked.

"Creutzfeldt Jakob Disease...I never understood why my father was so obsessed with it. It was unstable at its core, and the side effects from trying to develop it were severe. The disease itself is caused by prions. It deteriorates the brain, causes rapid memory loss and psychosis."

"Psychosis..." Brooklyn echoed.

"It was trial and error with the Surros. The virus was too volatile; it needed more time to adapt to the body to do what it was supposed to. When it was introduced to them, my father and his colleagues tried to speed up the process, make it immediate, but it didn't work. The prions corrupted the microbes like any bacteria would, and the result was a group of subjects that were physically enhanced but mentally broken." Porter cleared his throat and adjusted his glasses. "All of you were successful. You're mentally sharper, more accurate, and incredibly strong."

Julian rolled his eyes. "And all this? What for? To have a bunch of high school and college students pass a few tests? To fly off a few charts? What are we to them, a new record?"

"No," Porter said briskly. He looked at Brooklyn before his eyes turned toward Julian and Rayce.

"You're weapons."

Chapter Eleven

Brooklyn lifted herself off the floor of the tent and walked out. The air was bitter cold. It rushed past her lips, into her lungs, chilling her from the inside out. Her eyes felt as heavy as the conversation. Even though it had been cut short by her sudden departure, its impact would last a lifetime.

Human beings weren't meant to be weapons. Not to the earth, not to each other, not to the species they shared the planet with. Yet there they were, in the middle of the woods, trying to run from a fate they'd never chose. None of it seemed real. Not in the slightest. She looked down at her hands, blotched violet and blue from the weather. Her veins stood peeked through the olive skin on her wrist. It was difficult to look at them, spindly and thin, knowing that the blood coursing within them was tainted.

"Hey." Amber said, appearing at her side. "I didn't hear much, but I heard enough." She raked her fingers through her hair, shrugging her shoulders. The fire pit finally sparked to life. "You don't look good, kid." She wriggled her nose and poked Brooklyn in the arm.

"I'm not good," Brooklyn said blandly.

"Keep it together." Amber grabbed a small water bottle out of a bag next to the fire, shoving it against Brooklyn's chest.

Brooklyn rolled her eyes. "You obviously didn't hear shit if you're telling me to keep it together."

Amber was small with cropped black hair and broad shoulders. Her petite build wasn't at all threatening, nor was her mousy, grating voice. She shoved Brooklyn back with both her open palms, lifting her chin proudly. "I'm telling you to keep it together because, if you fall apart, guess what? Time-bomb blondie over there's gonna flip her shit. So is your cutie-pie traitor boyfriend if she doesn't actually kill him by then. So, woman up."

Surprise squirmed across Brooklyn's face. She stumbled back, catching herself on one of the logs adjacent to the fire. Snarling at Amber, Brooklyn snapped, "He's not my boyfriend."

Amber gave a wry smirk, accompanied by the arch of one of her thin brows. Her head lolled to the side, a challenge sparking in her dark eyes.

Brooklyn's face simmered red. She squirmed to get back on her feet. It would've felt good to blow off steam, to jet forward and back-hand the smug look off of Amber's face. However, in the end, she was right. Brooklyn needed to collect herself, and she needed to do it quickly.

"I'm gonna cook something," Amber said. "Are you hungry?"

"Yes," Brooklyn said.

"I'm not the one whose gonna tell you everything's gonna be a-okay, dollface," Amber's voice dropped to a soft whisper. "I been through too much shit m'self to lie to my friends, you understand?"

Brooklyn nodded. Even though she understood, she still didn't like being put on the spot.

"Where did Ellie and A.J. go?" Brooklyn asked.

"Getting more firewood," Amber pointed past the bus and into the woods.

"And Gabriel?"

"Dawson dragged her somewhere that way," Amber laughed. She gestured loosely over her shoulder, digging through a large duffle bag for cans of soup and a few loaves of bread. "If I were you, I'd let him calm her down, go back to that tent, and do some learnin'."

The look on Gabriel's face was still etched cruelly in Brooklyn's mind. She'd looked angry...menacing. She'd looked so scared.

But Amber was right.

"Tell those boys I'm cooking," Amber called to her when Brooklyn got up, heading back toward the tent.

Brooklyn nodded, hesitating for only a moment before she unzipped the front of the tent and stepped back inside.

Porter sat with his legs crossed in the middle of the tent. Rayce stood, but now Julian was sitting down at his feet with one leg pulled up against his chest.

"You okay?" Julian asked, patting the space next

to him.

She swayed awkwardly on her feet. "No."

"Oh, good. Come sit." He rubbed his hand in a circle and patted the ground again.

"Where do we go from here? Who are we running from?" she asked as she sat down.

Porter bit down on his lip. "I was just explaining to them that, at this point, I don't really know. They're not going to stop trying to catch us, and ultimately…"

"They will," Brooklyn finished. He nodded.

Rayce shrugged. "We'll kill them all."

"Down boy." Julian tilted his head back to look up at him, elbowing Rayce in the shin. "In all seriousness, though, where should we start? Do we hide? Do we fight?"

Soft pops came from Porter's knuckles as he cracked them nervously against the heel of his palms. "I don't have answers like that, and I can't tell any of you what to do or how to handle this. I can try to get a hold of my dad, but I doubt he'd trust me. After all, I helped destroy a few of his toys *and* assisted in the escape of genetically modified specimens."

"Don't say it like that," Brooklyn sighed. She mentally kicked herself for not having more control over her mouth.

"That's what you are, Brooklyn," Porter said. "You're smarter, faster, and stronger; you have an incredible memory and acute senses. All they see when they look at you are statistics. It's how we're all trained to look at you."

"I'm not a spreadsheet," she growled.

"No, you're not," he said through pursed lips, "but the best way to beat the enemy is to think like the enemy."

"And how do we know *you* aren't the enemy?" Julian piped, shifting closer to Brooklyn.

Porter stayed quiet, twiddling his fingers in his lap.

If she could have disregarded the entire situation as a whole, Brooklyn would have. She would've run away, only looking back once she was far enough that everything behind was a blur.

Somehow, it felt like her options had dwindled down to none. There was no way out of the cage that trapped her, and even if there was, she didn't know if she had the courage to leave her friends behind.

Porter kept talking of strength and speed—it didn't make any sense. A cluster of revelations had suddenly been dropped on all of their shoulders, and she wasn't strong enough to bear the weight of it. She wasn't fast enough to escape it.

"I don't expect you to trust me…"

Julian interrupted Porter with a loud laugh.

"But I want to help you as much as I can…I want the chance to earn your trust again." Porter looked up and peered at Brooklyn shyly.

It was silent.

Rayce exhaled a long breath. Julian tapped his fingers against the floor.

"We'll talk to Dawson and Amber," Rayce said.

Brooklyn felt relief slide off of her like freshly melted snow.

"We should eat," Brooklyn said.

Porter didn't move when the three got up and exited the tent.

"Hey," she stared at him over her shoulder. "I'll bring you some, all right?"

Porter's eyes were glassy. He looked away, hands twitching nervously in his lap.

"All right?" she repeated sternly.

"Yeah, all right," he said.

Brooklyn stepped out of the tent. As she fastened the flimsy makeshift door, she heard Porter swallow a small, exhausted sob.

Chapter Twelve

The soup was tepid. The taste of it was bland over Brooklyn's tongue even though it was filled with spices and vegetables. Still, she could appreciate its warmth.

Dawson and Gabriel emerged from the shadows beyond the trees.

They looked disoriented. Gabriel's cheeks were bright red. Her eyes were swollen. She had her arms folded around herself like a shield and shuffled nervously next to Brooklyn when she sat down.

Dawson was as fierce as ever. There was no fear in his eyes. He sat down next to Rayce, his back straight, chest lifting with every breath he took.

A boy named Jordan from Rayce's cabin took a piece of bread from the top of the duffle bag, which lay as a makeshift table.

"What're we doing?" Jordan asked timidly as he nibbled on his bread. He was tall with strong arms and long legs. He looked tired. He glanced around at each of them but never let his gaze linger, flicking from face to face before falling to the bread in his hand.

The camp had been small. They all knew of each other but tended to keep to their own cabins. Most exercises were done with the same small group day in and day out. The only time they all had the chance to really mingle was during breaks and meals.

"Resting," Rayce answered. He tried to give a convincing smile.

"Everyone wants to know what's going on and…" Jordan shifted his weight from one foot to the other, glancing at the tent where Porter was. "What we're going to do with him."

"Nothing yet," Dawson said.

"Is it true?" Jordan's voice cracked. "Ellie heard something about us being sick."

"We're not sick." Gabriel laughed sourly, reaching over Brooklyn to grab a piece of bread.

Dawson glared at Gabriel. "Rayce and I will fill everyone in. Just eat and relax, okay?"

Jordan didn't look like he was too fond of the answers he'd received, but he nodded anyway and headed back into the bus where the others were taking shelter from the cold.

The puffiness that swelled around Gabriel's eyes made her seem more fragile than she was. Her bony shoulders hunched up around her neck as she leaned over and rested her elbows on the tops of her thighs. Her tongue ran across the scar on her mouth, and she glanced at Brooklyn. "Sorry."

Goosebumps spread over the top of Brooklyn's arms, scaling the back of her neck, but she played along. "For what?"

"Trying to shoot Porter."

Brooklyn eased. "We need him."

"*You* need him."

Heat radiated through Brooklyn's cheeks, and she gritted her teeth. "Everything he knows could be useful in the long run, and he's a doctor. We need him in case someone gets hurt."

"Do you really believe that?"

"Do you honestly think I would jeopardize our lives for…" she waved her hands, trying to find the words she was looking for "—that guy?"

Gabriel's nostrils flared. She opened her mouth and took a deep breath. "No, I don't."

"After Seattle, we're going home," Brooklyn whispered. She reached over and snatched Gabriel's hand, squeezing it tightly. "Back to the beach, our eleven-month summer, street tacos, and…"

The way Gabriel ripped her hand from Brooklyn was devastating.

"You don't get it, do you?" Gabriel said, face twisting into a scowl.

Amber watched them from the other side of the fire. She bumped her knee against Dawson's to get his attention.

Brooklyn felt like she'd been kicked in the gut.

Gabriel stood up hastily, wiping her eyes. "We can't go home, Brookie! We can't. If we go home, those Surros, those *things* will find our parents, find my little brother. Then what?"

Her mouth was dry, and if Brooklyn could have hidden inside herself, she would have.

"We don't get to go back home." Gabriel shook her head and turned to stomp away. She was good at that, at getting away from situations until it was acceptable to ignore the things she didn't want to face.

Dawson turned to set his plastic bowl down, but Julian stopped him.

"No, no, just eat. I'll go get her," Julian said. He stood up to trot after Gabriel, who melted into the darkness.

Rayce watched Julian go while Dawson stared down at his bowl and chewed on his lip.

"We need a good night's sleep," Dawson said. "We need to collect ourselves and get everyone together to discuss what comes next."

"Isn't Seattle next?" Rayce asked.

"Yes, but I don't want anyone thinking this is going to be safe or easy. I don't want anyone to feel like they're being forced. So, in the morning, we'll get everyone else to sit down and talk."

After the situation in Portland, Brooklyn could understand exactly what Dawson was saying. The journey ahead, whatever journey it may be, could be a rough one. People could get hurt. It was no longer a game of hide and seek, and the letter he had come across in Terry's room wasn't a clue anymore. They were being hunted, and those who didn't want to run shouldn't feel obligated to. Those who didn't want to fight shouldn't be forced.

"That's a good idea," Amber said.

"It is," Brooklyn agreed.

Dawson stared into the darkness where Gabriel had gone. Rayce slapped a hand over his shoulder and said, "She's fine, D. Julian will calm her down."

"She's scared," Dawson whispered, more to himself than anyone else.

Brooklyn stood up quickly, brushing the dust off her pants. She reached out to get the last bowl of lukewarm soup and a hunk of bread before motioning toward the tent.

"I'm gonna take this to him," she said cautiously, almost asking for approval.

Dawson nodded. Brooklyn watched Amber give her a quick reassuring nod before she turned to unzip the tent and step inside.

Porter was sitting in the same exact spot he'd been in all night. His hands were balled up in his lap, and he was playing with the sleeves on his maroon sweatshirt. He didn't look up when she set the bowl in front of him. He didn't say anything. She decided to take a seat across from him on top of her bundled-up sleeping bag.

"Thank you," he said as he poked at the bread.

"Amber made it." Brooklyn pushed the bowl toward him. "It's still warm."

"You don't have to stay in here with me."

"Just eat your food," she grumbled.

He dunked his bread in the soup and took bite after bite until everything was gone.

It'd been a long day. Despite the many thoughts running through her head, Brooklyn could feel the tug of sleep pulling at her. She leaned back and stared at Porter, looking from the top of his head, which lolled lazily to the side, to his shoulders, slumped and weighted. His chest was strong. She could tell he was concentrating on each breath, the sound of his inhale, and the scratch of the air on his teeth when he exhaled.

"I can hear your heartbeat," Brooklyn said. "If I listen closely enough, I can hear it. You're nervous."

"That's incredible." He smiled and tapped on the space between his clavicles. "Harnessing something like that could come in handy. You could be a human lie detector."

"I don't want to be a human lie detector," Brooklyn growled.

Porter shrugged. "And you're right. I am nervous."

"Because you think we're going to kill you?"

"No, I don't think you're going to kill me."

"You're wrong. I am going to kill you, just not yet."

His lips twitched into a crooked smile, and he flicked the plastic spoon with his index finger. "I'm scared that I won't be able to stop them if they find us."

"Who?"

"Everyone associated with the project that's out searching for us right now."

"What will they do when they find us?"

"That's the problem," Porter said. "I don't know."

Brooklyn's stomach turned, and she closed her eyes. Her thoughts revolved around laboratories filled with gleaming silver tools, curious hands prodding at her like she was an animal. She imagined cages and needles, rooms with stark white walls. The image of a cold steel slab where doctors and technicians ogled her kept branding itself in her mind. All the things she'd read in books and seen in movies were the building blocks of her nightmare.

"You need to sleep," he said softly.

She shifted uncomfortably and gnawed on one of her fingernails. Her options were small, but they were there. Brooklyn could take her sleeping bag into the other tent, or she could climb into the bus.

But if she left him...

Her eyes flicked up to Porter's face. The urgency that consumed her when Gabriel pointed the gun at him still lingered.

Brooklyn kicked off her boots.

"You don't have to sleep here," Porter said.

"I know," she said through a yawn. She shrugged her jacket off so she could wad it up and use it as a makeshift pillow.

A battery-operated lantern glowed in the corner of the tent.

Brooklyn thought about Gabriel, thought about home. She thought about her friends and wondered if they would die running. Or, one day down the road, could they start over?

Porter sighed. Brooklyn listened to the crunch of the tent as he moved around.

Her eyes were closed when Julian and Rayce walked inside. They cracked open when chilly fingertips brushed a piece of hair off the curve of her cheek.

"Hey," Julian whispered. "Gabriel and Dawson are staying in the other tent with Amber; you wanna go with them?"

She shook her head.

"You sure?" he pressed, voice straining.

101

She nodded.

Rayce and Julian took turns staying up. Both lay on either side of her like warm, solid walls, blocking her from the sight of Porter, curled up on the opposite side of the tent.

Brooklyn fell asleep while Julian told Rayce stories of his mom's restaurant in L.A., and Rayce told Julian about growing up in Texas.

She didn't dream.

Chapter Thirteen

Two arms twisted around Brooklyn's front, settling on her lower back. Her eyes flew open, and she gasped, squirming backward to try and get away. When she saw golden hair and Gabriel's big clear eyes blinking back at her, she stopped struggling.

"It was weird not sleeping in the same place as you," Gabriel murmured tiredly as she scooted forward and buried her head under Brooklyn's chin.

Brooklyn took a deep breath. "Did you sleep okay?"

"Yeah. Dawson was there, and so was Amber, but it still didn't feel right leaving you alone in here."

"I wasn't alone." Brooklyn smirked. "Julian and Rayce were in here. So was Porter."

"Exactly," Gabriel growled and wrinkled her nose.

Brooklyn rolled her eyes. "He wouldn't hurt me."

"Yes, he would," Gabriel said, snuggling closer

into Brooklyn's space and hugging their bodies tightly together. "I mean, he's already hurt you enough. If he did any more damage, I would definitely have to kill him."

"No one's killing anyone right now," Brooklyn breathed whilst petting Gabriel's hair.

If anyone felt like home, it was Gabriel.

The air was cold and damp. Even in the tent, the younger girl shivered against Brooklyn's torso. They stayed like that for as long as they could. Sharing such a small space reminded them of the simplicity back at camp. Of routine and ignorance. Sometimes, Brooklyn wished they could go back. Sometimes, she wished they could rewind and never find that letter.

"Did you hear that?" Gabriel whispered suddenly, body stiffening.

Brooklyn opened her eyes and held her breath. She listened carefully to what was going on outside.

Dawson was walking back and forth between the bus and the tent.

Julian was helping Porter make coffee over a dimming fire.

Amber was in the bus with the others. Jordan, Rayce, but Ellie…

Ellie was screaming.

It echoed distantly through the trees along with the sound of her boots beating the ground. Twigs snapped. Her nails raked across the trunk of a tree when she passed it.

"They found me!" Ellie squealed and shrieked, "Run! They're here! They've found us. Run!"

Gabriel squeezed Brooklyn. "You're my best

friend, Brookie. You know that, right?"

Brooklyn couldn't breathe. She couldn't think.

Dawson's footsteps stopped and Porter's voice went quiet.

Rayce was the first to run toward Ellie.

"We need to get the guns," Brooklyn said quickly, scrambling to sit up and get her boots on.

Gabriel darted out of the tent. Dawson tried to reach for her, but she swung around the left side of him, sprinting toward the woods after Rayce.

"Gabriel, stop!" There was desperation in his voice. A sleek black gun was shoved at his chest.

Porter's expression was grim. "Let's go."

Julian tried to keep calm, piling as many bags as he could together so they were easier to grab. His eyes moved to Brooklyn when she came stumbling out of the tent. Her head whipped from side to side until she found what she was looking for: the slender curve of Gabriel's legs as she ran through the trees, with Dawson and Porter at her heels.

"We need to get everyone in the bus. We need to get out of here," Julian's voice shook.

The sound of bodies clashing came before the drowned, gnarled howling of the Surros.

Ellie bounded into the camp heaving in deep, burning breaths. Her hands were covered in black sludge, and her shirt was torn. She tripped trying to get to the safety of the bus, and tears came pouring out of her eyes.

Brooklyn rushed to her side and pushed strands of Ellie's hair away, peeling them out of the black blood on her face.

"How many are there?" Brooklyn asked.

Ellie couldn't stop crying, clutching at Brooklyn roughly, with her nails scrabbling to find purchase on her shoulders.

"Ellie!" Brooklyn shouted, "Talk! How many?"

"Too many," Ellie sobbed. "I couldn't count. I c-couldn't…"

"Go inside," Brooklyn said.

Ellie was taken inside by Jordan. He was pale-faced and sickly-looking.

Brooklyn looked over her shoulder to Julian, who was staring back at her. It was an unspoken agreement between close friends. No words were necessary.

I don't leave without you is what they said to one another in silence, eyes locking for a short moment. Then they were off, running faster than they ever had.

Straight toward the clatter just past the tree line.

Chapter Fourteen

Brooklyn thought about slowing down as the noises started to get louder. She expected her legs to falter, and give out before she faced the Surros again. But they didn't. She lunged past the trees with Julian at her side while the sun peeked through a thick layer of morning mist hovering low in the sky. They made a quick turn around a large oak, and suddenly, the blur of the enemy became clear.

The crash of a squirming body startled her into a skidding stop. Brooklyn caught herself before she could fall backward.

It was a Surro.

Its body writhed in the leaves scattered on the ground. Its back was broken, eyes bloodshot and protruding from their sockets while it wailed and clawed at her feet. Brooklyn gave it a blunt kick in the skull and turned back toward the chaos to find Julian running into the fray.

Ellie was right. There were too many—at least five Surros to every one person in the camp. They were everywhere, screaming and hissing. It was

Brooklyn's nightmare played out in real time, and the only thing that pushed her to move was a gunshot.

Porter struggled to reload as he shoved a larger Surro back with his fist. Black blood was splattered across his face. It speckled his glasses and dripped over the front of his shirt, accompanied by a patch of damp crimson bursting over his shoulder.

Brooklyn ran forward and tried to piece together a plan or an idea, anything that could help them get out of this alive. Maneuvers danced behind her eyes, every strategy Terry had forced on them, every combat simulation, and every fighting style. She kept it all on repeat and strained to keep focused and controlled.

Three closed in on Porter, only a few feet away. The nearest to him was the largest. When it reached out, he raised the gun to fire, shirt lifting to expose a gleam of metal shoved in the back of his jeans.

She saw it happen before she moved. Every particular play. Every intricate detail. It happened exactly how she predicted, exactly how she wanted, and all she had to do was concentrate.

As he pulled the trigger she slid on her knees behind him. Her fingertips latched around the sleek silver gun. She tugged it out of his jeans and slammed it into the jaw of a slender Surro to their left. It crushed the creature's jaw and left its mouth hanging open. Teeth dropped from its gums, rotted and sallow, while empty eyes stared out at them before it fell to the ground. Brooklyn swooped in front of him and aimed the gun over his shoulder, firing a bullet between the eyes of the third Surro that had been running toward them from behind the dense brush.

Porter's breathing was shallow, and he clutched on to her waist. "God, you're fast," he said, voice grave and low.

"Go back to the camp," Brooklyn said as she tore his shirt and revealed the wound on his shoulder. A deep gash, caked in drying blood and dirt. His shoulder had been filleted open, and unlike the rest of them, Porter didn't possess any radical healing powers. How he hadn't already passed out from blood loss was beyond her.

"I rubbed some dirt on it. I'm fine." Porter's voice wobbled.

"What happened to you?"

"A Surro got a hold of one of Amber's knives." He winced when she tugged on him. "I said I'm fine. Go help them!"

"I can't just...leave you, you idiot. You'll die." She grabbed his hand and kept it snug on her hip, demanding that he hold on to her.

He leaned against her, and she backed up, forcing him to take heavy steps backward as well.

"Well, I guess letting me die would leave you without the opportunity to kill me yourself," he said, almost laughing.

"Exactly."

Brooklyn focused on the orchestra of sounds. On each branch that was broken. Every yelp and shout. The cluster of voices melted together and made it nearly impossible to find her friends.

Her eyes finally came across Rayce with a Surro climbing up over his shoulder. He fisted his fingers in the back of the white cloth shirt it was wearing and smashed it carelessly into a tree.

Julian was with Dawson. They were back to back, shouting at one another about what they were supposed to do while another group of Surros descended from around a wall of pale green bushes.

Dawson's movements were quick and precise. He knew exactly where to put his hands, how high to kick, when to move just an inch or pivot a certain way to avoid unnecessary contact with the enemy. He was textbook. A prime example of what they'd learned in the camp.

Julian was good at deflection. He could use anyone's own strength against them and make it look like an art form. His body twirled around, and he ducked down underneath a Surro, snatching its arm and twisting it painfully until it snapped. Brooklyn almost flinched watching.

"Where is she?" Brooklyn whimpered, fingers dancing nervously against her palm.

Porter hissed loudly, "Brooklyn, on your left!" He tried to lift the gun, but the Surro was on top of them before he could even get his arm up.

Porter was knocked to the ground. Brooklyn's lungs jumped into her throat. Pale fingertips latched around her jaw, and jagged yellow nails stung when they dug into her cheeks. She squirmed and thrashed while its dark eyes stared at her, a face full of black veins and busted capillaries. Its breath was putrid, and she almost gagged when it leaned closer and snapped its teeth at her face. "Got the girl," it chirped horribly. "Got her, got her, got—"

There was a glint of silver and Brooklyn flinched

as the side of her face was sprayed with thick, black liquid. The hilt of a knife jutted from the Surros temple, cutting its proclamations short.

It fell toward Brooklyn, and she jumped away. The body slammed face first into the forest floor.

Amber knelt down and pulled the knife from the Surro's skull. "More are coming."

"More?" Brooklyn whimpered, glancing around to the already overwhelming amount of Surrogates and their bodies that littered the ground.

"Yeah, we gotta get," Amber said and bounced back to her feet.

Porter's eyes scrunched shut as he tried to lift himself off the ground. He whined under his breath and wasn't shy about reaching for Brooklyn when she offered to help him up.

"Where's Gabriel?" Brooklyn asked after she'd slung Porter's good arm over her shoulder.

Amber twirled two knives in each of her hands and bounced from foot to foot.

"That girl was everywhere," Amber said. She lifted her hand over her head with one of the small knives tucked between her knuckles and threw it hard at a Surro that was charging toward Rayce. It flew end over end until it met its mark and sank into the thin flesh of the Surros neck.

Amber took off running toward Rayce to retrieve her knife while Brooklyn lifted her head and wrapped an arm around Porter's waist to steady him.

"You're okay," she said and nudged him.

"I need stitches," he snorted.

The area around them sounded like a storm, but

one voice in particular demanded Brooklyn's attention.

"Get back to the bus!" Gabriel yelled, sprinting across the clearing toward Dawson. Her hair fluttered behind her as she leapt over the body of a dead Surro and spun around when another large creature lunged toward her from behind a tree. She was a machine, spinning, kicking, hitting, and crushing everything in her way. Her willowy hands wrapped around the wrists of the Surro, and she used it as a platform to vault herself over its head. Her feet hit the ground behind it, and she yanked its arms cruelly before slamming the sharp edge of her knee into the center of its back.

Another Surro tried to surprise her. She smashed her elbow into the bridge of its nose, tangled her fingers into its knotted black hair, and slammed its face into the trunk of a tree.

Brooklyn's eyes widened when she saw the hoard of Surros running toward them in the distance, a mass of bodies that blocked the light between the trees coming to retrieve them. Her heart was pounding, her mind going a million miles an hour, trying to find a solution or a way out. Something. Anything that could give them more time.

But this was the end of the line.

Porter sank heavily against her, and Brooklyn shook him as gently as she could. His eyelashes cracked open, and he swallowed hard. "Get outta here, Brooklyn. You need to get out of here."

"Gabriel!" Brooklyn shouted, leaning up on the tips of her toes to try and get her friend's attention.

Porter tried to pull away, but she tightened her grip and shook her head. "I'm not leaving you here," she said, glancing at him.

Three Surros clambered toward Porter and Brooklyn. One of them crawled, dragging itself toward them with a broken leg. The other two stalked toward them like predators closing in on prey. She was strong enough to kill them—she knew that. But Porter wouldn't be able to stand on his own. If she put him down, they could easily get to him.

Brooklyn growled and backed up, dragging Porter with her. She fumbled for the gun, steadied her breathing, and aimed. But when she pulled the trigger, a tiny click was all that came from the barrel.

"God dammit," she cursed and shoved the empty pistol into the back of her pants.

Brooklyn lifted her leg and kicked one of the nearing Surros in the chest. The other three snapped their teeth and muttered nonsense as they inched closer.

It seemed like there was no way out.

Porter kept apologizing to the base of her neck, asking her again and again to leave him behind. She kept backing up until they hit the stump of a broken tree, almost toppling over it.

The thought that maybe it wouldn't be so bad if they were taken flashed through her mind. A quiet whispered idea that it would be easier to give up, that fighting or running would only delay the inevitable.

A gunshot proved the thought to be fleeting.

Gabriel jumped in front of them. She grabbed the closest Surro by the throat and squeezed until its eyes rolled back and the veins in its forehead started popping out above its eyebrows.

Julian shot the other three and stumbled over beside Brooklyn.

"Let me help you," Julian said.

Brooklyn nodded, and they adjusted on each side of Porter so they could give him enough stability to walk along with them.

Gabriel was covered in black Surro slime, and she gagged when she looked down at herself.

A chorus of screams rose up through the trees. Julian gestured to the rest of the uncharted forest with his chin. "Come on, we need to go. They have the cars. They'll find us."

"We can't leave them!" Brooklyn shouted.

Julian's teeth set hard, lips drawn into a tight line. "He's dying, Brooklyn. We have to clean this shit out." He glanced over the parted skin on Porter's shoulder. The cut was deep enough to expose the pale yellow sponge of muscle tissue and a thin line of fresh blood wouldn't stop dripping down his chest.

"All the medical supplies are back at camp…"

"There's a river," Porter slurred and pointed over Brooklyn's shoulder. "I heard it last night."

"I heard it too…but we can't…" Brooklyn's voice trailed off when Gabriel started walking in the direction Porter pointed.

"They're coming!" Gabriel snapped. "Julian's right. Dawson will find us. We have to get out of here!"

114

Brooklyn didn't want to leave. She didn't want to hide. To wait. To surrender. But they were out of options. It felt so cowardly listening to the Surros sprint toward the camp while they snuck off in the opposite direction.

It was a hard pill to swallow, and all that Brooklyn could think of was the look on Dawson's face when he realized they were missing.

"They have all the guns," Julian said softly. "They're gonna be all right."

Their pace quickened as the hollow screech of the Surros echoed through the mist. Brooklyn's eyes started to burn. Tears dripped down her cheeks, betraying the strength she'd been trying to hold on to. She didn't want to cry. She didn't want to crumble.

The screams, the shouts, and the voices of their friends all faded away with every step they took.

Gabriel's hands trembled, and Brooklyn watched her clench them over and over again.

"There's a cabin up here," Gabriel said. "Looks empty. It'll be better to be inside. We'll look for the river once we've put him somewhere safe."

"Best we got," Julian said.

Chapter Fifteen

The cabin was large, with a dark cherry wood door and light cream-colored shutters on the windows. It stood alone in the woods with no trail leading to or from it. A broom was propped beside the door, and a couple cheap fold-out chairs were discolored and weather-worn on the porch. It didn't look lived-in. Gabriel cupped her hands around the window to look inside, but she couldn't see anything past the thick layer of dust.

"It's probably some old rental property," Julian said.

Brooklyn didn't trust it, but she didn't trust anything anymore. Julian was right; it was the best thing they had.

Gabriel jostled the doorknob. "It's open."

Julian handed Gabriel his gun, and she pushed the heavy door until it slid slowly against the floorboards. The hinges, thick with rust, creaked as the door came sliding to a stop. The air was littered with particles of dust that glittered when rays of muted sunlight beamed inside. The small pieces of furniture laid out as a living room looked old and smelt like expired dryer sheets.

Nothing about the place seemed harmful. The décor was eclectic, consisting of floral patterned drapes on either side of the shutters and old copper kitchenware in the open-facing kitchen on the right. There was a blue velvet recliner and a pale yellow couch embroidered with pictures of dandelions toward the center of the room, adjacent to a large stone fireplace. A red rug with frayed edges lay beneath a large wooden trunk that served as a coffee table.

"Get him on the couch. I'll sweep the second level," Gabriel said, creeping silently up the carpeted staircase next to the back door.

They tried to be as careful as they could, but Porter still whined when they set him down on the couch. His shoulder had stopped bleeding, but the gash was matted with dried blood and mounds of dirt. Brooklyn could only imagine the infection he would get if they didn't get him cleaned up.

"Think they'll really find us out here?" Brooklyn asked.

Julian was using a pocket knife to cut the remainder of Porter's shirt off so they wouldn't have it pull it over his arm.

"'Course they will," Julian said matter-of-factly. "There's no way Dawson would go anywhere without Gabriel, and I'd like to think we matter a little bit too."

There was a smile on his face, the kind that told Brooklyn he was trying to keep himself together. She wasn't going to dim his positive light with the dreariness of her worries. She tried her best to smile and absorb some of his hopefulness.

Porter's face was pale and ashy. His eyes were faint, like he was chasing after sleep each time he blinked.

Gabriel's feet made loud sounds against the floor, creaking and cracking as she walked into each room upstairs. She sighed when she jumped down the last two steps on her way back down the stairs.

"No one's here," she said.

Brooklyn nodded. She crouched down beside Porter to get a closer look at his shoulder. She chewed on her lip. "I don't know how to handle this," she confessed as Porter's gaze shifted toward her.

It was hard to watch him try and swallow, to listen to the way his throat clenched dryly.

The floorboards were old and wheezed under the weight of their feet. A soft whistle of wind flowed past the window through the screen on the top of the back door. Everything was natural. Appropriate. Nothing seemed out of place. Except for a distant drum that echoed like a dull record in Brooklyn's ear. It was off-beat, a dual set of repeating notes that continued on and on. Brooklyn closed her eyes, listening to each one. They were soft and warm, muffled by something, either miles or…earth.

Brooklyn's bright, curious eyes fanned out over the floor. They traced each crack and crevice until she found a notch just shy of the fireplace, peeking out from beneath the red Persian rug.

"What is it?" Gabriel huffed.

Brooklyn held up a hand to silence her before

118

she pointed slowly toward the rug.

They weren't drums.

"We aren't alone," Brooklyn whispered.

They were heartbeats.

Porter tried to get up, but Brooklyn pushed down forcefully on his chest to keep him on the couch. He yelped and cursed, slapped her hands and narrowed his eyes. "Let me up."

A smothered crash came from under the floor. Brooklyn strained the listen for the heart beats. They continued to drum, escalating rapidly.

"It's a cellar door," Julian hardly whispered as he took slow, hesitant steps around the trunk. He lifted the far edge of the rug to reveal an old cracked and rusted latch. It blended almost seamlessly with the rest of the floor.

Gabriel aimed the gun just shy of the latch and glanced between Julian and Brooklyn.

Brooklyn shook her head. "They might have seen the Surros and hid. They're probably just campers."

Julian nodded.

They moved slowly. Gabriel curled and uncurled her fingers around the gun. Julian rubbed his palms together. Porter was holding his breath and continued to struggle, but Brooklyn still held him down.

Julian pulled the latch and lifted the door in one swift movement.

Brooklyn froze when she heard a smooth voice wrap like silk around the stillness of the cabin.

"Now, now. It would be in your best interest to put that gun down, sweetheart."

119

Gabriel smiled despite the long barrel of a shotgun pointed at her from the top of the stairs that led down into the darkness of the cellar.

Julian was quick to step in front of her, showing the skin of palms. "Forgive us for intruding, but our friend is hurt. He's lost a lot of blood, and if we don't do something, he's not going to stay conscious for very much longer."

Heavy footsteps shook the floor. Brooklyn stood protectively in front of Porter while the keeper of their safe-haven appeared out of the cellar.

Long platinum dreadlocks sprouted from the top of his head, pushed back by a pair of dark navy goggles wrapped snug behind his ears. A short blonde goatee framed thin lips, and light grey eyes analyzed each of them carefully.

"We heard quite a commotion out in the woods," the stranger said. He gestured to the three of them with his shotgun. "Were you all a part of that?"

Brooklyn felt Porter tap against her hand and she inhaled a deep breath. "Yes," she said hurriedly. "We're on the run from some bad people."

"A lot of bad people claim to be on the run from bad people, missy."

Brooklyn's jaw clenched and her chest ached. "We need your help…We need to clean his shoulder and sew him up. Let us stay here one night, and we'll be out of your way, I swear. Just, please…"

"Go on and tell your friend to hand over that nice little .22, and we'll consider talking." He wasn't aggressive, but his eyes never left Brooklyn. The way he stared, unblinking and cold, made her rethink her cry for his help.

Porter tensed under her hand which was still resting on top of his chest. She nodded to Gabriel. "Give it to him."

"Brookie, I'm not going to give this freak our gun."

"Yes, you are!"

The man clutched his shotgun tighter.

"Gabriel, give him the gun. Now." Brooklyn's words tumbled out from between her clenched teeth.

Julian nudged Gabriel with his elbow.

"C'mon, Gabriel is it? Now, you all stumbled in on us unexpected, and if you wouldn't mind, I'd like to be sure of those I offer a hand in helping, you understand? I'll take that gun of yours and set it on the table. Then we can take a look at your friend." The stranger was insistent but lacked any real hostility.

The shotgun was raised, propped up toward the ceiling. He reached out and curled his fingers inwards, inviting Gabriel to place the gun in his hand.

"So, Gabriel and...Brooke?" he guessed, eyes flashing toward Brooklyn.

"Brooklyn," she corrected as politely and evenly as she could. "This is Julian and Porter..." She moved aside only a fraction, so the man could see their friend mangled by the fight.

"I'm Nicoli," he said.

"There's another person down there," Gabriel blurted defensively. "Make them come up here, and then I'll put the gun down."

Nicoli's smile was wolfish and dark, but he shrugged his shoulder anyways. "Fair enough," he mused.

The tan coat he wore was lined heavily in off-white sheepskin, and when he stepped aside, it tapped against the ripped-up bottoms of his blue jeans.

A heavy-set young woman with high cheek bones and fringe violet bangs emerged from the cellar, holding a dusty white box. Her skin was dark, matching her ruddy eyes, and a small golden hoop hung delicately from her septum.

"I'm Cambria." Her gaze settled on Gabriel.

Gabriel still held on tightly to her gun. "What's all that?"

"Medical supplies for your friend," Cambria answered, dipping the box forward so Gabriel could look inside.

"Gabriel!" Brooklyn seethed.

Gabriel's eyes rolled. She flipped the gun and handed it over by the handle to Nicoli. "Here. Sorry. I've got trust issues."

"Understood." Nicoli smiled sweetly. It was a comforting surprise.

It didn't quite make sense, but something told Brooklyn there was much more to Cambria and Nicoli than they imagined.

Chapter Sixteen

Cambria was quiet for the most part, but she hummed while she worked. Every so often, Porter would make a wise comment while she cleaned out his arm, and the gap between her teeth would show cutely as she smiled down at him. Porter's face was once again alive with color, cheeks flushed a deep red as Cambria used a soft sponge to dab at the inside of the gash. He didn't make much sound, but whimpered occasionally with his hands fisted in the couch cushions.

"I need more water," Cambria said.

The small bowl of water she'd been using to flush his wound was clouded, murky with blood and grime.

Nicoli nodded. "I'm guessing none of you are very familiar with the river about a quarter mile east of here, are you?"

"Porter mentioned hearing it at our camp, but we're not very sure where it is," Brooklyn said.

"It runs the length of these woods. We collect our water from there." Nicoli reached for the shotgun that was now resting by the fireplace and hoisted the barrel to rest casually over his shoulder. "I'll show you if someone wants to join me."

Brooklyn's attention was captured by Porter. Even if he did seem to be doing all right, she preferred to stay with him—that was quite clear to everyone in the room. Julian was the one who agreed to go even when Gabriel glared at him from her place behind the recliner.

Gabriel watched them go and chewed nervously on her lip when the back door shut quietly behind them.

It was hard for her to accept help from a couple of people they didn't know. Especially a couple of people who could very well turn on them at any second. But Brooklyn could see the relief hidden inside Gabriel's eyes. They were hooded, and her breathing was even, shoulders relaxed. Even if it wasn't the most ideal break they'd been given, at least they had a break in general.

"I'm going to stitch you from the inside out," Cambria said softly.

Porter nodded. "I assumed so. Seems to me you have a basic understanding of what to do. Are you a nurse?"

"Vet tech," she hummed.

Porter raised a brow. "Well, thank you, Cambria. For helping me."

"It's against our code to leave anyone in need without assistance. It isn't human."

"Your code?" he asked curiously.

Cambria smiled, but ignored the subject completely.

"The reason I told you I'll be stitching you up from the inside out wasn't because I assumed you hadn't already known that, but because I don't have any anesthetic. You'll feel everything."

Brooklyn's face squirmed as if she'd felt Porter's discomfort herself. The thought brought her back to Terry's cabin, to being held down on a table. Porter's wound was much more severe, but she could relate.

Porter's mouth twisted into a wrinkled frown. He gave a curt nod. "Do what you gotta do."

***

Julian kept up with Nicoli's brisk pace and catalogued his surroundings as they went.

There was an odd-looking tree, bent and warped with its roots hanging over the edge of a small divot in the earth. They jumped down over a cluster of rocks and looped around a bushel of pale pink flowers. Finally, they descended toward the banks of the river. This part of the woods felt different than the rest. It was secluded, rich with plant life, a place that Julian would have loved to explore.

The river was quiet and hardly moved except for the small ripple of waves that skidded across the top of the water when a small puff of wind blew against it.

"Are you and your friends out here on your own?" Nicoli asked.

Julian cleared his throat. "We got separated from the rest of our group."

"I'm assuming that happened when the bad

people Miss Brooklyn told me about came upon you in these peaceful woods?"

"Yeah." Julian handed over the clean bucket when Nicoli reached for it. "That's about right."

Nicoli dipped the lip of the white bucket into the river and collected a substantial amount of water.

"I know what it's like to run." Nicoli's words were blanketed in a throaty laugh. "Cambria and I, we've been running for a long time. We've taken in strays along the way, people like you and your friends. Only if they chose to stay and only if they were on board with our cause and with our code."

Julian's heart was beating faster than he expected. He nodded along, turning to walk beside Nicoli once they started to make their way back to the cabin.

"What is your, uh, cause...?" Julian asked timidly.

The taller man smiled, and his lashes closed around one of his eyes in a quick wink. "Revolt, my friend. Revolt."

***

Brooklyn jumped when the back door swung open. Gabriel tapped her nails against the window that she'd been leaning against.

"Bring it here," Cambria said, curling her fingers toward Nicoli.

Julian shuffled close to Gabriel, and her eyes asked him questions that he couldn't answer in the crowded room. But he did lean in and breathe against her ear, "We'll trust them for now." It was enough to allow her to relax a bit more.

"We have some menthol," Nicoli said with his eyebrows drawn tight and a grimace on his face. "It might make things a bit less...horrible."

"Save it for after," Cambria said. She was lacing a thin sewing needle with thread.

Porter's gaze was hardened and callous as he stared up at the ceiling. Brooklyn stood next to the arm of the couch and reached down to tap on his forehead.

"How long will something like this take to heal?" Brooklyn asked.

Porter pulled his bottom lip between his teeth and rolled it. "A few weeks. Less if I can get to my supplies."

Fresh water flushed the wound, and Porter winced, gritting his teeth as Cambria dabbed the inflamed rim of the gash with a clean cloth.

"Iodine?" Porter gritted when he spotted a small bottle of dark liquid on the trunk.

Cambria nodded. "Correct. Did you think I would use river water to clean you out without disinfecting it first? Please."

Porter smirked.

"Don't hold your breath, all right?" Cambria added quickly.

She didn't give him much time to prepare. Within seconds of speaking, she had the needle sliding into the flesh on the inside of the wound. His hips lifted up from the couch, and he dug his heels into the cushion. The shirt he was wearing was gone. A sheen of sweat started to form across his torso, which was clenched tight along with his jaw, his hands, and his eyes.

Brooklyn wanted to reach down and touch him, to reassure him that he would be all right. The person she used to be would have done that. The girl who was about to graduate high school and had a future to look forward to—she would have done it. But Brooklyn sat back and nibbled on her nail beds, torn between the compassion she had buried down under the rubble of distrust and the growling bitter voice that whispered "he deserves it" in the back of her mind.

The make-shift procedure lasted only a few minutes. Cambria's speed and nimble hands were impressive. Brooklyn finally felt somewhat at ease when she saw the clean white bandage wrapped snug around Porter's shoulder and chest.

Porter didn't look at all like he was relieved. His cheeks were blotched bright red, and his eyes were swollen from tears that ran down the edges of his cheeks. He pawed them away carelessly and adjusted his glasses. Not once had he made a sound. Not one cry or whine or plea.

Brooklyn thought maybe he looked at the pain as a punishment.

Nicoli placed a hand on Brooklyn's back and pointed through the window toward a cluster of trees on the left side of the cabin. "We have another camp out that way. More people, supplies, food and water. There's a room upstairs where Porter can stay, but the rest of you are welcome to share our space if you'd like."

Brooklyn glanced at Gabriel, who nodded back at her.

"That would be very much appreciated," she answered. "I'd like to stay with Porter, though, until he's doing a little better."

"I'll stay here so you can get some food," Cambria said softly. "Nicoli will have Plum whip up a healing remedy, and when you come back after dinner tonight, we can trade posts."

It was hard to agree to leave Porter alone. But Julian cleared his throat, and Brooklyn saw his eyes shift around nervously. He gave a slight shake of his head, a warning not to oppose their generosity.

"Thank you," Brooklyn said.

Nicoli smiled and hoisted the shotgun up over his shoulder again. "Follow me."

Brooklyn's fingertips trailed against the couch beside Porter. His hand brushed tentatively against hers. She took long strides out the back door behind Gabriel. Brooklyn glanced over her shoulder just once to see Porter's gaze lingering on them as the door swung closed.

Chapter Seventeen

The camp Nicoli spoke of was composed of a small slew of tents upright with old rugs and carpets set out in front of them like welcome mats. An old shed that had the same vintage feel of the cabin was the center point. It loomed eerily in front of a smoldering pit of almost burnt-out logs with four or five tents scattered around it. Some vibrant animal print fold-up chairs sat around the fire. An old clothes line stretched between a long pole and the shingles on the top of the shed.

Whoever they all were, they'd been out in the woods for a long time.

A wind-chime sang when the flap of a tent drooped open. It hung from the top of a small orange tent and a brightly stitched oriental rug was beneath it. A pair of dainty feet stepped out, toenails a glittery bubblegum pink.

"Plum," Nicoli said, arms open as he showed off Brooklyn, Julian, and Gabriel as if they were long-lost friends of his. "I've brought some wandering souls to our home. They'll be joining us for dinner tonight and perhaps tomorrow night as well."

The young woman who crawled out of her tent was lean and bony. Two long braids twisted out from the brim of a well-worn straw hat, and a thin white sundress hung over her body like a shirt that was two sizes too big.

"Hey y'all," Plum said. Her words were coated in a thick southern accent. "Seems a bushel of jumpy critters by the look of ya."

Nicoli grinned. "They are rather jumpy—I must say." He winked at Gabriel, and she couldn't help but roll her eyes and smile back at him.

"Well then, how 'bout I find somethin' for us to eat, and we get on with some cookin'?" Plum said.

"I'll actually be starting dinner myself tonight, Plum. One of their friends was badly injured, and I would love for you to whip up some ointment to help with the pain. Can you do that?"

She nodded and shrugged. "I sure can, Nic. Do any of y'all have names?"

Plum's eyes were almost too big for her face. They sat far apart beneath thick, unmanaged eyebrows and glowed prettily against her light lashes.

"I, uh…" Brooklyn cleared her throat. "I'm Brooklyn. This is Julian and Gabriel."

The other two nodded. Julian raised his hand in a friendly wave while he looked wearily around the camp site.

"What happened to your friend, then, hmm?" Plum asked. She was reaching back into her tent and rummaging around. A stone mortar and pestle rolled out on to the mat, followed by a few vials filled with different colored oils.

Brooklyn didn't know how to answer, how to make something terrifying and otherworldly seem plausible and realistic. She tried to sugar coat the words to herself but it just came out sounding wishy-washy and incomplete. Which, it was. Everything was still so incomplete. They had no real idea what they were fighting against, and they had no idea when whoever they were running from was going to find them.

Plum smiled, her legs crossed and her hands in her lap, watching them expectedly.

Gabriel flipped one of the chairs around and sat down. "We're running from some bad people. They found us, and they hurt him."

Her words floated around like ash, clogging up the space they all shared. Brooklyn almost choked on them.

"Bad people?" Plum asked slyly. "What kinda bad people are we talkin' 'bout? Because there's bad people who beat their dogs an' their wives, there's bad people who sell smokes to little ones, and there's bad people who steal from their mama. We talkin' bout those kinda bad people here? Or are we talkin' 'bout the kinda bad people who can throw you in a room and lose the room?"

Brooklyn's face tightened up.

"We're running from the government because they think they own us," Julian said.

His words came out slurred and rushed like the moment they had popped into his head he'd let them explode past his lips. The instantaneous regret that washed from his forehead to his slack jaw was brightened with a deep blush.

Plum tilted her head to the side and grinned. "Well, aren't we all? It's hard to come across likeminded folk. I'm sure Nicoli is jumpin' for joy over y'all's arrival if that's the truth."

Nicoli walked into the shed and started preparing something for dinner. Brooklyn still didn't know how far they could stretch the truth until it ran out of oxygen and deflated right in front of them. What Julian said hadn't been a lie—not in the least. But the details that went along with it could cost the people harboring them their lives and so far…well, so far, Nicoli, Cambria, and Plum all seemed like people Brooklyn might have called friends.

Julian looked relieved and nodded, eyebrows raised high on his forehead. "We've been on the run for a little while now. What about you? How long have you been out here with Nicoli?"

Plum stood up and walked into the shed, returning with a bundle of herbs and flowers in her arms along with a bag full of spices. When she talked, it sounded like butterflies tap danced on the edges of her lips. She was whispery and chirped at the end of some sentences while humming at the end of others. Everything about her seemed whimsical and dreamy, like perhaps she walked right out of a southern sunset.

"Used to live in Georgia," she started as she tore open the bag of spices with her teeth. "My mama died when I was a tiny thing, so my daddy raised me. He got himself cancer and died about eight months ago. So I decided to get in his car and drive it 'til I couldn't. I made my way out to these parts, but my daddy's old car crapped out on me before I could get to Portland. I hitchhiked up to Seattle, and that's where Nicoli found me. Some guys I thought were nice fellows offered me a ride back to the place I was stayin'. Turns out they weren't no nice fellows at all and tried to put their hands on me."

Plum paused to shove a piece of gum in her mouth and smacked it loudly. She grinded the dark star-shaped seeds up with the pestle then poured in half of one of the vials and continued to mix it all together.

"Those two good-for-nothing woman beaters almost got me in the back of their old town car. If it weren't for Nicoli bein' there to stop 'em, I'd probably be rottin' somewhere in a back alley, bein' rained on."

"What'd he do?" Gabriel asked.

"Oh, he shot one of 'em right there in the kneecap with a pistol," Plum said.

Brooklyn shifted to look at Julian, and he gave a half-shrug. Gabriel grinned ear to ear.

"Then he got me all wrapped up in a blanket and brought me back here. Told me I didn't have to stay or nothin' and that his way of life wasn't for everyone. I stayed, though. Didn't have much of anythin' to go back to anyways."

"What does he mean by his way of life?" Gabriel asked.

"Same as you, I s'pose," Plum said. "'Cept you're runnin' and we're fightin'. And when we're not fightin', we're plannin'."

Brooklyn was curious, but pressing the matter wasn't going to get them anywhere except into trouble. She opened her mouth and inhaled a sharp breath. "And what is it you're making? Nicoli said it was an ointment?"

"Mm-hmm," Plum hummed. "Peppermint leaves, aloe, cardamom, dried gotu kola and some marigold. I'm grinding it all together with some rose oil extract and coconut oil so it can be applied like a salve."

"Oh..." Brooklyn was taken aback by the impressive concoction. "That's...amazing. How do you? I mean, have you done this before or...?"

"Oh yeah, back home, I worked in a little flower shop on the edge of town. We did this for people a lot when they were sick or hurt. It was always nice bein' able to offer an alternative to the poison those doctors and such like to shove down our throats. They just love makin' us sick, makin' us die."

Julian clicked his tongue ring against the back of his teeth and nodded. "Oh yeah, Porter's a doctor. He's definitely good at poisoning people."

Gabriel kicked him in the leg.

Plum stopped stirring the murky off-white substance in the mortar and looked at Julian quizzically. "Your friend over there in the communications cabin is a doctor?"

Brooklyn wanted to reach over and clasp her hand over Julian's mouth before he could make another mistake with his words.

"Yeah, but he's a, uh, a good doctor. Still our friend. Still running from the bad guys with us," Julian said and shifted on his feet. He glanced at Brooklyn, but she was staring at the ground.

The dirt was dark and moist in the lush forest.

Brooklyn sifted the soil between her fingers. What Julian had said had hit a nerve that sent a ripple of unease throughout her bones.

Still our friend

Porter was still their friend. After everything, he was still important. Brooklyn had convinced herself that at one point in time she would be angry enough to do away with him, whether that meant aiming a gun at his head and pulling the trigger or leaving him for dead in the woods. She assumed that over time the distrust would evolve into hatred. She believed that maybe some things couldn't be forgiven.

Still running from the bad guys with us.

But he wouldn't leave her. Not even if she pointed a gun at him.

Porter wouldn't leave Brooklyn's side.

Something about that made her feel dizzy and sick and sweaty.

The door of the shed swung open, and Nicoli stepped out, holding a couple bowls filled with leafy greens, colorful strands of beet and carrot. "I'm sure you're all hungry, and it'll be getting dark soon. Eat; keep warm by the fire, and when night falls, make yourselves comfortable in any of the tents."

"They don't belong to anyone?" Gabriel asked as she took one of the bowls.

Nicoli nodded. "They do. But the rest of our company won't be back until morning."

Julian narrowed his eyes. "Where are they?"

"Gathering some supplies and investigating our next target operation," Nicoli said and smiled, offering up another one of the bowls.

"Target operation?" Brooklyn asked.

Plum nodded and started crushing up a gooey stem of aloe. "Gotta send a message, do what others won't."

"Exactly," Nicoli said. He shrugged his shoulder toward the shed. "I'll grab you some dinner, Brooklyn."

It was jarring, the way they spoke, like they were fighting an invisible war. Somehow, Brooklyn understood. As much as she wanted to pry, to push into their business and immerse herself, she didn't. They'd been kind. They'd been hospitable. Brooklyn was comfortable.

She looked down at her hands, at the dirt that was under her nails, and then at Gabriel, who was still covered in dried black blood and Julian, whose shirt was ripped across his chest.

Still, these new friends of theirs paid no mind.

"Tomorrow, I'll make y'all some sun tea, how about it?" Plum said. She smiled, tongue tucked between her teeth.

Brooklyn smiled back.

It was easy to trust them, to sleep among them. Because in the end, as she looked down at her hands, it didn't matter how dangerous these strange campers were. In the end, Brooklyn knew what *she* was capable of.

Chapter Eighteen

They ate raw vegetables and drank hot tea that was brewed over an open flame. The sun set only a short time after. Brooklyn stared off into the distance where the cabin was. She thought of the others, of Dawson, Rayce, and Amber. She hoped they were somewhere safe, maybe sitting around the familiar crackling of a fire or even better, in a bed with the covers pulled up over their chins.

Brooklyn could hope for them.

Nicoli's laughter was loud and cheerful; it distracted her from old memories and new worries.

"Okay, what? You think we're the people holding signs outside of aquariums, waving hemp flags, and throwing blood on celebrities? No. No, I can assure you that we are not *those* people." Nicoli sat close to Julian with a mug of oolong tea resting on his thigh.

Julian tried not to offend or to be too awkward. He shrugged nonchalantly. "So I guess the title "eco-terrorist" isn't necessarily all too fitting?"

Nicoli rolled his head from side to side and

shimmied his hand. "I don't like titles, to be honest. We fight for those who can't fight for themselves. There's a lot of shit goin' on these days. Our water's poisoned, our food is poisoned, pharmaceutical companies are keeping us sick, and we're running out of time. Mankind is starting to play god, and if someone doesn't take a stand...well, we're not going to have anything left to play god with."

"If you're non-violent, then why the gun?" Gabriel cut in from her place next to Plum. Her arms rested on the tops of her knees, and she was using a washcloth to scrub the dark remnants of the Surros from underneath her nails.

"Oh, now I never said we were non-violent, sweetheart." Nicoli barked another laugh, shaking his head. "Someone has to be a voice and a defense to those without one."

Gabriel nodded. "I like you more." She wrinkled her nose and dug at her hand with the washcloth. "Now that I know that."

Plum shifted and brushed a piece of hair off Gabriel's shoulder. "My now, you are a mess. What is all this stuff anyway?"

"Blood," Gabriel said.

"I ain't surprised." Plum clicked her tongue against the roof of her mouth and sighed. "You do need a bath, though. It's too cold for the river now that the sun's sleepin', so how 'bout we go down in the mornin'? I'm sure you'll feel much nicer when you're clean."

"Are you gonna try and wash me with tree bark?"

"Well, if you want me to wash you with tree bark, I can, but I think you might prefer a lavender dry soap I cooked up," Plum hummed.

Gabriel's lips creased into a smile on one side. "Yeah, that sounds good. Can I borrow some of your polish too?"

Plum looked down at her bare feet and wiggled her toes. "I don't have no big selection, Miss Gabriel, but I'd be more than happy to share what I got."

"You're lucky, you know," Gabriel said, deflated and soft.

"Oh, am I now?"

"You are." Gabriel nodded. "To have the luxury of being so free."

Plum laughed and swayed her shoulder into Gabriel. "Oh, honey, no. I don't have no luxuries here. I do have good friends, and we take care of each other just like y'all, but when it comes to being free, well...I fight for that every day. And you should too."

Gabriel's big jungle eyes flicked up and settled on Brooklyn, who was sitting on the ground against Julian's legs.

Brooklyn listened and watched. She smiled softly at Gabriel, who tried to smile back, but the attempt was solemn and small. It seemed that no matter how comfortable they became they knew that it was only a matter of time before someone found them.

All they could do was hope that the "someone" who found them turned out to be Dawson and the others.

Nicoli trailed his eyes down the expanse of Julian's arm, dusting his fingertips lightly along one of the many illustrations tattooed into his skin.

"What do they mean?" Nicoli asked.

Julian turned his arm over and opened his palm, showing the traditional Japanese art marked into his skin. A delicate temple curved up over his wrist and merged with a blooming lotus flower. A Geisha sat high on his shoulder, wrapped in different colored robes, and down one side of his back was the unfinished outline of a roaring tiger.

"My mom and dad left Japan when they found out she was pregnant with me. Totally cliché, but they chased their dreams of opening up a restaurant on the west coast. I never really understood how important it was to keep my heritage alive, because my parents and I, well, we aren't that traditional at all," Julian laughed. "I never saw any of my dad's tats until I was ten. He took off his shirt one night after a dinner rush in the back of the kitchen, full body suit, chest, back, stomach, the whole deal. I was hooked as soon as I saw 'em…when I turned nineteen, I started my arm then I waited a couple years and kept going down my back."

"Why didn't you finish them?" Nicoli asked as Julian lifted up his shirt to show off the thin black outline of the tiger.

Brooklyn's cheek rested against Julian's thigh, and she closed her eyes. She knew why.

Julian pursed his lips and shrugged. "Some shit happened. I wasn't exactly…able to get to my artist." He laughed bitterly. Chills rose up along Brooklyn's spine.

"I'm sorry to hear that," Nicoli said.

"Me too, man." Julian shrugged and ran the stud in his tongue against his teeth.

A dim glow blinked to life in the dark and got brighter as it closed in on the area surrounding the shed. Brooklyn heard Cambria's dainty footsteps as she approached. She saw her far off in the distance, walking around the bulky trunk of a tree.

"What's that?" Plum asked.

"It's Cambria," Brooklyn said.

Plum's eyes squinted and she huffed. "You must be some kind of cat, Brooklyn. I dunno how you can see her out there in that darkness."

"Yeah, I'll land on my feet if you drop me," Brooklyn joked. She stood up as Cambria got closer.

A cloth was draped over the rusty lantern in Cambria's hand. A small tea light candle was lit behind the glass, allowing only a miniscule amount of light to illuminate her path. She smiled and tried to hand the lantern to Brooklyn.

"I don't need it," Brooklyn said. "Is he all right?"

"Porter's doing fine, but it's a far longer walk when you can't see where you're going. Take the lantern with you and…" She leaned in close to Brooklyn's ear and whispered, "Go ahead and take a shower if you want. We usually don't use it, since we have the river, but I left a towel and some clothes out for you."

The thought of a hot shower sounded almost as good as eating a burrito on the beach in California.

"Did Plum get that ointment made up for him?" Cambria asked.

Brooklyn nodded. "Yeah, she did. I was gonna take him some dinner too if that's all right."

They walked together toward the fire. Nicoli stood up to retrieve something from the shed. When he returned, he was holding a bowl with some ground-up oats, warm and sweet, topped with berries. He handed it over to Brooklyn. "It'll be easy on his stomach," he said.

Plum also stood up and slid a mason jar half-filled with the homemade medicine into Brooklyn's jacket pocket. She smiled, but her gaze drifted past them up over the trees where the moon hung heavy in the sky.

"Uh oh, look at that." Plum whistled, pointing up at moon. An aura of deep red shined against the clouds. "Moon's got blood on it. Bad omen."

Brooklyn almost dropped the lantern. Her knees wobbled, and her chest clenched tight. She locked her legs in place and kept herself upright, holding on to the bowl with a shaky hand.

Plum reached out and rubbed her arm. "You okay, kitty cat? Looks like you've gone and seen a ghost."

"Y-yeah, yeah, I'm okay. I just...I'm curious. I've heard the term before, but what exactly is an omen?" Brooklyn tried to keep her voice from shaking and giving her away.

Gabriel was at Brooklyn's side within seconds and reached out to take the lantern from her.

Nicoli tilted his head to the side, shrugging one shoulder. "An omen?"

"Yes," Brooklyn said.

Plum walked back over to sit by the warmth of

the fire. Nicoli rubbed his fingers through the short scruff around his mouth.

"Well," he sighed, looking up at the sky, "an omen is usually a foreshadowing. It can be a clue or a curse, a message being sent. Just depends on who you ask, really."

"Most folks like to think they tell the future," Plum added. "And depending on the omen, you either get somethin' lovely happenin' or you get somethin' not so lovely."

Brooklyn nodded, slow and steady. "Oh," she squeaked, clearing her throat. "Thanks. That…makes sense."

Nicoli watched her carefully, lips curved into one of his dangerous smiles. He nodded in the direction of the cabin. "Get yourself some sleep, all right? We'll be here with breakfast for both of you in the morning."

Cambria touched Brooklyn gently on the shoulder. "No one's going to hurt you out here," she whispered.

Brooklyn felt transparent. They were looking right through her, and still, *still*, these people continued to help them. Either Nicoli was truly interested in nothing more than helping them or there was something far more sinister going on behind the scenes of their obscure forest company. Brooklyn couldn't make up her mind. She couldn't choose between trusting them and sleeping sound or packing up in the middle of the night and running off.

It seemed like most people who told Brooklyn she wouldn't get hurt ended up hurting her or her loved ones anyways.

"Hey," Gabriel soothed, stepping in front of her friend. "Relax, okay?"

Brooklyn nodded and swallowed.

"We're okay, Brookie. I know no matter how much I bugged you, you still wouldn't let me go hang out with Porter instead, would you?"

"Probably not," Brooklyn said.

"Even if I promised not to kill him?"

"Even then." Brooklyn smiled and let the breath she'd held flow over her lips.

"Go on. I'll be here with Julian, telling scary stories around the fire. Just yell if you need me."

Brooklyn nodded. "You too, okay? Yell or shout or..."

"If anything happened, it wouldn't be my screaming you'd hear."

The idea of something happening to them while she was with Porter in that cabin was daunting. But pieces of Gabriel's hair were still smudged black, her eyes fierce. It was a morbid reminder of her deadliness. She leaned in to press a quick kiss to Brooklyn's cheek and smiled.

"Goodnight," Gabriel said firmly.

Brooklyn turned around after giving a short wave and set off into the woods toward the cabin. The lantern was almost more distracting than it was helpful. Brooklyn could see just fine in the dark. She dodged the noisy crunch of fallen leaves and stepped up onto a log, walking across it with ease and finesse. The tension in her body seemed to vibrate as she moved, testing the strength in her legs and the sharpness of her vision.

It was crazy to think that she had been this way for so long. Advanced. Evolved.

An Omen.

The cabin came into view through the stretched shadow of the trees. It looked different bathed in darkness, haunted. Brooklyn glanced at the back door, the screen open and swaying on its hinges. A window on the second story was open, the wind whipping against a thin white curtain, a candle glowing dim and steady on the windowsill.

Chapter Nineteen

The rumble of a generator in the basement thrummed in Brooklyn's ears. She set the lantern on the top of the old antique trunk in the middle of the living room. The stairs creaked under her feet as she made her way to a narrow landing, facing a wide hallway. Paintings of different plant species filled the spaces between the doors on either side. Brooklyn admired them as she walked past. At the very end of the hall, the door to the master bedroom was cracked open.

Brooklyn paused, rolling the end of her shirt into her hands. She licked her lips and turned the corner. The air tasted like salt and mint. Light danced on the carpet from candles lit on the dresser opposite the bed that Porter was lying in. They cast shadows that jittered along the walls.

Porter's lips were parted, breathing faint with sleep. They looked inviting when they were relaxed and when lies weren't falling from between them. She watched him like that for a moment, remembered his face and how soft it could be when

147

they weren't fighting for their lives. His eyes twitched, dark, long eyelashes batting. The scratch of young stubble had started to rise up through his cheeks.

She set the bowl of hot cereal down on the nightstand next to him and put the ointment on the dresser where Cambria had left some fresh bandages.

The adjoined bathroom was open. Brooklyn's mouth watered at the sight of a pristine shower waiting to be used. She left Porter to sleep, assuming that the sound of the water running would wake him.

Two fluffy towels were on top of the toilet seat. A toothbrush with some mouthwash was on the sink, and when she peeked inside the standalone shower, it was stocked with travel-sized shampoo, conditioner, and soap. It was more than she was expecting, and it was more than she needed. But she was going to enjoy every single bit of it.

"Oh my god," Brooklyn keened, grasping the handle of a pink razor. She gave it a once over to make sure it wasn't rusted and was thrilled to find it hadn't been touched.

Cambria's kindness would not be forgotten.

She stripped out of her clothes as quickly as she could and stepped into the shower. The hot water was like something out of a daydream. It scalded away the black stains on her skin, along with the dirt and grime of their escape from the camp. She scrubbed her flesh with soap, lathered her hair, and scraped her nails across her body until it felt raw. Her hands moved over her hips, up to her belly button and then scrubbed at the smooth silkiness of her stomach. The place where she'd been shot was a plain canvas, no nicks or cracks, scars or blemishes. Just smooth, healed skin.

The shampoo smelled like lilies. She made sure to rake her fingers through her hair and detangle the knots that had grown together.

Brooklyn stayed in the shower until the hot water turned cold. She reluctantly twisted the knob and dried off, debating whether or not she would take a second in the morning. The last thing she wanted was to be selfish or disrespectful, but the thought of another shower before they set off again to who-knew-where was enticing.

"Cambria?" Porter called from the bedroom.

Brooklyn popped her head around the corner, a towel wrapped around her midsection and a toothbrush shoved in her mouth. "No, it's me," she slurred around the handle of the toothbrush, lips covered in foam.

Porter's eyes squinted. "I can't see a damn thing. My glasses are on the dresser."

She walked over, handing Porter his glasses, bare feet still damp as she tiptoed back to the bathroom so she could get dressed.

"Oh, hello," Porter said bashfully, watching her disappear into the steam-filled room.

"Be quiet," Brooklyn grumbled. "It's nothing you haven't seen before. We lived in the same cabin for like two years."

"One year and seven months."

Brooklyn rolled her eyes and shimmied into the gym shorts Cambria had left for her. She used the shampoo from the shower to scrub her underwear and bra, leaving them to dry over the top of the shower. A large black t-shirt was also folded up on the toilet seat. After she tugged it on over her head, she hugged herself, chin tilted down with her nose buried in the clean material.

"Hey, is this for me?" Porter called.

She walked out as he reached for the bowl of oatmeal. "Yeah, it's yours. How are you doing?"

He used his good arm to maneuver himself into an upright sitting position against the headboard. "It hurts, but I'm fine. Cambria's stitches will hold for a while, but I wish I had some of the antibiotics from the bus, though. I'm guessing we haven't heard from them…"

Brooklyn took a deep breath and shook her head. "No." Her voice was faint.

Porter's lips twisted into an uncomfortable frown.

"I'm scared," she confessed under her breath. "What if something happened to them? What if they got taken? I don't…I can't imagine not finding them, Porter. I'm freaking out."

"You should have gone with them and left me."

"That wasn't an option." Brooklyn stiffened.

Porter breathed through his nose, and even though it seemed like he wanted to argue, he stayed quiet.

Brooklyn wasn't going to fight with him over her decision to look after his safety. There was no use. She didn't have the heart to leave him for dead, but she was too proud to admit that.

"They're gonna be fine." The edge lifted from

Porter's voice. "I'm sure they're somewhere safe right now, wondering where we are and looking for a way to find us."

"I hope you're right," she said.

He ate his food while Brooklyn moved the drapes aside so she could look out the window. The woods were dense and wide. The trees were a cocoon around them, spanning out in every direction. She saw the fire in front of the shed blink in the distance. Far off past the tree line, a road curved up a hill that connected with a highway.

That's probably the direction Dawson, Rayce, and Amber had taken the rest of the group.

The empty bowl slid against the nightstand when Porter set it down. Brooklyn felt his gaze on her. She listened closely to the uneven beat of his heart. He licked his lips, took a deep breath, gearing up to speak.

"Let's get that ointment on you," she said quickly.

Porter shook his head, teeth set in his lip. He shifted to the side, giving her more room to work. She stooped over him, untying the small knot in the bandage above his collar bone. She was careful, making slow movements to remove the white cloth. The last bit was sticky with menthol and tugged at the stitches as she tried to ease the bandage loose.

"Sorry," Brooklyn mumbled, lips curling back in a wince when she finally pulled the remainder off.

"Don't apologize."

She used a warm washcloth to clean around the long row of black stitches and gently dabbed Plum's home-made remedy over his wound with her fingertips. The lower point of the cut curved down over his shoulder onto his arm, and the other end almost reached the base of his neck. It would take more time than they had to heal properly.

"How are you gonna travel like this?"

"Well, I'll use my two legs until we get to a car—then, I'll probably upgrade to wheels," Porter said, eyes rolling.

"You know what I mean."

"I have a few different medications in mind, but I have to wait 'til we find everyone to worry about that. Until then, I'll be fine. I'll keep up." He reached out and touched the top of her thigh. It was barely there, a sweeping brush of his thumb against her skin. Still, she stepped back after she'd finished wrapping his arm back up.

The night was placid, just as quiet as any other night they'd spent out in the woods. The home she remembered with warm beaches, authentic Mexican food, and suntan lotion didn't match the arms of towering trees or the cocoon of ferns and oaks. She'd spent enough time in the forest to appreciate it but not enough to be comforted by it.

Brooklyn moved back to the window and distanced herself from the room she was in by losing herself in what was outside. She focused on the hop and thump of a rabbit in the brush, the hoot of an owl, its talons tearing the bark off the branch it was perched on. Her eyes strained, vision sharpening around the image of a tiny mouse scurrying up a tree hundreds of feet away in the dark. Her heart skipped a beat. Excitement climbed up the stairs of her spine. She concentrated, eyes staring out into the darkness, and realized how crisp her sight could be. The clatter of a squirrel in a bush tapped on her eardrums, the sound of the air rushing past a pair of feathered wings.

"Cambria told me about Nicoli and their band of freedom fighters," Porter said, testing conversation.

Discovering the strengths that had slept peacefully inside her all this time was thrilling. Brooklyn smiled as she glanced back inside. The flame on the wick of the candle was clearer; the shadow it cast across Porter's bed was too.

"Yeah, they're pretty cool."

Porter's lips stirred into a grin. He narrowed his eyes as she turned her attention back to the window.

"Pretty cool? That's all I get? There must be something interesting going on out there for you to ignore my crippled sorry self."

"I can see everything," Brooklyn said. "I can almost see better in the dark than I can during the day. I can't explain it...it's like..." She played with her hands and mulled over how to efficiently describe it. "I can focus on certain things with my eyes and others with my ears. I can...I don't know. I don't know how I'm doing this, but it's amazing."

"Come here," he said, patting the empty side of the bed. "Let me see."

She hesitated for a moment, contemplating whether or not she could trust herself to be close to him. She brushed the thought aside and walked around to the other side of the bed. She sat down with her legs crossed, waiting. His heartbeat accelerated as he leaned in to touch her cheek. She heard it prang like a rock bouncing across a frozen lake.

"Incredible," he whispered over a stifled laugh, warm fingertips settling below her lashes.

Brooklyn's nose wrinkled. Her gaze shifted around to look at anything else besides Porter. "What?"

"You, in general," he said quickly. She rolled her eyes, fighting the blush rising into her face. "It seems to me that you've learned how to control your pupil dilation."

"And?"

"And that means you don't need to adjust to darkness or brightness. Your eyes continuously change throughout the day, I'm guessing. Like a cat."

Brooklyn heaved a sigh and shook her head. "Plum called me a jumpy cat earlier. Not really feelin' the label right now."

"Cats are one of the deadliest stealth predators in the world. You should be flattered."

She pulled her lips back and hissed at him. He grinned and let his hand drop away from her face.

"Why would, Plum…? Her name's *Plum?*"

"Yes, jackass, her name is Plum."

"Okay," Porter continued. "Well, why would Plum call you a cat?"

"Because I saw Cambria walking toward us in the woods. She said I had to be some kind of cat to see that well in the dark, and then she started talking about the moon and…" Brooklyn's voice trickled away.

Porter poked her belly. "And?"

She squirmed, brushing his away. "The moon is

red tonight, and she said it was a bad omen."

The tension between them spiked. She watched him lick nervously across his lips, and he sighed, rich caramel eyes staring up at the ceiling.

"Why did they choose to call us that?" Brooklyn whispered even though she wasn't sure whether she truly wanted the answer or not.

Porter's lips parted. "Are you sure you wanna know the details?"

He waited for her to nod and continued.

"Omens were regarded as powerful messages from the gods in most ancient civilizations. They could be anything from a vase breaking to a massive tidal wave washing away a village, but the people...the people listened to them. They feared them. Every omen demanded respect, and when they came they brought—" he shook his head until the right word came to mind "—chaos. But chaos always evolved into order even if it was only for a short time."

"So," Brooklyn said. "We're here to send a message?"

Porter tilted his head to the side. "Yeah, basically. But what's the typical message in tactical warfare?"

The realization was ice cold and branched out through the rest of her body. It froze her bones, chilled her insides, a distinct, dreadful presence that she couldn't swallow down.

"Assassination," Brooklyn said.

"Yes, a target is given; an Omen is dispatched. That's it."

"Just like that…"

"Yeah. Just like that."

Brooklyn wanted to run as fast as she could and as far as she could. She wanted to put her boots on and go, go until she couldn't go anymore. Nothing about what Porter said could possibly be linked to her. She wasn't a killer, much less a trained assassin…she couldn't be and she wouldn't be.

The generator in the cellar came to a rumbling halt, and the small lamp on the nightstand dimmed until it was completely out. A couple candles continued to burn, but the rest of the bedroom went dark.

"Cambria told me the generator was set to go off at midnight," Porter said.

"Oh." Brooklyn glanced around the room. "Okay."

"It's late, and we should probably get some rest. There are a couple other rooms with beds that Cambria said would be fine for you to sleep in."

Brooklyn sat stationary with her legs crossed and her hands in her lap. Her tawny eyes that usually held such distrust and hostility were lost in the sheets of the bed. Thoughts flew by in her mind, building scenes and pictures that she could never see herself in but were created just for her. Thoughts of what it would be like to be an occupational murderer. How had they chosen her, Brooklyn Harper, of all people? How had a doctor looked at her when she was a toddler, decided her life would be riddled with violence, and had handed her a lollipop on the way out?

"Or you could always sleep in here if you want," Porter offered.

Brooklyn didn't answer. She slid down under the covers and felt the mattress dip comfortably around her. Her toes flexed. She rubbed her cheek into the squish of a feather pillow.

Porter set his glasses down on the nightstand and lay down on his side to face her. They stayed like that, looking at one another in the dark until Porter reached out and touched the line of her jaw with his thumb.

"You're gonna be okay," he whispered.

She closed her eyes and waited for the brush of his lips against hers.

But it never came.

"I promise," he added. His breath, warm, stained with the scent of berries, drifted across her cheek.

She didn't remember falling asleep, but when sleep did come, it was peaceful.

Chapter Twenty

Birds sang in the trees outside, and the smell of fresh pine filled the air. They'd left the window open, letting the chill in overnight, but Brooklyn was burrowed underneath the covers, feeling impossibly warm. Her heavy eyes refused to open even as her good night's sleep started to fade away. Lean legs stretched out, and her hips moved slightly until she felt the press of Porter's torso against her back.

She stopped moving altogether and cracked her eyes open to look down at the large hand resting comfortably on the top of her stomach. His arm tightened around her—his breath ghosted along the back of her neck.

"Awake already?" Porter rasped.

Brooklyn melted back into his embrace. "Not really."

Her shirt was rucked up and bundled at her ribs with his hand gripping bare skin just beneath. The press of something cold and small rubbed against her hairline. Brooklyn whined in protest.

"Your hair smells good," Porter said.

She smiled and tried to twist around to face him, but a loud, shrill, very familiar voice startled her into pulling the comforter tighter around them.

"Okay, gross! I'm going to gag, and then I'm going to shoot both of you," Gabriel hollered from her place in the doorway. She twirled a small silver gun in her hand, craning to look around the room. She stepped inside and gasped when the bathroom came into clear view.

"You guys have a shower! That's not fair! How…?" Her words trailed off as she spotted Brooklyn's dry under garments hanging from the top of the glass shower door.

"Gabriel! What the hell are you doing here? We were sleeping!" Brooklyn seethed.

"Holy shit," Gabriel said, lips curled back. Her hair whipped over her shoulders as she spun to face the bed, gun high and pointed at Porter.

"Are you *naked*? Is she naked, Porter? If she's naked, I'm going to shoot you in the throat."

Brooklyn sat straight up, swatting Porter's hand away so she could pull down her shirt. A hot blush tinged her cheeks, and her lips set in a tight line. Not only was she thoroughly humiliated, but she was fuming with anger.

"I'm not naked, Gabriel! You're being ridiculous—put the gun down!"

Porter lifted his hands and showed his palms. "This is not how I saw this morning going."

"Oh, yeah? And how *did* you see it going? Please, enlighten me, you vile piece of…"

"Gabriel!" Brooklyn interrupted with a loud shout. She walked in front of Gabriel's outstretched arms, blocking the gun. "Give that to me. Now."

Brooklyn held her hand out and waited. Her whole body quivered; adrenaline pumped fast through her veins, clouding the overwhelming amount of anxiety that constricted her lungs.

Gabriel stared at her for a long minute before she finally handed the gun over. Brooklyn manhandled her inside the bathroom, slamming the door behind them.

"I want to strangle you," Brooklyn whispered as she set the gun down on the edge of the sink. "Why would you do that? Why would you come storming in here? I can't even...I can't believe you! I was fine!"

"Did you sleep with him?" Gabriel laughed. Her eyes widened, and she wore a nasty grin.

She didn't think her face could get any more red, but Brooklyn felt her cheeks beam with even more heat. "No! I did not sleep with him!"

"Did you want to?"

Gabriel's whispered prying took Brooklyn off guard. She stuttered over an answer that she didn't know how to give. She stared back at her friend, mouth open, fingertips twitching. It wasn't that she couldn't say "no;" she could have. But if she was lying, Gabriel would know—she always knew.

"I don't know." Brooklyn bit down on her lip hard.

Gabriel threw her head back and laughed, which in turn made Brooklyn extremely self-conscious.

Brooklyn shoved Gabriel aside, reaching for the clothes she'd left there. She stripped off the shirt and gym shorts so she could put her now clean underwear back on followed by the tight beige tank top and jeans.

"You can't want to sleep with him—he's Judas." Gabriel rolled her eyes. She grabbed the shampoo bottle from inside the shower and popped open the top, inhaling the sweet scent.

"Can we please not talk about this right now?" Brooklyn groaned.

"I'm your best friend, Brookie! I'm supposed to be your voice of reason here, okay? Like, let me help you *and* him because if he touches you I'll be forced to rip his tongue out."

"Stop it."

"Oh, come on. I'm joking, sort of."

"I'm going to brush my teeth, and you're going to apologize to Porter," Brooklyn said sternly.

Gabriel arched a brow. "No."

"Yes!" Brooklyn yelled, shoving the toothbrush in her mouth before she swung the door back open. "I don't give a shit about what happened. I'm done wasting my time trying to hate him, so do this one stupid favor for me, and get along with him!"

Gabriel looked like a toddler who'd been sent to time out. Her plump pink lips folded down into a bitter frown, and she crossed her arms over her chest defiantly. Brooklyn glared at her from the mirror until she finally gave up and stomped out into the bedroom.

Porter blinked wide, confused eyes at her as Gabriel sucked in one of her cheeks and chewed on it.

"I'm sorry," she said coldly. "You're still a dick, though."

"You don't have to apologize to me. That's the last thing you should be doing," Porter said.

"Whatever. Breakfast is ready, so get your asses out of the love shack, and meet us at the shed."

Brooklyn tried to throw a boot at her, but Gabriel dodged it, laughing all the way down the hall.

Brooklyn stayed in the bathroom for as long as she could and chomped on her nails the whole time. She kept looking in the mirror, hoping the dark blush would fade from her cheeks, but it was still there, plaguing her with embarrassment.

The cushioned squeak of the bed alerted her to Porter's movements. His bare feet padded toward the bathroom, but he stopped just outside and tapped on the open door.

"Are you okay?" he asked.

Brooklyn brushed past him as she walked by. "Yeah," she lied, "I'm good."

Porter didn't press her, which she thoroughly appreciated.

He slid in front of the sink and started brushing his teeth while Brooklyn sat down on the bed and laced up her boots. They avoided speaking to each other for the rest of the morning. It was easier that way, but it wasn't hard to pick out the giant white elephant poised in the corner of the room. Once they were both fully dressed, they headed down into the woods. The walk back to the shed was tense and quiet. Brooklyn felt his gaze on her and the silent questions he asked, but she ignored it.

Plum spotted them approaching as she adjusted some clothes hanging on the line. She gave a toothy smile. "Well, good mornin'. You must be Porter,

I'm guessin'?"

"Yeah, that's me," Porter said and extended his hand.

She gave it a dainty shake. "Good to see you're up and movin'. I'm Plum."

"Nice to meet you, Plum."

"Same to you, sweetie. Nicoli's at the territory line, waitin' for everybody to get back from the city." She swept her hand toward the door of the shed. "Go on in, and get somethin' to eat. I'm sure Cambria made some real nice breakfast."

Brooklyn heard Julian laugh from the shed and walked inside with Porter at her heels.

Plants hung from the ceiling in woven baskets. Their vines tickled Brooklyn's cheek as she dipped her head around them. A small, round wooden table was in the middle of the room accompanied by three matching chairs. A long table was pushed against the left wall. Shelves filled with vials, books, plants, and flowers hung on all four walls, and an old metal radio sat on the ground under the table next to a space heater.

Gabriel drank tea and picked sliced fruit out of a large communal bowl in the center of the table.

Cambria pointed to a few pieces of seedy bread on the table and smiled to them. "Have some bread and fruit salad. Did you two sleep okay last night?"

Brooklyn nodded. "Yeah, thank you for everything."

"You're very welcome," Cambria said, offering a quick wink.

"How are you feeling, man?" Julian walked over to Porter and gave his wrapped shoulder a once over.

Porter sighed. "Better now."

"Good, we were worried."

"I'm fine, really. I'd like to get to our medications though. There's a serum that might...speed up my healing a bit."

The distant crunch of the forest floor under several pairs of shuffling feet stole Brooklyn's attention. She stopped chewing on a piece of ripe pineapple and listened closely. They weren't far, walking from the direction of the river toward the camp site. She didn't know if it was Nicoli or if it was someone else. Something else.

Gabriel kicked her foot. "You hear that too?"

Brooklyn's nostrils flared. "Yeah."

Plum's voice rang out from the other side of the door. "Them boys are back! Y'all might wanna come outside and introduce yourselves."

Brooklyn breathed a sigh of relief, looking from Gabriel to Julian and back again. The weariness of meeting new people wasn't as prominent as she thought it might be. Maybe it was because they felt a little bit safe, maybe because they felt powerful enough to not care about safety. Either way, it didn't matter; these people that they were about to meet had been in the city.

Maybe, just maybe, they'd seen Dawson and the others.

Chapter Twenty-One

Three men followed Nicoli into the camp. All but one seemed young, the youngest in his teens, but the man in the far back was old enough to be Brooklyn's father.

Brooklyn prepared herself for an introduction, repeating what she'd say several times in her head. Nicoli walked right past them. His sheepskin coat brushed over her boots as he walked by, and his gaze flicked past them. The only words spoken were between Cambria and the short, slender one with a lengthy beard and bright red hair. He handed her a box filled to the brim with fresh food and muttered something under his breath that Brooklyn didn't catch.

All four of them disappeared through the trees in the direction of the cabin.

Cambria looked taken aback. That alone was unsettling.

"What's going on?" Julian asked.

Plum's mouth twitched. "Don't know, but whatever it is they found out there in that concrete jungle isn't good."

"Should we be worried at all?" Porter said.

"No." Cambria was quick to answer. "Just let me get this haul into the shed, and then we can go down to the river for a bath. They'll meet us there."

Gabriel licked her lips. "I don't like this."

"I don't either, but it's none of our concern, so we should probably just go with it," Julian said.

Brooklyn agreed with Julian. If anything, they would leave by mid-day, which was only a couple hours away, and get on the road toward the city. She knew that if it came to a sudden departure she could count on Cambria for directions to Seattle. The hope that perhaps one of those men had seen their lost friends loomed over her.

"C'mon, let's head down to the water and get clean!" Plum said enthusiastically. She held a small basket with a couple towels, some oil, and a canister full of dry soap.

Porter walked close to Brooklyn, his shoulder brushing against hers every other step. Julian was just as close on her other side. Gabriel was busy jumping off large protruding tree roots and darting along the edges of boulders like they were gymnastic beams.

"These people have been really good to us, but I think it's time to go," Julian whispered.

"Porter needs more time to heal," Brooklyn said under her breath. "We need at least one more night."

"I'm fine," Porter hissed.

"You're not fine. Besides, I need to find out if they saw Dawson, Amber, or Rayce. Or any of our other friends that we abandoned, all right? Just keep it together. It's one more day."

"One more day with a group of violent eco-terrorists who live in the forest, Brooklyn!" Julian said.

She snorted. "No more violent than us."

They came upon the sleek river and helped Plum lay out the towels in a patch of sun that beamed down from between the tree branches.

Brooklyn decided to stay on shore with Porter while the rest of them waded into the water.

Julian was hesitant, laughing nervously when Cambria took off all her clothes and walked naked into the lake, followed by Plum. He made a strangled noise. "So like, they are completely naked, and I am guessing they expect me to be completely naked, and then when those guys get back they will also be…"

"Completely naked, yeah," Gabriel said. She kicked her boots off, letting the heavy jacket she wore fall from her shoulders. "I figured you'd be a little excited to be naked in a body of water with Nicoli anyways."

"That is—" Julian pointed a finger at her while she reached around and unclasped her bra "—completely inappropriate! Besides, I don't think I'm available. So. No."

Gabriel scoffed. "Oh, yeah? Who has your panties in a wad then? Because I was sure you were gonna jump all over tofu king."

Porter gave a breathy laugh, averting his eyes when Gabriel finally kicked off her underwear and stood confidently in front of them. Her hands were on her hips, head held high, toes curling into the dark soil.

"Doesn't matter," Julian said.

"It really *does,* though. Who is it?" Gabriel prodded his chest with her finger.

Julian stared up at the sky.

"It's Rayce, isn't it?" Brooklyn asked.

"N-no! No, absolutely not. I mean, he's not even into all this." Julian's voice cracked while he gestured down the expanse of his body.

"It's Rayce," Porter confirmed.

"Excuse me, but how would you know anyways?" Julian's hands were on his hips, and his jaw was set tight.

Porter shrugged, still staring at the ground. "You guys slept in the tent with me, remember?"

Gabriel cackled and reached down to fish through her jacket. Julian didn't have anything to say—he just rubbed his hand over his mouth, bashful and embarrassed.

Brooklyn wanted to laugh, to ask Julian all about his short-lived courting with Rayce, but all she could imagine was talking about it, making it real, acknowledging it, and then never having the opportunity to see it in real time.

Because they might not find their friends.

Her throat tightened. She shifted so that she could lie down on her back in the sun, shielding her sour expression with her arm.

"Well, anyways," Julian sang, taking off his shirt. "Let's just not bother with my non-existent love life and take a hippie bath."

"Hippie bath?" Porter laughed.

168

Plum splashed the water toward them from far out in the river. "C'mon, y'all smell bad. Get in!"

Gabriel had the pink-handled razor clutched in her hand that she'd apparently borrowed from the cabin and made her way into the water.

Brooklyn and Porter could hear Julian yelp as he tried to tiptoe into the water, whining about how cold it was.

"Whatcha got there, Miss Gabriel?" Plum asked as she waded over toward her.

Gabriel had one of her legs stretched out and was shaving carefully around her knee. "I found it in the cabin. It's okay that I use it right?"

"Course it is. We have the communications cabin set up mostly for us girls anyhow."

"Why's that?" Gabriel asked, eyeing Plum carefully as she scrubbed herself with some kind of strange powder soap from a jar.

"Well, we're the only ones who bleed on a schedule 'round here. Whenever we need time to ourselves or the freshness of a shower and a bed, we can go off into the cabin an' have some peace."

"That's pretty cool," Gabriel said. "I've never really had any need for all that. I had some issues when I was younger, and they took my uterus out when I was fourteen."

Plum frowned. "I sure am sorry to hear that."

"It's not a big deal. It happens."

"You're so damn pretty, though...woulda been nice to pass that on to a little one, wouldn't it?"

Gabriel laughed and shook her head. "My mom used to say that to me all the time, but I don't want kids."

169

"Really?" Plum gasped.

"Really. There's too many of us on this planet anyways."

"Well, I can't argue with that." Plum waded closer. She reached out but stopped inches from the slope of Gabriel's neck. "Oh, may I wash your back for you, sweetie?"

Gabriel was apprehensive, eyes searching Plum for any ulterior motive, but Plum was kind and genuine. She waited patiently while Gabriel considered it.

"I…I guess so," Gabriel mumbled.

"I ain't gonna bite ya, just wanna help."

Gabriel gave another slow nod. "Go ahead."

Plum rambled on about how beautiful the weather was and how she wasn't expecting September to go by as fast as it was. Her hands rubbed up over Gabriel's shoulders, scrubbing off the sweat, dirt, and blood. Gabriel smiled contently. When Plum finally went quiet, she turned and glanced over her shoulder. "You keep calling that cabin the communications cabin. Do you guys have meetings there or something? Why do you call it that?"

"There are some computers and such in the cellar that we use from time to time. I'm guessin' that's what them boys are up to right now."

"I see." Gabriel's gaze drifted around the river.

"Speak of the devil, there they are," Plum said and waved.

The four men walked out of the woods, bumping into each other casually and talking amongst themselves. They set their towels down on the ground next to Brooklyn and Porter.

"Sorry about earlier. We had to transfer some files over," Nicoli said.

Brooklyn sat up. "Is everything okay?"

"Yes, everything's okay. We were just going over some information that they gathered in Seattle."

"Did they…?" Brooklyn paused and shifted her gaze to the three men stripping off their clothes. "Did they happen to see a group of people in a bus just outside the city?"

"There's a lot of buses out there." One of them spoke up. It was the same guy that had spoken to Cambria. His bushy red beard shined in the sunlight, and his hair was tied back into a small bun. He sighed, tossing his shirt aside. "Can't really say we saw anything out of the ordinary."

"They have to be here somewhere…they wouldn't have gone on without us, would they?" Brooklyn asked, looking beside her where Porter sat.

Porter cleaned his glasses with the bottom of his shirt and took a deep breath. "I don't know, but we'll find them."

The red-haired man paused before he stepped out of his jeans and extended his hand. "I'm Freddie."

Brooklyn shook his hand. "Brooklyn."

"It's nice to meet you. You are?"

"Porter."

He walked away after that and followed Nicoli into the water.

Porter tried to roll his shoulder but winced and gritted his teeth. He sat back and rested his arms over the top of his knees, watching Brooklyn pick grass out of the ground at her feet.

"We'll find them," Porter said.

His tenderness was appreciated, but Brooklyn wasn't in the mood for coddling.

"You don't know that."

"I do know that. We're gonna find them, or they're gonna find us—there's no other options."

"We have to get to Seattle. That's exactly where Dawson would have taken them, and he probably thought that's where we would have gone too," Brooklyn said.

"Who are you two after?" A thick, raspy voice came from just behind them.

It was the older man that Brooklyn had seen with Nicoli before they came down to the river. His eyes were creased with fine lines, and he had a large red birthmark that spanned the left side of his face. It was raised like a scar, the edges dark and spotted. Large calloused hands rubbed together, and a towel was draped over his shoulders.

"Our friends," Brooklyn said. "We lost them yesterday."

"How'd you lose them?" he asked. He was still wet from the river. The jeans he'd put back on were damp against his freshly washed skin. He plopped down in front of them and reached over to grab a water bottle from Plum's basket.

"We had to run," Brooklyn said. She chose not to go into much detail. "But we had a plan on getting to Seattle together, so Porter thinks that's where they probably are."

"Had to run, huh?" The stranger laughed, taking

172

a long drink off the water bottle. "I have a feeling you don't want to tell me what you're running from, and to be honest, I don't really care. I do care that you've brought your problems here, though. We have a job to do, and if whatever it is you're running from catches up to you, you best know you're on your own."

Brooklyn narrowed her eyes, head tilting to the side. She wanted to breach the small distance between them and smash his face into the damp soil they were sitting on.

Porter's hand moved to sit gently on the top of Brooklyn's knee.

"We don't have any intention on staying longer than we need to. You don't have to worry about that." Porter's voice was cold and defensive.

"I'm not worried, kid."

He was gone after that, carrying his shirt and towel back to camp.

Chapter Twenty-Two

The day crawled by at a snail's pace.

They returned from the river after everyone was done bathing. The food collected from the market in Seattle was cleaned and put away in the shed while Plum offered to help them wash their clothes. Cambria gave each of them some of what she had extra to wear while their jackets, pants, shirts, and socks hung to dry on the clothes line.

Brooklyn was given an ankle length sun dress decorated in swirling colors and patterns. She tugged at it uncomfortably and constantly pushed her legs together, trying to remember how to sit appropriately in a dress. It'd been far too long since she'd worn one.

Brooklyn changed Porter's bandages in the afternoon, right before the fire was started. Julian helped Cambria cook up a pan full of sizzling vegetables and drank cup after cup of hot tea.

As peaceful as it was, Brooklyn couldn't help but notice how secretive Nicoli and the other men were. They kept to themselves, disappearing to the cabin often throughout the day. It was unusual to say the least and left the camp under a cloud of palpable unrest.

"Hey, Cambria." Brooklyn touched the woman's arm.

Cambria turned from her place at the table in the shed. "Yeah?"

"I know that something is going on, and I understand that you guys don't want to share everything with us, but I have a feeling we might be able to help."

A defeated sigh drifted out of Cambria's mouth. She set the large green pepper down beside the knife she'd been using to cut it. "I don't even know all the details, but what they're working on is going to affect a lot of people, save a lot of lives. Nic hasn't even told me everything about it yet."

"Okay, but are we safe here? One of those guys said some nasty shit…"

"Let me guess, the old guy, right? Chester?"

"I don't know his name, but yeah, the older guy with the red mark on his face."

"Chester," Cambria rolled her eyes. "He's been with us for a short time, maybe four or five months. He means well, but he can come off harsh at times. Don't worry about him."

Brooklyn didn't need to know the ins and outs of their relationships, but she did need to know that her friends would remain safe.

"Will Nicoli talk to me if I ask him about all this?" Brooklyn asked in a hushed whisper.

Cambria pursed her lips and went back to cutting the veggies on the table. "You can try, but don't expect much."

Brooklyn walked out of the shed and took off toward the cabin. Gabriel was shouting after her, but she didn't turn around. If taking them off guard with curiosity was what it took to get a straight answer, then that's exactly what she would give them. She knew that they didn't owe her anything, especially answers, but if she didn't go out on a limb now, something bad could happen later, and then it would be too late.

Too late for what? She wasn't sure. Too late to warn them, too late to be aware of everything going on, too late to get away before their own hell infiltrated these people's lives.

She didn't bother knocking on the door, just opened it and walked in. Her boots were loud against the floor, and she could see down into the open cellar.

The audible slide, click, hitch of a shotgun being prepped alerted her to speak. "It's me—it's Brooklyn!"

Nicoli popped his head out of the darkness of the cellar and stared at her. "What're you doing in here?"

His dreads were all bundled into a bun on the top of his head, and he wore thin reading glasses. Brooklyn couldn't help but chuckle softly. "I'm curious. I wanna know what it is you guys are obsessing over."

"Don't laugh at me," Nicoli warned, amused.

"You look adorable," Brooklyn said and laughed harder.

Nicoli's eyes slanted, and he bypassed her

comment. "Now, we're still developing some things down here, and I don't exactly think you and your crew will be sticking around to help us out with it. Why are you so concerned?"

He wasn't being aggressive, but he did watch her carefully and moved his arms to sit over the top of the cellar door.

"We're probably leaving in the morning, but maybe we can help until we take off. If you don't want to tell me, I understand but…what we're running from, it's big. It's bigger than us. You guys might be dealing with the same thing."

"Brooklyn, I can guarantee you that what we're on to right now has nothing to do with you."

"Please," Brooklyn sighed. "You don't have to tell me everything, but give me something."

Nicoli shook his head, looking down into the cellar where the other men waited. He gave a few glances back and forth until finally stepping down, waving his hand for her to follow.

She was nervous, and her heart fluttered when she dropped down into the darkness. It wasn't what she expected in the least. A table top lined with computer screens shone bright against the barely-there light of a lantern on another far table. A few chairs were folded out, which Freddie and Chester occupied. The other man, who Brooklyn hadn't been introduced to, sat in one of the chairs in front of a computer screen.

Nicoli took a seat next to him. "This is Brooklyn."

He was the youngest of them all—she guessed maybe sixteen or seventeen—with a crooked front tooth and a handsome face. His head was shaved, and he was tall enough to have to slump in his chair so he could see the computer screen.

"Oh, hey. I'm Lance." He also seemed the friendliest, with a welcoming smile.

She didn't pay mind to Chester's boiling glare and did her best not to look at him while he snarled at her from his place next to Freddie.

"Did you get his name?" Nicoli asked when Lance clicked on a series of pictures. Most of them focused on a man, his face obscured by a pair of sunglasses, skin freckled and pale, wearing a black suit.

"No," Lance said. "He was constantly in a group. Obviously government. They didn't ask many questions, and the ones they did ask were strange. The whole recon was bizarre."

"Almost like they were hunting aliens," Freddie snorted.

Nicoli shook his head and drummed the tips of his fingers against his lips. "Did they have badges?"

Lance shook his head. "Naw, not anything like that. I did get…" He paused, clicking through some more of the pictures. "These though."

He zoomed in on a label sticking out of a thin blue binder that a woman was holding. Across the orange tag in bolded black letters spelled out: ECHO

Brooklyn kept her composure. She kept breathing. Kept blinking. Kept standing. But the word, bold and familiar, sent shivers into her bones that shook her from the inside out.

"Any idea what it means?" Nicoli asked.

Freddie spoke up from his seat behind them, "It has to be an operation of some kind. Gene therapy. Animal and human trials. It would make sense with everything else we've collected on the Omen project."

Brooklyn stumbled and caught herself on the stairs leading back up to the cabin. Her eyes were wide, and even though she wanted to breathe, she couldn't. She struggled to swallow, to stop her lips from shaking.

Nicoli tilted back to look at her. "You okay?"

She tried to nod, but it came out short and barely there.

"Can't handle a little investigating there, girly?" Chester said snidely as he picked at his teeth.

"What are they looking for?" Brooklyn asked, keeping as calm as she could.

"We never acquired that information," Freddie said. "But they did question a few store owners and some tenants in the area—said they were looking for some voluntary test subjects that hadn't come forward, made it seem like they were looking for people who were doing trial runs for new prescriptions."

Brooklyn wanted to be sick.

"That's weird," she said and rubbed her sweating palms together. "Is that all you found out?"

"Yeah, pretty much," Lance said. "We're trying to tie it to another case we've been working on. Genome splicing. Cybernetic upgrades. The kind of shit the human race shouldn't be messing with."

"Yeah, that sounds crazy," Brooklyn said. "I'm gonna head back to camp and get some tea."

"You sure you're okay, now? You seem a little shaken?" Nicoli asked.

Brooklyn made her way up the stairs and called back down to him. "Yeah! Just tired, thanks Nicoli!"

He didn't follow her, and she was thankful for that, because her feet moved fast against the ground as she ran out the door and into the woods.

Chapter Twenty-Three

Brooklyn found Porter pacing around the fire. She grabbed him by the arms, causing him to yelp. He tugged away and clutched his bad shoulder. "Relax! What is it? What's wrong?"

"Sorry! I'm sorry. Are you okay? I didn't mean to—I just…" She shook out her hands, shifting from foot to foot. "There's a lot going on, and I think we should go. I think we should go right now."

"What'd you find out in there?"

She looked around before she leaned in closer, bouncing on the balls of her feet. "There are people in Seattle looking for us, and they're carrying around a bunch of shit labeled ECHO, just like the empty document that we found on Terry's laptop."

"That's not possible," Porter snapped. "ECHO was never a go. They demolished the idea within months after my dad pitched it to the board. There has to be a mistake."

"I saw it!"

Porter's nostrils flared. She could see the gears

turning in his head. His blood was pumping fast, increasing his heartbeat.

"Dawson's in Seattle…they're in Seattle. I know they are. We have to get to them first, Porter. We have to find them," Brooklyn whimpered.

"You don't understand." Porter reached out and grabbed her hand. "The ECHO campaign is extreme. It's more than I can explain right now, and I don't want you thinking I had anything to do with it."

"I don't care about your involvement anymore, okay? I care about our friends who are going to get taken by these people if we don't hurry up and get moving. You can explain everything about that after we find them."

Brooklyn turned swiftly to find Gabriel, who was in the shed with Julian, Cambria, and Plum. She walked inside and found them picking at a salad of vibrant peppers.

"Why'd you just take off like that? I was worried," Gabriel said.

"I just wanted to talk to Nicoli," Brooklyn said. "Are our clothes dry?"

"They should be. Hey, look at what Plum did for me." She wiggled her fingers out in front of Brooklyn and showed off the pretty nail polish adorning her nails.

Brooklyn couldn't help but smile. "They look really nice. I like the light blue."

"It's periwinkle," Gabriel corrected.

Brooklyn rolled her eyes.

"I thought we'd be staying another night," Julian said.

"Yeah, well, I was thinking we should get going sooner than later." Brooklyn was trying to get her point across without having to say much in front of Plum and Cambria, but that seemed to be near impossible.

Gabriel frowned. "We probably shouldn't be traveling in the dark though."

"I…I know that, but really, just…I think we should go. Let's get dressed, okay?"

"Y'all can stay," Plum whined. "I like you guys. You're funny an' nice. Please, stay?"

The last thing Brooklyn wanted to do was run out on the people who had given them shelter, and even though they hadn't spent much time with them, it seemed like Plum, Cambria and Nicoli were important. The group of forest dwellers pulled at Brooklyn's heart strings. If she lived a normal life, things could be different. She could leave a phone number, an e-mail. She could promise to visit, make plans. But she didn't live a normal life, and the hardest part about leaving was the fact that she may never see her new friends again.

Julian cleared his throat. "I'm sure we'll see you guys again, Plum."

"Of course we will," Brooklyn said. Her heart sank.

Porter took the clothes down off the wire. Gabriel walked out first with Plum at her side, and Julian followed. Brooklyn hurried after them, but Cambria grabbed her arm and waited for the door to shut before she spoke.

"You've got something to do with the Omen operation, don't you?" Cambria asked.

Brooklyn didn't want to lie. She didn't think she could have if she tried, especially not to Cambria.

"It's okay. You can tell me," Cambria added.

Brooklyn searched Cambria's face. She printed it in her mind, the woman's pretty high cheek bones and the gap between her front teeth as her lips fell loose, waiting. Brooklyn wanted to remember the kindness in her earthy brown eyes.

"Yeah," Brooklyn confessed, shaking her head, disappointed with herself for even accepting their help and putting them in danger. "We do. We need to go before this gets out of hand."

"I'm going to get you a backpack with some water and food. Keep the clothes, pack them if you need to, and stay off the main roads."

"Cambria, you don't have to do all that."

"We're not the kind of people who will send you off with nothing but a memory and some good luck, all right? Take what I'm giving you." Cambria nodded slowly and reached out to rub the top of Brooklyn's arm.

Brooklyn didn't know whether to say thank you, to hug her, to cry, or to deny everything and just run. Run as fast as they could away. So she stood there, wearing an expression that lingered somewhere between disbelief and the utmost gratitude.

"I don't know how to thank you for all this. For everything," Brooklyn said.

Cambria huffed. "You don't need to."

Brooklyn was lost for words, and her stomach started to turn upside down. She tried to walk out the door, but once again, Cambria's hand stopped her.

"I just have a question," Cambria whispered. There was a tremor in her voice that clued Brooklyn in on what she was about to ask. "Are you one of them?"

Brooklyn's fingers curled into fists, and she turned to look over her shoulder at Cambria. The woman looking back at her shrank, eyes clear and curious, like a seal looking at a shark. Brooklyn said nothing as she pushed the door to the shed open and walked outside toward the fire.

Chapter Twenty-Four

It wasn't dark yet, but the sun was starting to set over the horizon and turned the sky into a palette of watercolors. Oranges melted into purples, and rose golds collided seamlessly with dark navy blues. It was beautiful. Brooklyn wanted nothing more than to climb into a tree and watch it while her friends cooked dinner over the fire. But that wasn't an option. They'd had their rest, and now they needed to move.

Brooklyn had changed out of the dress Plum had leant her, but when she'd tried to give it back, Plum had insisted that it was a gift. Gabriel shoved the pair of decorative lace shorts she'd worn into the backpack, followed by a pink crop top, substituting both with jeans and a long sleeve shirt.

Cambria handed them the backpack while they laced up their boots. "I put fresh bandages and some of Plum's ointment in there as well. Keep the jar airtight so it stays fresh."

Porter smiled. "You're a lifesaver."

She winked down at him and looked out past the

trees toward the cabin.

"You need to find Nicoli. He'll never forgive me if I let you guys leave without saying a proper goodbye," Cambria said.

Julian shrugged the backpack over his shoulders and adjusted the straps to fit snug.

Brooklyn shoved the only gun they had in the back of her pants and gave the camp a onceover to be sure they weren't missing anything. "Okay, let's go to the cabin, and then we'll try to get a clear trail before nightfall."

They made their way toward the cabin with Plum and Cambria guiding them. Plum held Gabriel's hand the whole time, swinging it playfully and laughing about the short time they'd spent together. She was one of the sweetest people Brooklyn had ever met. It was a shame to have to say goodbye.

Cambria walked next to Brooklyn and didn't say much but turned and gave her a once-over. "You're strong. You know that?"

Brooklyn shrugged. "Not really. Not as strong as I should be."

"Yeah, well, you're strong enough." Cambria hummed. "Came into a pretty dangerous pack and lay with them just fine."

"We're a lot alike, I guess."

"You're a lion among wolves, Brooklyn. It's not that we're alike at all—it's that you're more deadly."

Brooklyn took in a deep breath and felt Porter bump gently into her shoulder. He was right next to her, listening to the entire conversation.

"You'll always have a home with us," Cambria

concluded.

Brooklyn mustered up a thankful smile.

They walked in through the back door of the cabin. Cambria leaned over the edge of the cellar to call down to the boys. They'd already heard them coming. Freddie walked up the ladder so he could see them all.

"Hey, you guys taking off already?" Freddie asked.

Brooklyn had it all planned out. Everything she was going to say. The words were right there on the tip of her tongue. She wanted to speak. She wanted to say goodbye and be done with it. She opened her mouth, smiled, but as soon as she tried to speak, the sound of feet slapping the ground silenced her. She looked up at the back wall and held her breath. Her heart raced; her chest tightened.

The leaves that littered the forest floor were picked up and tumbled along the ground in the wake of several pairs of feet. They hit the earth sloppily and quickly, again and again. A group was running. Their breath was moist and clogged with blood. She could smell it, the sickness of it. The sourness left a taste like something fermented on her tongue.

They were too late.

Gabriel realized it too and shoved Plum toward the cellar. "Get in! Get down there now!"

Plum's eyes narrowed. She resisted, squirming in Gabriel's grasp. "What's a matter with you! Lemme go!"

Julian was the first one outside and stared off into the woods in the direction of the noises.

"Cambria, get everyone inside. Lock the door. Do not come out until you don't hear anything for at least an hour. Do you understand?" Brooklyn snapped, pushing Cambria toward the cellar as well.

"What's happening?" Cambria squeaked.

"They found us. Just go. They don't have any interest in you. Please, please, go." Brooklyn was on the verge of tears.

The danger, the destruction, everything Brooklyn wanted to shield their new friends from, all of it had followed them.

Freddie ducked down, and Brooklyn heard him speaking quickly with Nicoli.

"Go!"

Cambria took Plum and hustled into the cellar.

Brooklyn grabbed the edge of the door and tilted it closed. She glanced between them, their eyes wide from the bottom of the stairs. Nicoli looked up at her, concerned and confused. Cambria's arms wrapped tight around Plum.

"Stay alive, girl," Cambria said.

Brooklyn closed to door over them.

The Surros moved fast, feet pounding the ground. Their breathing was accompanied by loud grunts and hollow growls. They sounded like a herd of rabid animals. Just before their silhouettes could be picked out among the trees, Brooklyn heard the first wave of ear-splitting screeches, warped and carnal.

As they took off toward the river, Brooklyn fished the gun out of the back of her pants and shoved it at Porter. "Take this."

"You should hold on to it," he said as he hopped

over a large rock.

"I don't need it, remember?" Brooklyn slammed it into his chest.

Porter winced but grabbed hold of the pistol and held on to it tightly.

The Surros were just behind them. Brooklyn could hear the wetness of their breath and the cracking of their bones as they closed in. There was no way to outrun them, not with Porter being hurt, and there were too many of them to fight. Their options had dwindled.

Gabriel spun around suddenly and took Brooklyn off guard as she sprinted back toward the group of Surros. She bared her teeth and yelled over her shoulder, "We have to pick some off before we can ditch them!"

Brooklyn admired her fearlessness.

Ten Surros were running toward them. They spat and snarled, clanked their teeth and tried to grab at them with long, bony fingers.

The sunlight faded, and the shadow of night dropped down over them. Brooklyn gave in to her senses, allowed her eyes to adjust and her ears to tune in to the vibrations around her. It felt like the world was rotating in slow motion, every precise movement, every instinctual dip or dodge. It all came to her as easily as breathing. Her fingers flexed, the muscles in her legs hummed. Her body wanted to move, and somewhere in the back of her mind, a primal part of her fed off the urge to fight.

A Surro, large and masculine with black blood oozing from its mouth, reached for Brooklyn, but she spun effortlessly and snatched its arm. She twisted, hurling the heavy body across her back before she sent her boot down into its face. Her heel crushed the bridge of its nose, leaving a wide, gaping cavern in its place.

Gabriel was messy. Her movements flowed together in time with each oncoming Surro, but that didn't mean she was executing the combat the right way. It wasn't an act of survival for her; it was a challenge. A test. Her lips turned up crudely. She laughed when a Surro gagged and gasped for air as she tightened her grip around its throat. She reveled in their death, teeth bared in a grin, eyes narrowed.

"Brooklyn! Behind you!" Porter yelled, firing a bullet into the chest of a Surro coming up on her flank.

The sound of the bullet cut through the air. The smell of bloodstained soil mixed with hot metal and charcoal.

Julian was busy with two others. He spun around, dodging the tangle of arms that tried to grab him. It seemed like no matter how many they took down the Surros just kept coming.

"We have to run!" Julian shouted as he tossed one of the smaller Surros against a tree, sweeping the legs out from underneath another.

"Go!" Gabriel yelled as she jumped up and bounced off a tree, kicking one of the Surros straight in the cheek. "I'll hold them off!"

Brooklyn pushed another Surro back with both her palms and dodged the prying, nasty hands of one on her left side. They were surrounding them, slowly but surely. Julian was right—they had to run.

Brooklyn felt Julian's shoulder brush against

hers as they tried to back up, taking careful steps backward toward the river. Porter was being wise with his use of the bullets. He cracked the gun down over a Surros skull that reached for him and kicked another out of the way.

"Get in the water!" Porter said quickly as if he'd had some sort of revelation. "They might not follow! The river could confuse them!"

Julian leapt in front of Porter and backed up toward the river banks. The ten Surrogates that they'd been dealing with had multiplied, and no matter how hard they fought, it seemed impossible to make any progress. They were more lethal, but the Surros were like ants, swarming around them. Soon, they'd be overpowered, and Brooklyn wasn't ready to give up even if not giving up meant running.

Brooklyn stood up on her tiptoes, scanning the area. She couldn't leave without Gabriel and ran back out to find her. She twisted and spun around the broken bodies of every Surro that tried to grab her. She slid across the damp grass and lifted her leg high in the air, kicking one backward. She used the darkness to her advantage and grabbed a sharp rock from beside a tree, slicing into two pale arms that tried to wrap around her midsection.

Gabriel was only a few feet away, fighting like it was a dance. She was right there, just within reach. Brooklyn opened her mouth to yell, but the crack of a shotgun broke through the misty air, distracting her.

Plum's petite body shook, but her hands were wrapped tight around the double-barreled gun. It looked much too big to be held by such a small woman. Tears ran down her cheeks. She wretched, gagging at the sight of the Surrogates. Brooklyn never wanted this; she never wanted any of her new friends to see the nightmarish creatures that'd been hunting them. Plum fired another shot at a group of Surros who were running out of the trees, and she sniffled, trying to catch her breath.

"Plum! Get the hell out of here now!" Gabriel yelled desperately. She ran forward while Plum struggled to reload the shotgun.

Brooklyn tried to follow, but two damp hands clutched her arm and swung her around. The Surro attacking her was quick, snapping from left to right as she tried to squirm away. It mumbled her name under its breath again and again. Greasy black hair was plastered down the blocks of its protruding spine.

Brooklyn lost sight of them just as Gabriel pushed Plum away

"Go back!" Gabriel shouted.

Plum cried and choked as she tried to catch her breath. "I ain't leavin' you guys!"

"You have to go!" Gabriel said, turning to shove another Surro away.

The distant call of Plum's name echoed through the woods. Nicoli and Cambria were searching for her, and if they didn't get her to go back soon, the entire group would be exposed. It was exactly what Brooklyn wanted to avoid. It wasn't Plum's battle, and she shouldn't have been fighting it.

"What are these damn things?" Plum sobbed as she swung the shotgun at a Surro running toward them.

It caught the barrel in its hand and ripped it from her grasp, tossing the weapon far out into the woods. Plum's eyes went wide, and she stumbled to get away, hiding behind Gabriel, who once again demanded that she go back to camp.

Brooklyn broke free from the Surro's grasp and looked back to find Porter and Julian holding their ground at the riverbanks. She turned and sprinted toward Gabriel and Plum. Her head was clouded with the thought of their forest friends, the ones who had saved Porter's life, losing their own.

Gabriel was close by, fighting as hard as ever. She snapped a Surros neck like it was a wishbone, gouged at their throats with her nails like she was just as wild as they were. Her emotions showed in the way she killed them, brutally, cruelly. Gabriel was sending a message to whoever was watching, and whatever it was she wanted to say was spelled out in black blood on the forest floor. The thought tickled the back of Brooklyn's mind that maybe Gabriel enjoyed killing.

When Brooklyn finally got close enough to reach Plum, she dragged her out of the fray and pointed toward the camp. "You need to go right now. Go and stay in the cabin!"

"What's goin' on? How are you movin' so fast?"

Brooklyn snarled fiercely. "Run, Plum!"

Plum shook her head, lips trembling as she whispered, "I'm sorry," turned on her heels, and ran.

The shrieking from the Surros grew louder and more frantic. They were scrabbling toward

Brooklyn with bloodshot eyes.

There wasn't a way out. Not to her left or to her right. She heard the gurgle of one breathing behind her, the rotten smell of another on her left. Brooklyn stood on her tiptoes, glancing at Porter and Julian a few yards away. They both yelled to her, blind from the bodies of Surros that surrounded them. Porter stood on his tiptoes, trying to find her while Julian continued to fight off the straggling Surros that had pushed them against the river bank.

The choice was an easy one to make. To let the Surros take her and ensure that her friends live. She didn't fight, not when they clawed at her. Not when they tore at her jacket or her shirt. Brooklyn held her breath and waited. Waited for the sounds of her friends to dwindle, waited for the Surros to drag her off somewhere unknown. Clammy hands gripped her shoulders—wails and screams echoed in her ears. If they took her, it would give Gabriel time to run to the river. It would give them time to find the others.

That was most important.

Brooklyn closed her eyes. She thought of things like ocean water against her toes and nachos on a hot summer day. She thought of Porter's hands on her bare hips and the smell of the old thrift store two blocks from her mom and dad's house.

It was easy to dive into her memories and let the rest go. It'd always been easy.

But something soft grabbed her wrist. It ripped her from her memories, from the moment she'd prepared for, and tossed her away, out of the Surro's grasp. Brooklyn's eyes flung open, and

Gabriel stared back at her. Black slime dripped down Gabriel's face. Her lips quivered as she tried to catch her breath.

"Get to the river," Gabriel said. Her voice was stern, but her eyes were gentle.

"Gabriel, don't—" Brooklyn's words were cut short when Gabriel used both her hands to push her backward.

It happened fast, like when lightning streaked across the sky and only a glimpse of its light shone through the window.

The sound of bones breaking was something Brooklyn knew all too well. But the sound of Gabriel's bones breaking would stay with her for eternity, of them cracking around the Surro's fist when it plunged into her back and pushed straight through her ribcage. The sound of her gasp, of her skin as it ripped open, of her trying to breathe. The sound of her dying.

Julian's scream was a distant echo.

Brooklyn didn't know how long she stood there, staring at Gabriel. Her mind went blank—her arms hung heavy. She couldn't fall to her knees; they were locked in place. She inhaled a sharp breath, watching as blood leaked over Gabriel's lips, as her eyes, green like jungle canopies, rolled back.

Suddenly, hands were on Brooklyn's hips.

"We have to go," Porter said against her ear. His voice was far away, like it was being shouted across a football field. It didn't register, not until the Surros started to carry Gabriel away.

"No." It started as a whisper, and then Brooklyn's voice escalated into wretched screams and sobs. "I'm not leaving her! No, let me go! God dammit, let me go!" Her voice was hoarse. She thrashed against both of them as Porter and Julian tried to pull her away. "I'm not leaving her!" She clawed at their arms, kicked her feet, screamed and cried and writhed.

Cold water washed up over her head as Porter and Julian dragged Brooklyn into the river.

Gabriel was gone.

Chapter Twenty-Five

Porter was right. The river stopped the Surros dead in their tracks. The demented creatures ran to the edge of the water and howled at them as Brooklyn, Julian, and Porter swam their way to the other side. The water was the kind of cold that sank deep into the bone. A numbing, merciless cold that Brooklyn wanted to float in until what she'd witnessed stopped being real.

The drowned gasp of Gabriel's last breath played on a loop in Brooklyn's head. It happened again and again, overlapping until it was the only thing she could hear.

"We'll walk the tree line close to the main road until we find somewhere to rest," Julian said. His voice was clogged and solemn.

Brooklyn sat in the grass and watched the Surros pace along the river bank. They snarled like vicious dogs. She wanted to rip every last one of them to pieces.

"What the hell are we doing?" Brooklyn whimpered, and her face crumbled. "You said those things were sent to collect us, not to kill us!"

Porter tried to reach for her, but Brooklyn pulled away.

"I don't know what's going on anymore. Nothing…nothing makes sense," Porter said. His voice wavered.

"We have to keep moving," Julian said, wiping his nose with the sleeve of his wet jacket.

They were like ghosts moving through the night. Empty of purpose. Void. No matter how far away they got from the maddened voices of the Surros, it still seemed like they were right there, nipping at Brooklyn's heels. The reality of what she'd been running from had swallowed her whole.

It felt like there was hardly anything left to fight for because Gabriel wasn't there to fight with them.

They walked for two hours in silence, staying close to each other, shoulders touching. Their feet started dragging after a while, boots filled with water, clothes sopping wet and icy cold in the chilled night air. The forest no longer seemed like a beautiful place, and Brooklyn wanted to get far away from it by morning. She wanted to shove her fingers in her ears to stop the repetition of Gabriel's voice from going on and on in her head, wanted to tear her own eyes out so she could forget Gabriel's blank, expressionless face. But there was no way to make it stop.

Through the trees came a clearing to a road that connected with the shoulder on the highway. City lights glinted in the distance not far past an old truck stop at the next exit. A green sign hung above the road. It read: **'SEATTLE 5 MILES.'**

"There has to be a motel at that stop up there," Porter said. His teeth chattered.

"We don't have any way to get a room. No IDs, no money, nothing," Julian sighed.

Without a word, Brooklyn started to trudge forward toward the truck stop.

"What're you doing? How are we supposed to get into a room?" Julian asked as he trotted up beside her.

She shrugged. "We'll figure it out."

"Okay, but how? How will we just figure it out?"

Brooklyn continued on without saying much of anything besides "hurry up" or "we're almost there." There was no reason to try and come up with a plan anymore. It seemed like whatever plan they did come up with would get compromised anyways.

The feeling of concrete beneath their waterlogged boots was strange after spending time traveling on nothing but soft soil. Porter almost tripped when they stepped onto the sidewalk. Julian caught him, and Brooklyn turned to glance over her shoulder as they followed quietly behind her. The path beside the highway was barely lit, and every time a car sped by, a gust of strong wind followed.

Porter was too cold. His lips were cracked and dry—dark navy circles started to develop below his eyes. His fingernails were translucent, and his cheeks were bruised from the air, cherry red and blue. They had to get somewhere warm and somewhere dry, not only so that he wouldn't come down with hypothermia but also because his bandages were sopping wet. They had to be crawling with bacteria from the river.

200

"Take off your jacket," Brooklyn said. "You should have taken it off before we even started walking."

Porter flinched, trying to get his bad arm out of the sleeve. "Do you have any ideas on how we're supposed to get into a room?"

The streetlights in the parking lot were mostly burnt out, and the lights over most of the doors on the second floor of the motel were flickering. It was run-down to say the least, but it was something. Only a few cars were parked in the abundance of spaces, and the adjoining gas station was out of order.

"Come on," Brooklyn said, walking toward the far staircase that led up the second floor.

She listened closely as they walked past each door. The slow sleeping heartbeat of each patron was easy to pick out. She heard their snores, the static of an infomercial playing on a television, the rattle of the one person who was awake rifling through their belongings.

They came across room number 174, and Brooklyn stopped. "Cough," she said.

"What?" Julian said, face twisting up with confusion.

"Just cough," Brooklyn said again.

Julian looked to Porter, who was too busy hugging himself for warmth to have anything constructive to offer. Julian coughed once and then loudly a second time.

Brooklyn's palms pressed around the doorknob. She gave one hard twist.

When Julian heard the snap of the lock breaking,

he smiled. "Good idea."

The room smelt like an antique booth at a flea market. The brown carpet was dull, and the two small beds pushed against the wall had cheap floral comforters folded down neatly on top of them. There was an old dresser and a small television. A mini-fridge hummed beside one of the nightstands, and a couple outdated magazines were laid out on the table.

It wasn't much, but it would suffice.

"We need to get you in the shower," Brooklyn said as she guided Porter through the dark toward the bathroom.

"I'm f-fine," Porter quivered and tucked his hands in his armpits.

The bathroom was tiny with a decrepit pale pink tub and a dinged-up shower head. There was some complimentary soap on the sink and towels on the back of the toilet.

Brooklyn turned the handle to the hottest point and helped Porter peel the almost frozen shirt off his back. His bandages were barely hanging on to his skin and gave way at the seams where they'd been tied around his chest. She was as careful as she could be, but her hands trembled. When she finally pulled off the last bit of bandage, it snagged on one of the stitches.

Porter hissed, "Ah! Shit, that hurt like a bitch."

"I'm sorry," she said under her breath. Brooklyn bit down on her lip and turned away when he discarded the brown leather belt wrapped around his waist. "C'mon, get in, and get warm. Take as long as you want. Just say my name if you need me. I'll hear you."

Porter brushed his hand against her arm. "I don't know what to say to you, Brooklyn...I don't know how to comfort you or be there for you. I don't know how to do this."

"You don't need to do anything," she said. "Take a shower, and I'll fix your stitches when you're done, okay?"

He was lost for words, and she didn't bother giving him time to answer anyways. She closed the door and leaned against it, holding back the urge to cry or scream or break the lamp that was on the nightstand between the beds. He didn't need to know how to comfort her, because there was nothing that could make what she was feeling disappear. She didn't even know if she was feeling anything at all. There was a knot in her chest that grew tighter and tighter, a cinder block of emotion that she refused to acknowledge. It sat there, right on her lungs, and reminded her every time she tried to breathe that her best friend was dead.

Julian sat on the edge of the bed and stared down at the backpack that was open at his feet.

"What're you doing?" Brooklyn asked as she pawed at her eyes.

He swallowed, but his gaze never left the backpack. "The clothes...they're all wet, and Porter's bandages are wet. I was gonna just lay them out to dry, but her stuff...Gabriel's clothes are in there."

The knot in Brooklyn's chest swelled—she choked it down and smothered it until it was a dull throb.

"It's okay," she said. "I can do it if you don't want to."

Julian let his head drop into his hands. "This wasn't supposed to happen," he wheezed. "She should be here."

Brooklyn didn't know what to do. She didn't know if her arms around him would make Julian feel less alone or if they would only make him shatter. Tears dripped off his chin, and he wiped at them roughly.

She knelt down on the floor beside him. "Let me do this."

"Are you sure?"

It wasn't worth answering, because Brooklyn wasn't sure of anything. She grabbed the bottom of the damp backpack and dumped the contents out on to the carpet.

The jar of ointment was still sealed, and she set it to the side followed by each of the clean bandages. A couple pairs of jeans were wadded up with the dress Plum had given her. She untangled them and laid them out one by one. Next were the bottles of water and a couple apples that Cambria had packed for them. Finally, at the very bottom of the backpack, was the neatly folded pair of lace shorts and the crop top Gabriel had worn.

At first, she laid them out like an outfit, shirt above shorts, but the more she looked at it, the more she pictured Gabriel wearing it, and she decided to place them in different areas on the floor. It seemed ridiculous to scramble around, separating pieces of clothing, but it was the only thing she could do to erase the image of long, pale limbs occupying them.

"Someone should stay awake," Julian said as they continued to stare down at the clothes laid out on the floor. "Just in case."

"Go to sleep. I'll take the first shift," Brooklyn offered.

Julian looked confused, like he'd been punched in the stomach. He ran his fingers through his damp black hair. "How are you doing this, babe…?"

"Doing what?"

"*This*," Julian repeated, waving his hand toward the bathroom door where Porter was and then down to Gabriel's clothes.

She ignored the comment and shook her head. "Go to sleep."

"You can talk to me," Julian said.

The shower stopped running. They both heard Porter stepping out of the tub.

"I know," she whispered, reaching out to touch him lightly on the knee. "Just get some sleep, please."

Julian's frustration with her was obvious. He heaved a sigh and threw his wet shirt down to the floor with the others. He shimmied out of his jeans and slid under the scratchy comforter, wrapped up tight in the clean sheets.

Chapter Twenty-Six

"Do I need to do anything for these?" Brooklyn asked as she took a look at the stitches holding Porter's skin closed on his shoulder.

He shook his head. "No, they're okay for now."

They stood next to the bathroom in front of a tall mirror. Brooklyn dabbed the ointment over his wound with the tips of her fingers. Porter's body was warm again, and even though it was clear he was exhausted, the discoloration beneath his eyes had brightened.

"We should probably wash those bandages and dry them out before we wrap you up again," she muttered. "The last thing we need is you getting an infection."

"I'll be okay without them for the night."

Brooklyn nodded.

"You should take a shower." He reached up to pull her hand away from his shoulder. "I can take care of myself for now."

"I'll start washing those bandages, then." She tucked a strand of loose hair behind her ear and walked toward the front of the room where their clothes were, but Porter caught her arm before she could make it too far.

Brooklyn tensed and pulled away, holding her hands snug against her chest.

"I can wash the bandages," Porter whispered, glancing to Julian who was asleep only a few feet away. "Go take a shower."

Her gaze darted around, settling on everything except for Porter. She shrugged, bottom lip quivering as she rolled it up and pinched it between her teeth. There was no way to capture how empty she felt, no way to make Porter understand that constant movement was the only way to keep the weight on her chest from sinking in any further. He stared at her, defeated, eyes warm and knowing. She hated it. She hated that he knew her as well as he did.

Porter sighed. "Go…"

Gabriel's face flashed through Brooklyn's mind, her scarred lips curled back as she yelled to them, "Go! I'll hold them off!" It was impossibly clear, like a film of her might have been playing on the television. That fight, the way Gabriel flew into battle like a Valkyrie, crawled behind Brooklyn's eyes like an old video.

She flinched and shied away, afraid to close her eyes but weary of keeping them open.

Porter moved toward her, but she put her hand out to stop him, fingers stretched out wide from her palm.

"I'm…gonna take a shower." Brooklyn hiccupped on her words.

"Yeah...just, if you need me—"

"Yeah, okay," she interjected. Her eyes refused to meet his.

Brooklyn dragged herself into the bathroom and shut the door. She turned on the water and didn't wait for it to heat up. She peeled her clothes off, shirt, then pants, bra, then underwear, letting them drop away into a pile on the floor. She stepped under the rush of cold water; it washed down her back, jolting her senses, but warmed up gradually and chased away the goosebumps that rose on her skin.

Nothing hurt. Her muscles weren't sore; her legs weren't tired. The scratches and bruises she'd sustained earlier had vanished. Brooklyn was stagnant, floating inside herself, trying to feel something that wouldn't seem to come. There were no bones to realign, no scabs to pick at or bullet holes to mend.

All she had was the weight of Gabriel's death like an anvil on her chest.

The shower wall was smooth as she slid down it and sat underneath the hot water. The steam was thick, and her lungs ached when she tried to take in a deep, long breath. Her arms posed as a shelter that she hid her face in. She felt secure with her legs, long and thin, pulled up against her chest.

It was like being trapped in the haze of a dream—the point where the body had convinced itself to wake up but the mind still clung to sleep. The free falling.

She used the tiny bar of soap to scrub her hair and face and stayed under the spray of the shower head until her skin pruned.

Brooklyn glanced at Porter when she stepped out of the bathroom with a towel wrapped around her torso. He held a fluffy white robe in his hands and handed it to her. "I found this in the closet. Didn't think a place this shitty would supply robes, but…"

The first thing she thought to do was to reject it and tell him to wear it instead. But her skin crawled with anticipation as she stared at it. She took it without saying anything and walked back into the bathroom to slip it on.

The robe was warm and roomy. She tied it tight and combed through her hair with the disposable brush they'd found in the vanity drawer. Once she felt comfortable enough, she walked out and sat down on the edge of the empty bed. The sheets were cold and stiff. She glanced at Julian asleep a couple feet away, watching the steady rise and fall of his chest.

"I'll stay up while you get some sleep," Porter said, walking over to sit in a large green chair pushed against the flimsy wooden desk.

"Will it be too hard for you to stay awake if you're in the bed?"

"No…" He looked taken aback and adjusted his glasses nervously. "Do you want me to lay in the bed with you?"

"I don't want to sleep alone," she confessed.

Brooklyn waited, watching Porter as he took his time climbing in beside her. He was slow and careful as he slid under the covers and made no point to reach for her until she was situated next to him. The pillow felt nice, cradling her neck.

Brooklyn lay on her side, facing him, eyes cracked open, scanning the delicate ridges of his face, neck, chest, his busted shoulder.

Her throat closed when she spotted a small cut spanning the curve of his jaw and a welt darkening his chest. Bruises fanned up the side of his neck, blossoming patches of navy, muted yellow, and ivy. The black stitches on his shoulder still held the skin tight together, but the area around them was red and swollen. Black and blue bruising faded into dark yellow blotches that broke up the freckles she was so fond of down his side, covering some of his ribs.

He took his glasses off and set them down next to a dusty bible on the nightstand.

She reached out and touched the mark on his jaw. "What happens if they take us?"

"I don't know anymore. After combat training, everyone in the camps was supposed to be transferred to headquarters for interrogation techniques and moxie training. But after everything that's happened...I don't trust what I was told."

"Do you think they found Dawson and the others?"

Porter hesitated but ended up shaking his head. "No. I don't think they did."

"Do you think they'll find us?"

"Eventually, yeah, they will."

"You could leave, you know. You could call your dad and get out of this. You don't have to stay and keep getting hurt."

He was quiet, eyes flicking around her face. The cold tips of his fingers moved to brush along her knee, and then he shifted his arm over her waist and tugged her closer.

"I think I'd rather keep getting hurt with you guys than pretend that I'm safe with my father."

Brooklyn shuffled against his chest and let him engulf her. It was nice to feel small and weak for a moment. To feel his chin resting on the top of her head with his arms wrapped protectively around her. Not that Porter could protect her, but that he would try. That was what mattered.

She closed her eyes.

"I was supposed to take Gabriel home," Brooklyn whispered, fighting back the lump in her throat.

Porter pulled one of her legs between his knees and tangled them together. His heart was kicking loud and steady. He didn't say anything, and she didn't expect him to.

Chapter Twenty-Seven

Brooklyn woke up alone.

She didn't open her eyes but instead stayed still, listening to Julian and Porter whisper to one another. The dusty smell of old wallpaper mingled with cheap, stale coffee. She craved the bitter warmth of it, of something that reminded her of normalcy.

Julian sighed. "It's shitty coffee."

"It's better than nothing," Porter said.

"You're awake!" Julian kicked the bed with the sole of his bare foot.

Brooklyn huffed and cracked her eyes open. "How'd you know?"

"Super powers, remember? Your breathing changed."

She sat up and nodded her chin toward the old coffee pot. "Is there any left?"

"Yeah, I'll get you some."

"Thank you," Brooklyn mumbled as she pawed at her eyes with the back of her hands.

The mug that Julian handed her was chipped and

decorated with doodles of cats. She didn't expect the roadside hotel to have anything nice, and the mug was just dinky enough to make her think of home. She smiled fondly down at it, the powdered cream rising to bubble on the top of the rich brown liquid.

She glanced up, noticing that Porter's shoulder was wrapped in clean bandages, and the clothes that had been laid out to dry were now folded on the table.

Brooklyn sipped at the coffee and wrinkled her nose. "We still have the apples that Cambria packed for us, right?"

The coffee wasn't good. It would have been nice to wake up to Plum's mint green tea with honey.

"Yeah, I washed them this morning after I took a shower," Julian said.

"Seems like I slept through a lot..." She shifted her gaze to Porter.

Porter shrugged his good shoulder. "You needed the rest."

"Did you eat?" Brooklyn asked, glancing back and forth between the two of them.

Julian shook his head. "We wanted to wait for you."

She slid off the edge of the bed and walked over to the table where her jeans and shirt were folded. Her jacket was draped over the back of one of the chairs, still damp from the river, and their backpack was hung open upside down. The gun was laid out alongside the water bottles and apples.

Brooklyn grabbed one of the apples and tossed it to Julian.

"I'm guessing there's nothing in the mini fridge?" Brooklyn asked.

Julian shook his head. "It's broken. There's gotta be some vending machines around here though. Think we could stock up if we found one?"

"Yeah, we'd just have to bust it open," Brooklyn said. "It'd be something we did on our way out."

Julian nodded. "That's what I was thinking."

"Eat this." Brooklyn handed Porter one of the apples.

"What about you? You need to eat too," Porter said.

She glared at him and took her folded clothes into the bathroom so she could change. Her jeans felt loose around her hips, and the tank top she'd had on since they left the camp was no longer tight. It wasn't alarming to notice a bit of weight loss, seeing as they were no longer receiving three square meals a day overflowing with protein. She stared at herself in the mirror and poked at her stomach, pinched the meat on her thighs, and flexed her arms. She was thin but still okay, still alive.

Brooklyn walked out of the bathroom after securing her hair into a ponytail and glanced at Julian as he shrugged the backpack on.

"I left a water bottle and an apple out for you," Julian said. "I got everything else packed."

Brooklyn gave a weak smile. "Thanks."

Porter shoved the gun in the back of his pants and slid his glasses up on to the bridge of his nose.

A part of Brooklyn didn't want to leave the motel. It was safe and small, with a way for them to stay clean and beds for them to sleep in. They could keep the drapes drawn and the door closed. The thought of hiding was more than tempting—it chewed on her, begged her. But she couldn't let the daydream of a little comfort stop her from finding the rest of their group. This was about survival, and surviving wasn't comfortable.

"You ready?" Porter asked.

Julian nodded and turned to Brooklyn. "We can make it to Seattle in a few hours if we speed walk. Hopefully it doesn't rain on us."

Brooklyn pushed the door open halfway and looked around outside. There was a man standing by a Volkswagen bus in the parking lot, a couple of scrawny people sauntered around by the stairs, and the concierge working the front desk flipped through a magazine in the lobby.

They walked down the hallway to the far staircase that led out to the side of the building. There was a soda dispenser on the first floor, and behind the building next to a fire escape was a dilapidated vending machine. Bags of chips, candy, and pastries packed with preservatives sat behind the cracked glass. The old yellow buttons on the selection panel were hardly readable.

"Should we even bother with this shit? It looks gross," Julian said.

"I want those doughnuts," Brooklyn snapped. "And those cheese puffs."

Julian's eyebrows pulled together as he took a step back. "Okay, warrior princess, you go ahead and get your cheese puffs."

Brooklyn's elbow shot back, and her fingers curled into a fist, but before she could punch a hole in the front of the vending machine, Porter croaked out a weak protest.

"Hey!" He tapped on her arm and shook his head. "I don't really like the idea of your bare hand going through that glass."

"I'll heal," she said and shrugged. She raised her fist, but Porter persisted, grabbing her arm.

"Yeah, I know you'll heal, but can you just kick a hole in it instead of slicing your hand up? Please?"

Brooklyn rolled her eyes and brushed him off. "God, fine."

"She really wants those puffs, man." Julian chuckled.

Brooklyn kicked her foot up and sent the bottom of her boot through the front of the vending machine. It shattered around the force of her leg, and she stumbled to catch herself before she fell all the way through it. Julian grabbed her around the middle and hoisted her out.

Porter craned his neck around the corner to see if anyone had heard the loud crack of the glass shattering, but the people wandering around seemed to pay no mind.

Brooklyn winced and reached down to roll up her pant leg. A sharp piece of the glass had ripped through her jeans and bitten into her ankle. It wasn't a deep cut, but it bled steadily into her boot. She hissed at Julian when he reached down to put pressure on it.

"Get me one of the shirts out of the backpack," she said through gritted teeth.

Julian fumbled to open the backpack and blindly grabbed for something soft that she could wrap around her foot. He shoved a shirt at her, and she smashed it down against her ankle without a thought. The light pink color of it took her off guard. Brooklyn swallowed painfully when she realized it'd been Gabriel's.

Brooklyn tied the crop top around her ankle and pulled her pant leg back down. She tucked the bottom of her jeans into her boot and flexed her foot.

"You okay?" Porter asked.

"Just a scratch."

She stepped over the pile of glass and reached into the vending machine to grab a few different bags of chips. She handed the majority of them to Julian to put in the backpack and opened up a sealed assortment of powdered doughnuts for herself.

The first bite was more than she ever expected it to be. Sweet, almost stale, processed grocery store goodness. It was something she'd almost forgotten. The powdered sugar was all over her lips, and the dough stuck to the roof of her mouth. It was sad how often she would sneer her nose at a poorly packaged doughnut years ago, but now she was moaning around the taste of it.

"Here," she slurred around a mouthful of doughnut, handing one to Julian. "Eat one."

"Ew, no. You couldn't pay me." Julian stuck his tongue between his teeth.

"Eat it!" Brooklyn laughed, shaking the doughnut at him.

Julian grinned and grabbed the powdered doughnut from her. He took a small bite and closed his eyes, savoring the sugary dessert.

"You too," she said, holding one out to Porter.

Porter smirked and lifted his hand to her face. "Got something right here." He paused, thumb rubbing over her chin.

"Take the stupid doughnut," Brooklyn mumbled, rolling her eyes.

"I haven't had one of these in years," Porter said as he took a bite and wiped his mouth with the back of his hand.

Brooklyn's lips lifted into a smile, and she let the empty wrapper fall in the mess of glass on the ground.

Julian zipped up the backpack and tightened it on his shoulders as they walked back around to the front of the motel. There was a sidewalk that ran parallel to the highway; it would be easy to keep sight of it if they decided to take the tree line.

They walked toward the parking lot. Brooklyn heard a seat belt being pulled across someone's lap; she heard the squabble from the couple by the stairs and water running on the first floor. Then she heard light footsteps and a rapid heartbeat, the crash of something being thrown, the swing of a door on its hinges.

Brooklyn turned on her heels and looked up to the second floor, where the door of their room was wide open.

Chapter Twenty-Eight

"We should go," Julian said. He fiddled with his fingers, shifted back and forth on his feet, and chewed on his lip.

The three of them stood in the middle of the parking lot, staring up at the second story. The door to the room they'd spent the night in swayed back and forth on a broken hinge. The heartbeat of whoever was rummaging around inside was frantic and fast.

"What if it's one of our friends?" Brooklyn never stopped looking at the door and caught glimpses of the shadow darting back and forth beyond it.

"I don't think we should risk it," Porter said.

"I can't just walk away without knowing who's up there." She started walking back toward the stairs.

Julian groaned. "This is reckless, Brooklyn! We should just keep going!"

Brooklyn shushed him over her shoulder and crept as soundlessly as she could up the staircase. The boys followed behind her. Porter's hand rested over his back pocket, close to the gun.

The closer they got to the room, the crisper the sounds became. There was heavy breathing and a muffled growl, the mattress springs squeaked as the bed was flipped on to the ground. It was clear what they were about to walk into, but Brooklyn wasn't going to leave a stray Surro hot on their trail, not when they had the chance to kill it.

"I told you," Julian whispered. "We should've just hit the road!"

Brooklyn hushed him again.

The movement from inside the room came to an abrupt stop. Brooklyn nodded as they rounded the corner and came face to face with the creature inside.

Porter stumbled into the frame of the door. Julian gasped, his breath caught in his throat. It seemed like every drop of adrenaline rushing through Brooklyn's body spilled out of her. She refused to blink, refused to breathe. It was a nightmare—it had to be. Her eyelashes fluttered. Her breath was cut short. She rolled her ankle and felt pain bite into her foot, but still, the sight before her didn't fade.

The Surro stood in the middle of the room. Long, pale fingers twitched, and petite nostrils flared. Knotted locks of blonde hair fell in messy waves over its shoulders, and the outline of sunken ribs showed through the dirty top stretched tight across its torso.

"Gabriel?" Brooklyn whispered.

Large bulging eyes stared at them long and hard. It cracked its neck, flexed its jaw. A thin stream of black blood dripped steadily from its right ear.

Brooklyn was paralyzed. She tried to ignore the dread welling inside her. The weight on her chest slammed down into her heart and wrapped tight around her lungs, squeezing every ounce of air out of them.

"Is that you, Gabriel?" Brooklyn squeaked, taking a step forward.

The Surro looked up. Its lips curled back. The resemblance was uncanny. There was no way that what they were looking at wasn't Gabriel, but everything about it was wrong. Everything. From the tips of its broken, yellow nails to the sallow color that tinged the whites of its eyes. A distinct smell of rot mingled with its breath and the wracked, sharp movements…somehow Gabriel had become one of the monsters.

It yowled, loud and deep, before lunging forward and swiping at Brooklyn. Porter shoved Brooklyn out of the way, and in the process came in direct contact with the Surro's fist. It knocked him to the ground, sending the gun sliding toward the door, where Julian stood frozen in place.

"It's me! Gabriel, it's me!" Brooklyn gasped, rolling out of the way when the Surro charged forward again.

Its mouth opened. Its teeth slammed together over and over as it bit at her. Large mossy eyes were dull and empty, void of any sympathy or life. The veins in its arms splintered under the paper-thin skin like dark grey thread and spread all the way up its throat on to its cheek.

Even as Brooklyn hopped over one of the beds to get away, it clawed at her. She choked back a sob.

"Gabriel, please! It's Brookie! Listen to me. We can fix you, okay? We can get you help! Just…"

She pushed the Surro back with her hand and tried to dodge its flurry of attacks. It continued to howl and shout. Its hollow voice trembled with rage, dirty fingernails leaving angry red welts down Brooklyn's arm.

"Stop! Please, don't make me do this, Gabriel! I'll fix you!" Brooklyn shouted, batting at the Surro's hand as it clasped tight over her shoulder, trying desperately to get to her throat.

Brooklyn fought and squirmed. She pushed as far as she could and held the Surro at bay. It writhed, bones cracking, mouth open. Its savage screech rang in Brooklyn's ears. It was too close, only inches from Brooklyn's neck. The image of the Surro, so familiar, coaxed tears to spill down her cheeks. Her stare bore into the Surro, into Gabriel, and she sobbed, blinking through her tears. The Surro stared back at her, face screwed into an expression of hatred and agony. One hand dug into her shoulder, the other ripped through the air trying to get a grasp on Brooklyn's free arm.

It was too late. Gabriel was gone.

The words left Brooklyn's mouth in a hurry. She closed her eyes as she said them. "Shoot her, Julian! Shoot her!"

Julian's breath came in short bursts, and his eyes were swollen from crying. His arms quaked, fingers clutched around the gun. He tried to pull the trigger; his index finger danced against it. But when he attempted to press down, an exasperated breath was all that came from him.

"Shoot her!" Brooklyn shouted again. She gasped, stumbling backward as the Surro finally snapped forward and dove for her throat.

A loud crack split the air. Brooklyn winced when a shower of black blood sprayed the side of her face. She caught the Surro's expression when the bullet entered through its temple, the animalistic anger suddenly shifted into sadness and then faded into nothing. Its body folded forward, falling against Brooklyn's knees as it toppled into a heap at her feet.

Julian tried to catch his breath. He stared down at the gun, confused and bewildered, because he hadn't pulled the trigger.

Brooklyn steered her eyes away from the body that lay atop her boots.

And found Dawson in the doorway with his gun raised.

Chapter Twenty-Nine

The carpet cushioned Brooklyn's knees as she knelt down in front of the Surro's body and cradled its head in her hands. The same long hair, the same sharp bone structure, the same plump mouth. It was all the same. Brooklyn stroked her hand across its cheek.

"How...?" Brooklyn whispered as she traced the line of the Surro's jaw up to the small bullet hole in the side of its head. "How did this happen to her?"

The floor creaked under the weight of large black boots. Brooklyn looked up at Dawson as he knelt down beside her. It felt like so long since they'd seen one another, and in any other situation, she would have thrown her arms around him. But Dawson's attention was submerged in the body on the floor. He reached out and touched the Surro's shoulder, brushed a piece of hair out of its face.

"Dawson..." Brooklyn's voice cracked. "I don't know how to explain. I don't know what to do. I..."

"We gotta go," Dawson said. "We found something, and we don't have a lot of time."

"But we can't just leave her here."

"We have to. You can tell me about what happened later." Dawson's fingers wrapped around the Surro's lifeless hand and squeezed.

Julian and Porter slumped against the wall, catching their breath. Julian's eyes softened when they laid on Dawson, who walked over, grasped him by the arms, and hauled him into a suffocating embrace. Julian's fingers dug into his shoulders, holding on. He sputtered, choking on his words. "I don't know how this...D, I don't know what happened to her. She..."

"We backtracked around the woods after we got split up but ended up heading into Seattle after a few hours. Rayce figured you guys would go in that direction too," Dawson said, ignoring his comment about Gabriel.

Porter cleared his throat. "It's my fault we didn't find you guys sooner. I got hurt, and we found some people that helped us out in the woods."

Dawson turned toward him, "You good now?"

"For the most part," Porter said. "I need that duffle bag, the one we packed the medical supplies in. Did you guys grab it?"

"We have it," Dawson said. "But we have to go. We have a lot to discuss."

Brooklyn stared down at the body. Her fingers flexed over its sternum, the place where she'd seen the Surro's fist go through Gabriel's chest. She touched the space between its eyes, trailed the tip of her ring finger down its nose. Brooklyn's heart was broken, and there was nothing that could justify what she'd witnessed in the last two days. There was just a pool of black blood and a creature that looked like Gabriel's twin lying dead in her arms.

It couldn't be her. Could it...? Would that happen to all of them when they died? Brooklyn needed to know. She was thirsty for answers to questions she never thought she'd be asking. Did being an Omen mean that becoming a Surrogate was inevitable? It couldn't be. It went against everything Porter had told them.

Maybe this was another one of Juneau's tests. Maybe Brooklyn was already dead.

"Brooklyn," Dawson said sternly, pulling her out of her thoughts. "Let's go."

It was hard for her to stand, to not look back. But she did. Brooklyn rose to her feet and walked out of the room with Porter just behind her.

She had never thought that this would be the way they found their friends.

***

The truck was at the bottom of the stairs. Rayce leaned against it, pushing off as they approached. "Is everything okay? I heard a shot."

"We lost Gabriel," Dawson said. His eyes stayed straight, his gaze cold as ice as he climbed into the driver's side and turned the key roughly in the ignition.

Brooklyn swept away the stray tears clinging to her lashes. Porter reached for her hand, but she didn't budge. There was no time for consolation, and she didn't want to make any time for it. They just had to keep going. They had to keep moving. If they didn't, then she would fall apart, and none of them had the time or resources to put her back together.

Rayce's strong expression fell into something shocked and forlorn as Dawson's words clicked into place. He reached out and grabbed Julian's wrist, twisting the other man to face him.

"What happened?" Rayce asked, giving a light squeeze.

Julian shook his head. "We'll talk later. You okay?"

"I don't...I don't really know, but you don't look like you're all right."

"I'm not. But we have to go. Where's everyone else?" Julian's slate eyes focused on Rayce's boots. Nervous energy was captive in his arms and legs, causing his fingertips to rub together, his ankles to weaken.

"We found another camp in a closed-off site just outside Seattle, ended up crashing there, and then moved on to an empty warehouse by the port. Not everyone made it out, though...the Surrogates took Ellie and the others that were held up in the bus before we got separated. There were just too many of 'em...Amber got Dawson and me in the truck. We took off before they could get us too."

Julian chewed on the inside of his cheek and opened the back door.

Rayce kept hold of his wrist a little longer. "I went lookin' for you, ya know?" His eyes searched for recognition, to know that Julian wasn't under the impression that they'd been left behind.

It was a mutual feeling.

"I know." Julian swallowed. "I looked for you too."

They piled into the car with Brooklyn situated between Julian and Porter. Her throat was raw—her head spun. She sniffled and wiped her nose with the sleeve of her jacket. Porter rested his hand on her knee, thumb swiping back and forth along her thigh. She didn't bother brushing him away.

She looked out the back window and saw that the concierge in the lobby was jabbering on the phone. The couple that stood by the stairs had shrunk behind the soda machine. They were on a cell phone too, probably with the police, reporting a gunshot and a dead body.

Dawson didn't pay mind to what they'd seen. The truck rumbled on toward the highway as they left the motel behind.

"So, it's just you guys and Amber left?" Brooklyn asked.

"Yeah," Dawson said. "It's us and a couple people from Camp Fourteen."

Brooklyn closed her eyes. A sour taste spanned the back of her throat as relief and regret battled in her stomach. She pictured it, the Surros dragging Ellie, A.J., and Jordan away. She imagined what it would've sounded like, their screams for help. She'd always thought of the leaders, Dawson, Amber, Rayce…And somewhere along the way, she'd forgotten about the others. Somewhere along the way, she'd given up on them without realizing it. A stray tear dampened her cheek, and she cleared her throat. "Camp Fourteen? Like, another camp like ours?"

"Yes, exactly like ours. One of the girls in the camp was already figuring shit out before we got there. She ended up coming with us."

"What happened? How many people were there in the camp?" Brooklyn pressed, leaning forward in her seat.

Dawson sighed. "There were seventeen of them at the beginning. Apparently we arrived right after the majority had been re-directed."

"Re-directed?"

"They were air lifted somewhere else for the next level in their training. That's what they were told at least. We would have had a chance at getting some answers if their camp supervisor didn't off himself in his cabin," Dawson said.

Brooklyn poked Porter's hand and turned to look at him. "What does that mean?"

"Means they were taken to Denver for desensitizing and mental enhancement," Porter said. He looked out the window, far off somewhere in the rain.

Brooklyn listened to his heartbeat, shallow and steady. She leaned closer, nostrils flaring. Sadness smelt sweet, like cotton candy or packaged sugar. It poured off him in waves, clogging up her senses. Sometimes, Brooklyn forgot that Gabriel wasn't just hers, and she reached out to take his hand.

"Figured as much," Dawson said. "We also found their mole. We have her cell phone and laptop at the warehouse. Amber's keeping an eye on her."

"Did she tell you her name?" Porter blurted.

Dawson rolled his eyes. "Yeah, we got her name.

229

Savannah Kingston. Did you guys do some studying together before you were sent to spy on us?"

Porter tensed and stared down at his lap. "I know her if that's what you're asking."

"Good, maybe you can get her to talk," Dawson hummed.

***

Seattle was wet, grey, and cold. Tall buildings erupted on all sides of them, and lush greenery spanned on the outskirts of the city. Rayce's window was rolled down, letting in air that reeked of coffee and salt. The people of the city weren't in a hurry. They strode from shop to shop; some dined in cozy cafes.

Brooklyn boiled with jealousy.

She was supposed to be one of them—she was supposed to be enjoying her twenties, traveling the world and making mistakes. But instead, she was being hunted.

The warehouse that Dawson found was on an old fishing dock. The building itself wasn't impressive. Broken windows were covered in newspapers or boarded up, unlike the other adjacent concrete warehouses that harbored the hustle and bustle one would expect from a busy port. They parked the truck down an alley next to the side door. Brooklyn got a good look at her surroundings and found workers going about their business and delivery trucks being unloaded into the other open garages. She narrowed her eyes as they passed a shiny white Escalade with a crown of lights on the roof next to the back gate.

"Where'd you get that?" she asked.

"We took it," Rayce said. "Courtesy of Camp Fourteen."

"Good, we'll probably need it."

Dawson opened the side door, and they walked inside. The concrete floor was cold, and their boots echoed into the large open area. Some old palettes were stacked up and posed as a nice distraction that they could hide behind if anyone stumbled across them. The group followed Dawson toward the back of the warehouse behind another wall of palettes.

The moment they turned the corner, Amber scrambled to her feet. "'Bout time!"

Brooklyn couldn't smile even if she wanted to, but she accepted the warmth of Amber's arms wrapped tight around her.

"We thought you guys'd been taken or somethin'," Amber said. Her big hazel eyes examined everyone in turn before she took a step back. "Where's Barbie?"

"She…" Brooklyn's breath caught, and she settled for shaking her head instead of explaining.

Amber's mouth fell open as she searched for something to say. Her lips twitched, and she gave Brooklyn's shoulder a hard squeeze. "I'm glad you're here."

Dawson kicked a large duffle bag toward Porter and then sat down on the edge of one of the wooden pallets.

"All the medical supplies we have left are in there," Dawson said.

Porter's relief was prevalent as he unzipped the

bag and dug through its contents. "Good, thank you."

Julian sat down on the ground with his back against the wall, and Rayce sank down beside him. They whispered to one another under their breath, probably details of the time they'd spent apart. Dawson wandered in his own thoughts. He swayed his feet and closed his eyes, jaw held tight, head hung heavy. Brooklyn wanted to sit next to him and beg for his forgiveness. But her attention was stolen by an unfamiliar pair of muscular legs and a sassy voice.

"You found your friends, Dawson?" The girl asked as she approached from behind a blockade of unused boxes.

"Yeah," he said, eyes flicking up. "Everyone, this is Charlie. Charlie, this is everyone."

"Hi." Charlie gave a short wave.

Brooklyn looked Charlie up and down. She was tall, as tall as Dawson even, with ruddy espresso skin and braids that dangled to her waist. Her eyes, rich like the famous black beaches of Iceland, matched her full lips, which twisted into a dainty smile.

"I'm Brooklyn." She took a step forward and offered her hand, which Charlie took in a firm shake.

"Heard about you, Brooklyn," Charlie said. "Did Dawson tell you about the situation we've got goin' on around here?"

"As in the situation with Savannah?"

"Yes, and some other pretty important details." Charlie cleared her throat, turning her attention to

Dawson.

"Like?" Brooklyn prompted sourly.

Dawson inhaled a sharp breath through his nose. "The mole is dying."

"And why is she dying?" Brooklyn hissed. "We kind of need her."

"Yeah, we do need her. And that is exactly why I need Porter to do some explaining."

Porter adjusted his glasses nervously. "Explain what?"

"Explain why Savannah has black blood coming out of her nose," Dawson said calmly.

Brooklyn's heart skipped, and all the heat in her body rushed quickly to her face.

Porter sighed. He gave a short nod and reached down into the duffle bag again, rifling around until he pulled out a sleek black tube. The case was slim, void of any sharp edges or locks. He was careful, and he took his time popping it open.

"I think I know why." He plucked out a syringe filled with murky charcoal liquid. It looked thick like tar. He turned it into the light, revealing specks of grey and white floating stagnant in the black substance.

"What is it?" Brooklyn asked.

"A derivative of the virus that you guys were given as children. All of us had one of these in our bug-out bags in case anything went wrong, in case our identities or operations were at a high enough risk to put our lives on the line. An irreversible alibi."

"And what exactly does that do?" Dawson growled.

"It depends on the person. It'll either make us like you or make us like the Surrogates."

"That's it?" Brooklyn said as she walked forward to get a better look at the syringe in Porter's hand. "That's the virus?"

"Basically, yes."

"We should destroy it, then," Julian said from his place against the wall.

"We're not destroying it."

"Why not?" Julian scoffed, his voice bouncing off the high walls.

Porter flicked the glass tube and said, "Because I'm going to use it."

Chapter Thirty

Brooklyn trembled. Anger pulsed in her veins, leaked like fumes out of her pores, and her eyes narrowed. She stared at Porter, and he stared right back as the rest of the room fell into uncomfortable silence.

"You're going to use it on yourself?" Brooklyn asked. Her voice was even and controlled. She strained to keep her heartbeat from running away with itself. Her fingers curled into fists, palms slick with sweat, and her stomach squeezed into a tight, tempered ball.

"That's the plan," Porter said.

She watched him slide the syringe back into the black case and tuck it into the inside pocket of his jacket.

There was a lot that she wanted to say, but all she could come up with was "You can't."

Porter zipped up his jacket and turned to look at Dawson. "Let me see if I can get something out of Savannah. If she's already showing signs, then we don't have a lot of time."

Brooklyn gritted her teeth. She took another step forward into his space. "Don't disregard me like that," she fumed. "You can't be serious about injecting. You could die, or you could turn into one of those things, and then…"

"Then you'll kill me." Porter cut her off, biting down on the words as they left his mouth.

The brash impact of his statement felt like a sledgehammer right to Brooklyn's gut. She didn't blink or breathe or move.

"There's a lot on the line right now, and we don't have time to argue about this," Porter said. "Where is she?"

Dawson waved them over to the wall of boxes where Charlie had just come from and showed him to the other side. The warehouse was nearly empty, but whoever had occupied it before had left a few chairs, a small desk, and stacks upon stacks of pallets and boxes behind. They were built up like a wall, dividing the group from the area where they held Savannah.

Brooklyn didn't follow at first. Her feet stayed planted. She tried to hold back the violent urge to throw her fist against the wall. Everything was spiraling out of control, sliding through her fingertips like grains of sand. Her fixed fortitude was dissolving, and she struggled to keep a reign on her fluctuating emotions. Control was all she had left, and she was losing it.

Brooklyn took a long, deep breath and followed them after she'd hog tied her emotions. She was ice cold and took the time to extinguish any abrupt flare or outburst that piped up inside her. It would be easier that way. It would be easier not to feel.

Behind the wall of boxes was Savannah, sitting on the ground. Her wrists and ankles were zip tied. Long brown hair was pulled back into a ratty ponytail, and a bitter expression turned her lips into a frown. The girl's nose was raw as thin trails of black liquid made their way down over her lips. Even her eyes, red from crying, were beginning to look sallow and sickly.

Savannah grinned. "Look at you, Porter. It's fairly obvious you've jumped ship, huh?"

"Yeah, seems that way, doesn't it?"

"Figures," she spat. "You never did follow the rules anyways, always had a way out of it."

"What's going on with ECHO? I need to know. I need you to tell me." He spoke slowly and was strategically calm.

She boomed with laughter, spit flying from her mouth. "You know I'm not telling you anything. You're a sick sympathizing traitor. I never..." Savannah paused, licking her cracked lips, eyelids twitching. "I never thought you'd go along with the project, but I didn't think you'd actually try to sabotage it."

"You don't seem to be in any position of power here. How about you just talk to me so we can be done with this? I need to know about ECHO, I need to know if the other Omens are in Denver, and I need to know right now."

"No, no, none of that matters! It doesn't matter anymore—it's done! All of you, every single one of you, you're all accounted for and screened and ready to be processed, so don't think just because you feel safe that Juneau doesn't have eyes on you!" Savannah was crazed. Her pupils swallowed any color left in her eyes. She picked at herself, pulling up the skin on the edge of her cuticles.

"It does matter, Savannah! Please, we used to be friends back at the lab. I just need you to tell me about ECHO. I need you to tell me what I'm getting myself into!"

"Getting yourself into...?" The mole whispered, leaning forward slightly. Her mouth opened, and her eyebrows pulled down toward her nose. "You think you're one of *them*? You're Porter Malloy, Juneau Malloy's son! You think you can flip sides? You think you can run? Please...they know your every move. They know where you are, and they know what you'll do before you do it."

"I'm already one of them," Porter said. "But when I inject, I'll become a priority to ISO, and my company-wide immunity will be washed. I made my choice a while ago. Now, will you help me or not?"

Savannah spit at his feet. Her lips pressed into a black-smudged line. "You'll never be a priority."

Dawson tried to step forward, but Brooklyn moved swiftly passed him, kneeling down in front of Savannah. There was no reason to play by the rules. Brooklyn was done trying to find the good in people.

"You're Savannah. Is that right?" Brooklyn said.

Savannah was silent.

"My name is Brooklyn Harper. I need you to answer every single question I ask you. Do you understand?"

Silence. Savannah's jaw slid back and forth. Utter silence.

Brooklyn gave her one last chance. She scooted forward only to have Savannah recoil further into the corner.

"I watched my best friend die," Brooklyn whispered. The words tasted stale and coppery; they branded her tongue like lit matches. "I watched a Surro rip her heart out. If you think I won't do the same to you, then you've underestimated my training."

"You can't do shit to me," Savannah hissed. Black blood spewed from between her lips when she coughed. "Killing me would be a favor."

Brooklyn snatched Savannah's left hand and grasped the length of her index finger, holding it tight. "Tell me about ECHO."

Savannah squirmed but didn't speak.

Brooklyn snapped Savannah's finger to the side until the bone splintered and broke. Savannah shrieked, gasping as Brooklyn clutched the now swollen digit.

"You have nine more," Brooklyn said as Savannah choked back a sob. "And when I'm bored with your hands, I will move on to your toes. Do you understand?"

There was nowhere for Savannah to escape, but she still tried to kick and crawl away. Brooklyn reached up and grasped her cheeks with one hand, squeezing hard until her mouth went slack and trembled.

"You have fifteen seconds to start giving me answers, or I move on to this one," Brooklyn pinched the knuckle of Savannah's middle finger.

Porter rushed forward, but Dawson held him back with an outstretched arm.

"Let her do this," Dawson whispered.

Savannah whimpered and tore her face free from Brooklyn's grasp. "Porter knows everything about ECHO! It's exactly what it was in the beginning when Juneau started the project. The only problem was the backlash from certain...*compassionate* partners." Her voice was slimy and sarcastic.

"These are people we're talking about, Savannah!" Porter shouted.

Brooklyn continued to bend her finger. "Keep talking."

"People? You think that these things are people? They're weapons, Porter!" she yelled, leaning forward toward him. Brooklyn grabbed her face again and tugged Savannah's head toward her.

"You talk to me," Brooklyn seethed. "What is the ECHO campaign?"

The whites of Savannah's eyes were dull and yellow. The skin around them crinkled when Savannah smirked. "Some of the big brains on the board didn't agree with Juneau's vision. He knew that when the Omens developed, when *you* developed, that there was no hope for any breeding to take place."

"I'm not a blue-ribbon poodle." Brooklyn snapped Savannah's finger to the side.

"All I'm saying is that you can't have children!" She squealed.

Brooklyn wanted to kill her right then and there, but she just moved on to Savannah's ring finger and bent it backward. "Go on."

"And if you can't have children, then you can't pass on the gene, which was a good thing, but at the same time, it opened up the discussion of how exactly your organs worked. How they would heal themselves, how we could preserve your shelf life after you'd been deployed. We don't have the luxury of transplants from typical donors when it comes to the Omens."

"What are you trying to say? Is there a fridge in your lab somewhere with a duplicate set of my kidneys?" Brooklyn asked.

Savannah almost laughed, but she ended up choking on a mouth full of blood. "A fridge? No, we have different sectors for each of you. And we have over one hundred clones of every single Omen that was harvested two years ago."

Brooklyn dropped Savannah's hands and took a step back.

"An echo," Savannah sang the word. "The replica of something rippling again and again through time and space."

"You have clones of us?" Brooklyn heaved in a deep breath.

"Juneau decided to go against the board and continue with the project. He received funding from the NSA, and there was nothing anyone could do about it," Savannah bragged.

Porter looked sick. He stared down between his feet, shoulders hunched up around his neck. Brooklyn didn't know how to swallow the information. The idea of clones made her skin crawl. She turned back toward Savannah, breathing even, and regained some composure. "Where are they?"

"The clones? None of us are given that information."

"Are they exactly like us?"

"No," Savannah said and shrugged. Tears streamed down her cheeks, clouded black, and her nose ran. "You're the original hosts. No matter how much we tampered with the microbes, we couldn't get them to do what they've done with you. We can program them with basic tasks like we have with the Surros, but all in all, they're just donors that we keep in a state of neurological sedation. I know some of them have been given the extended dose of the Jakob's disease to trigger the bleeding, which allowed for more access to disposable Surro activity, but other than that, they're only used in an emergency."

"The bleeding? So…you have a name for what's happening to you right now? Explain it to me."

Savannah stayed quiet until Brooklyn reached for her mangled fingers.

"Okay!" she yelled, clutching her bound hands against her chest. "The Jakob's disease attacks the brain. It causes hallucinations, memory loss, and psychotic attacks. When we tried to reprogram the genome, we noticed that the microbes weren't reacting properly in most of the trials. That was before my time, though. Juneau didn't bring me on until after I graduated medical school four years ago. He recruited me based on good word from a professor of mine." Savannah was rambling. The psychosis was clearly taking hold, prevalent in her chattering teeth and quick, darting voice. "We don't really have an answer for why the blood turns black, but it has something to do with the way the microbes circulate through the bloodstream. Once the disease itself is compromised and reverts back to its primal instinct, we no longer have control of what happens to the mind."

"So, the Surros really are just sick people?" Brooklyn asked. She started to shake. "You infected these people with two viruses, and when one didn't work like you wanted it to, you just...rolled with it?"

"It's more complicated than that," Savannah said. "When the Jakob's disease went against our programming, it got stronger, and the symptoms developed more quickly. The Surrogates are like you, strong and adaptable, but they lack depth."

"It is astonishing how proud you are of something so cruel."

Savannah's jaw slid from side to side. "Natural selection doesn't always do its job, honey. We gave things a kick-start when we created you."

Brooklyn spun around and walked over to Porter. He looked like a frightened dog, cowering before the one who'd kicked him. He averted his eyes. She reached around and pulled the gun from the back of his pants.

"Brooklyn! Wait, hold on!" He tried to snatch the gun away from her, but she was already in front of Savannah again. Dawson grabbed Porter, pulling him away for his own safety. The boys waited, listening as Brooklyn pressed the barrel of the gun against Savannah's forehead.

Savannah closed her eyes. "Go ahead. It won't change anything."

Brooklyn took a moment and swallowed down the urge to pull the trigger. "How does it feel to know your life is in the hands of one of your little experiments?"

"It feels like accomplishment," Savannah said confidently.

Brooklyn bit down on her lip. "And what's it like to forget the color your mother was wearing on the day of your high school graduation? Or the song your father used to sing to you before you went to sleep?"

Savannah's eyes, muddled with black blood and bulging from her skull began to soften.

"I'm sure it's already started, the memory loss, the psychosis. I bet you can't even remember the last thing you had to eat, can you? Or the last time you blew out candles on your birthday? The last time someone kissed you?"

The mole chewed on her lip, bare feet shuffling against the concrete, toes curling until they popped.

"When the voices start eating away at everything you want to remember, I hope you think of me," Brooklyn said. "And when the last shred of sanity you have disappears, I hope all you do is wish I was here with this gun. I want you to pray for me to come back and end it for you. But I won't. Do you know where I'll be, Savannah Kingston?"

Tears dripped down Savannah's cheeks, and she clutched her tied hands deeper into her chest.

Brooklyn tilted her head to the side, twisting the gun brutally against Savannah's flesh.

"I'll be destroying everything you've worked for, and I'll be killing all your colleagues," Brooklyn said as she pushed the gun hard against Savannah's head.

Brooklyn stood and tossed the gun back to Porter, who fumbled to catch it. Dawson and Porter stared at her, shocked by the display. She walked back toward the larger part of the room, where everyone else had been listening.

The sound of Savannah begging for death bounced off the walls of the warehouse. Brooklyn didn't feel an ounce of pity.

Chapter Thirty-One

A few hours passed by, and Brooklyn decided to keep to herself for most of it. She sat against the wall beside Julian and Rayce, who continued to discuss what had gone on while they were apart. Amber brought her a washcloth and some water so that she could wipe off some of the blood from the hotel room and offered up a package of dry noodles to eat.

Everyone kept their distance, and Brooklyn appreciated that. She picked noodles out of the plastic wrapping and put together plans in her head. Plan A. Plan B. Plan C. They needed something to hold on to. Even if her plans always seemed to fall apart, at least they would have a direction to go in.

Charlie was the one who approached her first. She sat down with her legs crossed in front of Brooklyn and took a sip off a canteen filled with water.

"Clones, huh?" Charlie asked.

Brooklyn nodded. "I guess so."

"You think they know how to talk and all that?"

"I don't really want to think about whether or not

they're cognitive. Savannah said they weren't, but I don't think anyone knows the truth."

"You got any ideas on how we can deal with this?" Charlie pressed her thumb against the base of her jaw and cracked her neck.

"I have to talk with everyone before we can move forward with anything, but yes. I think I have an idea."

"Well, whatever it is, I'm in," Charlie said through a sigh.

Brooklyn raised an eyebrow. "And what if it puts your life in danger?"

Charlie shrugged, playing with the end of one of her locks. "I'm from Detroit. Danger's not a foreign concept."

Dawson and Porter stayed behind the wall of boxes with Savannah. Brooklyn wanted to intrude on their conversation a number of times, but it would have only caused problems. She kept her mind wrapped around the details Savannah had given her and tried to think of some way to escape the inevitable. They'd been on the run for four days, and now that they were in Seattle, it seemed like everything was coming to an undeniable halt.

Juneau was going to find them. Realistically, he probably already knew where they were.

Brooklyn chewed anxiously on her fingernails.

She perked up when Dawson and Porter walked around the boxes, into the room. They were still talking quietly to one another, and despite her anger Brooklyn couldn't help but smile when she watched Dawson pull Porter into a tight hug.

Porter made his way over to Brooklyn and took a

seat next to her. Charlie glanced between the two of them and then shuffled over toward Amber, who was napping like a cat against Rayce's legs.

"I never thought they would go through with it," Porter said.

Brooklyn stopped chewing on her nails. "You don't have to explain yourself to me. I know you never would've been a part of something like that."

"I was a part of something just as bad, though."

"Yeah, you were, and then you came clean, and you stayed with us. It's been hell, and you're still here."

He nodded and watched her over the top of his glasses. The old black beanie still hung on to the back of his head, and his smile was still a little crooked. They hadn't even been gone a week, but Brooklyn felt like they'd had so much time to relearn each other.

"Please don't inject," Brooklyn whispered.

Porter's nose twitched. "I'm sorry," he said, shrugging his good shoulder. "But I already did."

The sadness was instantly replaced by anger, and Brooklyn's face showed it clearly. She grasped his wrist and lifted his arm, shoving the sleeve of his jacket over his elbow. The grid of veins under his pale skin rose like thick deathly grey walls. They pulsed as the virus spread like toxic sludge through Porter's body.

"Why?" she hissed. "You won't be able to have kids; you won't be able to start over! You've dumped any chance of a life after this in the trash."

"If there was a chance for me to be more of an asset, then I had to take it," Porter said.

"You're not even twenty-four…" She wanted to cry, but she couldn't; the tears wouldn't come. "You had so much to look forward to. You could've gone to any hospital with your experience. You could have saved lives."

"I already have some lives I need to save," Porter said. "And one that I couldn't."

She almost flinched at his blatant mention of Gabriel. The thought of her made Brooklyn want to be sick.

"I don't need you to save me," Brooklyn growled between her teeth.

Porter rubbed his fingers together and nodded. "Trust me—I know you don't, but I'm gonna be here in case you change your mind."

She felt his hand on her arm and then the drag of his fingertips across her wrist to the top of her hand. He poked at her fingers until she allowed him to interlace their hands together. She couldn't deny that it felt nice to have him so close, to know that he was willing to give everything up for his friends. But it wasn't necessary. She wished he would've run off and done something with his life. Brooklyn wished he would have forgotten about all of them, left it all behind, and *lived*.

Dawson sat back down on the edge of the palettes and cleared his throat.

"Did all of you hear the conversation Brooklyn had with Savannah?" he asked.

Everyone nodded. Amber piped up from her place on the floor. "So there's a bunch of flippin' copy cats out there, huh?"

"I guess there is," Dawson sighed. "But we also

have Juneau and his people chasing us. They're in Seattle, and I'm not convinced that they don't know where we are."

"Well, let's just get rid of 'em, then. We've got enough guns," Amber said.

"I would say that was an option, but it seems like they have no qualms about disposing of us if they need to." There was a shake in his voice that Brooklyn could feel in her bones.

"What are we lookin' at, then? We gonna just let 'em take us?"

"I don't know. That's why I wanted to talk to everyone. We need to come up with a plan. A good one," Dawson said.

"I've thought of a few things," Brooklyn said.

Dawson turned and opened his hand to her. "A few things are better than nothing. Shoot."

Chapter Thirty-Two

They argued until nightfall.

Brooklyn tried to come up with something that everyone could agree on, but it wasn't happening. Amber wanted to bait them into a full-force attack. Rayce wanted to try and track them down and pick them off one by one. Dawson was unsure of everything that anyone presented, and Porter was against anything that put them in direct danger— even though danger wasn't something they could avoid at this point.

Charlie sided with Julian when he mentioned staying on the road. They were both sure that in time their trails would be lost.

Porter was the one who shut them down. He rolled his eyes and tried not to laugh when they mentioned running again. "My dad is funded by the National Security Agency. They can log into any camera on any street in any city. They'll tap every single phone line for voice recognition. They'll send helicopters. They'll send Special Forces. They will send everything…"

Julian's face tightened into defeat.

251

"We can't just keeping running. If we do, more of us will die," Porter said painfully.

"What about the laptop?" Brooklyn said.

"What about it?" Porter asked.

"If they didn't have time to wipe it, then why don't you try to reach your father? You might be able to talk some sense into him or to at least, I don't know, buy us some time?"

"He's not gonna listen to anything I have to say."

Brooklyn's shoulders slumped. "You don't know that, though. It's all we have; it's the only thing that might be able to slow them down enough for us to either make a move or get out of here before they find us."

"ISO will find us anyways," Porter said.

"But maybe you can give us some time!" Brooklyn said sternly.

Porter looked like he wanted to crawl into a corner and fade away. His face was pale, and his thoughtful eyes held a tinge of fear that Brooklyn hadn't seen before. Someone who wasn't scared of Surros or of injecting himself with a deadly black cocktail was apprehensive about speaking with his own father. That alone made Brooklyn wearier of Juneau Malloy.

Dawson rapped his knuckles against the wood palette. "I think it's a solid idea."

Porter groaned.

"Just try to get him off our tail for a little while, Porter. It could do a lot of good," Dawson said.

"Or it could make everything a lot worse," Porter mumbled.

Dawson held his arms out to the empty

warehouse and said, "Couldn't get much worse than this. You'll do it in the morning, okay? Tonight, we should all get some sleep."

They hadn't agreed on much, but at least they'd agreed on something.

***

"Hey!" Gabriel whispered to Brooklyn while they hid behind Cabin A.

It hadn't been long then, maybe six months since they arrived at the camp, and the two girls were attached at the hip. The night sky had been full of stars, the summer air was warm and dry, and things had started to feel real again. That six-month mark: that was when the earth started to spin the right direction after winter formal.

"What?" Brooklyn laughed, a faint blush brushed on the apples of her cheeks. "Did you guys like, make out or…?"

"What? No! Well, yes. Actually, we did," Gabriel grinned, and the two of them almost toppled over laughing.

"What was it like?" Brooklyn asked, wide doe eyes peeking out from underneath her lashes.

Gabriel's brows furrowed. "What? Sneaking off with Dawson or kissing him in general?"

"I don't know—all of it, I guess."

"Oh, come on. You were varsity soccer…you were the cool older girl in high school…"

"I'm eighteen. Don't make fun of me because I was held back a year," Brooklyn pouted.

"No, I'm just kinda shocked. Are you…have you

253

ever hooked up with anyone before?" Gabriel asked, mouth agape as she stared at Brooklyn.

Brooklyn stammered and glanced around to make sure no one had found where they were hiding. "It's not like I haven't, okay? I just like never really met anyone interesting enough. I don't know."

"Oh my god, you're a virgin!"

"Be quiet," Brooklyn hissed. "I'm not a virgin! But it wasn't...great. Like no fireworks or whatever, so..."

"So you've never had an..."

"Would you stop it!" Brooklyn swatted Gabriel, who was still laughing.

Gabriel dabbed at her eyes and snorted, "So, what? No good kiss either? Nothing? Nada?"

"Nada," Brooklyn confirmed through a defeated groan.

Brooklyn watched Gabriel's grin fade, mischief danced playfully behind her eyes. She felt the stiff wall of the cabin as she backed up into it. She held her breath and contemplated trying to break away when Gabriel leaned in and slotted their mouths together. The kiss was soft, though, comforting.

Brooklyn's mind short circuited. Her bones hummed, her chest ached. Kissing Gabriel felt like tumbling in the ocean under rolling waves and breaking the surface for a deep lungful of air.

It shouldn't have lasted as long as it did. Gabriel shouldn't have grabbed Brooklyn's face; she shouldn't have kissed her like that.

But she did. And when she pulled away, Brooklyn's eyes were still closed, and her mouth was still open.

"Now you can say you've been kissed properly,"
Gabriel purred and ruffled Brooklyn's hair. "And
you know what to do when you get around to
hooking up with Porter."

Brooklyn wanted to hit her, but she could only
smile and roll her eyes. "I don't even like him!"

"You totally like him," Gabriel said and turned
to walk away.

Brooklyn's heart had been beating fast. Fast
enough to scare her.

It was beating just as fast when she jolted awake
on the floor of the warehouse.

Porter's arm was tight around her waist, and he
pressed his nose against the back of her neck. He
was still asleep; she could hear the light rhythmic
drum of his heartbeat, the steady inhale and exhale
of his breath.

That visceral memory tied around her ribs and
pulled, striking like a lightning bolt into the pit of
her stomach.

"Hey," Dawson whispered as he watched her
from his place against the wall. He smiled when she
glanced up. "You look comfy over there."

Brooklyn wasn't sure how to get up without
rousing Porter. She did the best she could and slid
slowly from underneath his arm. Porter's eyes
cracked open a sliver, but she hushed him and
pulled the jacket they were using as a makeshift
blanket up to his neck.

"Where ya goin'?" he slurred and tapped on her
hand as she sat up.

"Just to get water. Go back to sleep."

Porter closed his eyes and snuggled into the jacket.

She looked around the dark room and spotted a mass of bodies all pressed together by the wall. It was Julian, Rayce, Amber, and Charlie. Brooklyn smiled as she picked each of them out. Julian was slumped against Rayce's chest, and Amber was lying across both their laps with Charlie curled up against her thighs.

"It's cute isn't it?" Dawson whispered to her.

She stifled a chuckle and nodded. "It's adorable."

He patted the space next to him.

"Are you first watch?" she asked, taking a seat against the wall beside him.

"Yeah, I couldn't sleep anyways. What about you? You kind of got up in a hurry."

She bit down on her lip. "Just a dream."

"Yeah...I'm scared of what I'll dream about too," Dawson said. "What you said to Savannah about watching Gabriel get killed...that happened?"

Brooklyn bristled but gave a short nod.

"How did she come back, then?"

"Who knows," Brooklyn said bitterly. "All I know is that there's a gaping hole in my chest that I can't fill. I feel empty without her."

Dawson looked down at his hands and his nose twitched. "I was gonna tell her I loved her if we got out of this," he said under his breath. "I was gonna ask her to move to New York with me."

"She loved you, Dawson," Brooklyn said almost too quickly. "God, she did. She loved you."

The back of her throat started to itch, and tears sprang to her eyes, but Brooklyn refused to cry. She swallowed again and again until the feeling died down.

"You loved her too," Dawson whispered, the words ghosting over his lips.

Brooklyn smelt the salt in his tears as he looped his arm around her and pulled her in against his chest. Dawson was supposed to be the strong one, the fierce leader. He'd taken on that responsibility without anyone asking him to, and in the end, the only person he wanted to save was the one they had lost. She rested her head on his shoulder, listened to his heart drum on, and ignored his tears. Dawson didn't grieve; he just kept moving, so she pretended not to notice as he cried and allowed him to use her as a shield. It was the least she could do.

They stayed awake in the dark together for close to an hour until Dawson wiped his eyes and shooed her away.

"Go lay back down with him," he said.

"I can stay with you."

Dawson shook his head. "He shouldn't have to wake up alone."

"Neither should you," Brooklyn protested.

"I won't. I'll be right here. And when I get tired, I'll wake Rayce up and go join the puppy pile."

They laughed, and he wiped his nose with the back of his hand after he sniffled.

"Thank you for not giving up on Porter."

"You should be thanking yourself," Dawson said and leaned his head back against the wall. "He's always been our friend, Brooklyn."

"I know," she said softly.

Brooklyn crawled back over to where Porter was sleeping and nudged under his arm once again. He stirred and cracked his eyes open, blinking at her. "Hi," he rasped, smoothing his arm up the back of her shirt. His chin rested on top of her head, and he drew circles with his fingers on her lower back.

The sound of a room full of familiar heartbeats lulled her back to sleep.

Chapter Thirty-Three

Hushed chatter was what woke Brooklyn the next morning. She stretched her legs out and felt Porter twitch his foot when her toes rubbed against his ankle. They were twisted up in one another—her knee was tucked between his thighs, and his arm was wrapped snug around her waist. She could taste the sweat on his throat where her mouth was pressed, and he hummed when she continued to squirm, alerting him rather quickly that she was awake.

"If you get up, that means I have to call my dad," Porter mumbled. "So don't move."

His arm tightened around her, and he pushed the palm of his hand up the back of her shirt, feeling along the expanse of her back.

"We have to get up," Brooklyn said.

Porter yawned and backed up a few inches so he could get a clear view of her face. "We can stay right here, actually."

"No," she said. "I need to take a look at your stitches anyways. C'mon, wake up."

Brooklyn unwound herself from Porter's long limbs and sat up. Julian was eating an old pastry from the vending machine they'd broken into, and Amber was scrounging around through the bags for more food. Rayce was around the corner, checking on Savannah, and Charlie was against the wall with Dawson. Everyone looked exhausted. Drained. Dirty.

"I would kill for some deodorant right now," Amber grumbled as she got her hands on a granola bar and tore the wrapper off.

"Don't talk about it," Julian said as his face crinkled up into a displeased scowl.

Brooklyn tried to untangle her hair with her fingers to no avail and opted to tie it back into a ponytail with an old rubber band. She would have loved to trek back into the woods and find Nicoli's cabin—steal a nice warm shower, scrub her skin with some of Plum's dry soap. But that wasn't going to happen. As gross as it was to deal with, they had bigger things to worry about than being clean.

"Good morning," Dawson said as he watched Brooklyn adjust the belt around her jeans.

"Morning, did you get some sleep?" she asked.

"A few hours."

She tried to smile but it was small and hardly visible.

"You need help with his shoulder?" Dawson asked as he gestured to Porter.

"No, we'll be fine," she said.

Porter's hair was sticking up in all different places. He didn't bother with trying to tame it and covered his head with the ratty old beanie before he slid his glasses up his nose. He squinted for a moment and then took them off again to inspect them, turning them around in his hands.

"Are my glasses scratched?" he asked and held them out to Brooklyn.

She gave them a once-over and shook her head. "No, it doesn't look like it. Maybe they just need to be cleaned?"

"Yeah, maybe. I'm surprised they've lasted this long," he said.

"You can clean them while I get these bandages off." She tugged on his shirt until he took it off and tossed it aside.

The bandages still looked clean enough, and they hadn't slipped much since the hotel. Brooklyn carefully stripped them away one by one until only a single layer was left. Her hand hovered just above his shoulder. She inhaled a rickety breath. It was terrifying. All Brooklyn could imagine was black blood seeping out from between his stitches as the virus ate away at what was left of him. His personality falling away day by day, his voice becoming unrecognizable, his honey eyes shifting into muted yellow voids. She thought of the memories they'd built together, of his arms around her, and knew that if the bleeding started, those memories would peel up and float away like ash. Porter wouldn't remember her.

"It's okay," Porter said. "Take it off."

Brooklyn shifted her gaze to the ground when the bandage dropped away. She didn't want to be a coward, but she also didn't have the courage to deal with Porter becoming a Surrogate. She held her breath and stared at the concrete.

"Would you look at that," Porter said lightly. He pinched Brooklyn's arm and rolled his shoulder around. "I guess it worked."

She looked up and analyzed the space where his wound was. Fresh silky skin surrounded the small indentions from the stitches. The wide jagged cut from days ago had faded overnight into a tiny sliver of what it used to be.

"You healed…" Brooklyn was breathless. The relief pouring off of her was evident in the smile stretching across her face.

"Yeah, I guess I did. Everyone that was deployed to the camps was injected with a dormant dose of microbes that would only activate if they were prompted by the derivative. I guess the microbes had been in my body long enough to be recognized efficiently."

"So, you're like us now?"

"Yes and no," Porter said. "I'll be like you; I'll become stronger and some of my mental capacity will expand, but you're the hosts. I'll never be as developed as you are."

Porter stumbled to catch himself when Brooklyn threw her arms around his neck and bracketed her knees over his waist. She sealed herself against his body and held on, fingers raking through the short hairs on the back of his neck.

"Remember a couple days ago when you wanted to kill me?" he whispered against the shell of her ear. His hands were large and firm as he held on to her.

Brooklyn wanted to tell him that she'd cared for him for too long to ever go through with it. But instead she said, "Maybe I still will."

"Maybe," he parroted.

She let him get to his feet while he complained that the stitches were starting to pinch.

"Do we have any of the medical scissors?" Porter asked as he looked over to Dawson.

Dawson pointed toward the duffle bags. "If we do, they're in there."

While Porter dug through the bags and went to work removing his own stitches, Brooklyn found the laptop in Rayce's backpack and started clicking through different files. There was so much hidden away. Folder after folder labeled with the names of different people all stuffed with notes on progress and capability.

"Charlotte White..." Brooklyn read the name out loud.

Charlie sat straight up and almost tripped to get next to Brooklyn.

"That's me," Charlie said as she pointed to row after row of documents.

"You're name's Charlotte?" Brooklyn asked.

"Yeah, but I've gone by Charlie since I was five. What's this?" Charlie tapped the screen.

Brooklyn clicked the folder she was pointing at and opened a detailed spreadsheet. Starting at the top were sectioned-off fighting styles followed by different kinds of weapons. From what they could see, their camp supervisor had caught on to just how good Charlie was with a knife.

"Are those his notes? 'Deadliest when using

tactical knives and/or garrotes,'" Charlie read what was written out loud and smirked. "Guess that asshole was payin' attention after all."

"Garrotes?" Brooklyn asked.

"Yeah, Davey used to let us practice with them on staged mannequins. You guys didn't get those?"

Brooklyn's eyebrows arched up high on her forehead, "No, no, we did not."

"What else does it say?" Charlie asked. She reached out and turned the screen.

The rest of the notes were about Charlie's specialties, her fears, and her behavior. Everything was documented in perfect synchronism from the time she'd arrived in the camp to the time the document had been sent to Juneau.

"Why did Davey kill himself anyway?" Brooklyn asked.

Charlie looked torn. "I don't even know," she said. "He was a really weird guy, but I never thought he'd do something like that. Once Amber and everyone found the camp, he ran off, locked himself in his cabin, and wouldn't respond to anything we were saying. Dawson yelled at him, said he was gonna kick down the door, and the next thing you know, we heard a gunshot."

"You were the only one left?"

"Me, Savannah, Gina, and Phillipe," Charlie said. "We caught Savannah injecting herself. That's when Dawson figured out who she was. Gina and Phillipe got scared and took off on their own instead of joining up with everyone else."

"I'm sorry to hear that...I hope they're okay," Brooklyn said.

"It was their choice."

Charlie didn't seem to be affected by the loss of her camp-mates. Brooklyn could relate, seeing as she'd hardly even thought of Ellie or Jordan or A.J....she could only hope that the Surros had been gentle when they took them. The thought left a sour taste in her mouth. She felt like a monster for leaving them behind and felt even worse for ignoring the thought of them.

Brooklyn clicked on another tab that led to a screen full of folders labeled ISO 1, ISO 2, ISO 3 and so on all the way to ISO 274.

"Videos?" Brooklyn hummed.

She clicked on one, and the folder opened up to half-screen. In the video, an older gentleman wearing a pair of circular glasses took notes in a binder. His hair was tucked back into a blue hairnet, and his hands were covered in latex gloves. The skin around his eyes had started to sink with age, fine lines and wrinkles spread out around his nose and mouth. He looked oddly familiar.

"Turn on the audio," Charlie said.

Once the volume was up, they heard the eloquent voice come through the speakers:

"This is Doctor Malloy with test subject number three for sector one of Isolation, short name ISO. Subject has shown no signs of aggression but has displayed adequate motor functions and the ability to mimic verbal phrases. We ran several tests on neural function. All came back at one hundred percent. Growth is standard; organ development standard and reproductive status is standard as well.'

The camera panned to the left, where an exact replica of Charlie stood. The clone was perfect, from the color of its lips to the shape of its nailbeds. Everything was in Charlie's likeness.

"That is the creepiest thing I have ever seen," Charlie said.

Everyone in the warehouse had made their way around the screen of the computer and was watching intently as the camera inspected every inch of the clone's body.

The only person who chose not to watch was Porter.

"There are 274 of these videos?" Julian asked.

"Yes," Brooklyn said.

Dawson pushed the screen down and closed the laptop. "That's enough of that for today. Porter needs to get ready to try and contact his dad anyways."

"The only way I'll be able to get through is if I can beam into the video chat on his phone," Porter said reluctantly. "And if I do this, there's a good chance he'll trace the call."

"Let him trace it," Rayce huffed from next to Dawson as he folded his arms over his chest. "We'll either fight or run."

"Get everything packed," Dawson said to Rayce. "We need to be ready in case things get messy and we need a quick getaway."

Brooklyn hadn't believed that there were really clones, not until she just saw one alive and breathing on the screen of that laptop. The only thing that came to mind was how hard it would be to get rid of all of them and whether or not it would be cruel. Did those things think? Did they feel or speak or have any inkling that they might be alive?

Did those clones have a soul?

She shook the thought away just as quickly as it had come. Whether the clones had a soul or not, they had to be destroyed.

Every last one of them.

Chapter Thirty-Four

Savannah started to scream when Dawson brought her a bottle of water. Her demands for freedom were vicious and loud, but after a while, they disintegrated into pitiful blubbering. She whined empty apologies and made promises that they knew she would never be able to keep. Her veins were starting to show through the skin on certain areas of her arms, and the bleeding had spread to her ears.

"I don't know how much longer she's going to be…normal," Dawson said as he walked around from the back area of the warehouse. A worried look twisted his lips into a frown.

Porter changed into some of the clean clothes they had left and was using his finger to scrub his teeth with some of the mouthwash from their duffle bag.

"We have about another day until she really starts to freak out," Porter said.

Dawson looked a little relieved. "We'll be gone by then."

"We're just gonna leave her here?" Porter said.

"We can't do anything else with her besides put her out of her misery…"

"No," Brooklyn interrupted. She slung the backpack Cambria had given them over her shoulder. "We leave Savannah here. There's no need to waste a bullet on her."

"We don't have to use a gun," Dawson said.

Brooklyn's jaw tightened. "We're leaving her here. Juneau can clean up his own mess."

She walked out of the warehouse and threw the backpack into the backseat of the truck. Rayce packed the Escalade. He sighed when she walked over and leaned against the side of the large vehicle.

"I know this is a weird question, but with things going the way they're going…I just wanna know. When they took Ellie and A.J. and Jordan, did you see what the Surros did with them?" Brooklyn asked.

Rayce was compassionate, and even though he didn't show his soft side all that often, she could tell that the question was a hard one for him. He closed the trunk and licked over his lips. "They pulled them out of the bus and pinned their arms, grabbed their legs and hands. It happened too fast. I was trying to shoot the ones I could still get to when Amber started to drive. I could hear 'em yellin' for us all the way down the road and couldn't get to 'em. We aren't supposed to hear that shit, girl. We aren't supposed to hear the people we couldn't save."

His words were leathery and heavy. They flapped like wings in her stomach. Rayce was right, though—no one should have to listen to their friends scream for help. No one should have to hear what they've heard, see what they've seen.

"I'm sorry," she said. "I shouldn't have asked."

"Don't worry about it. I know why you did."

It was hard to look at him.

They walked back inside together. The warehouse was starting to suffocate her. It's tall concrete walls and cold floor was beginning to remind her of a cell. Brooklyn crawled on top of a stack of palettes and sat down.

Porter sat in the middle of the room with the laptop open in front of him. He had his glasses on, but they were balanced on the very tip of his nose so he could see over them. His eyesight was changing. Things that were once blurry had started to clear, lines that weren't defined were now sharp. Brooklyn had lived with the abilities since she was a toddler. She could only imagine what it would be like to get a grasp on them now.

She scanned his face, the concentration settled in the pinched area between his eyes. It was difficult to distinguish how deep her feelings for him went. He was all long arms and even longer legs with an attitude that'd been large enough to catch her attention right off the bat when they'd first met. The evolution of Porter and Brooklyn might stay in the space between the concrete walls of the warehouse. Maybe too much time had passed. Maybe it was best that they stay right where they were, with Brooklyn taking sanctuary in his arms at night and him holding on to her.

It would be easier that way, but it was too bad

Brooklyn wasn't one for easy.

"I'm dialing in," Porter said. He looked up at Dawson first and then over to Brooklyn.

Amber and Charlie sat on the floor by Dawson's feet with Julian. Rayce walked over and took a seat next to Brooklyn.

Dawson nodded, and Porter exhaled a deep, long breath.

The laptop beeped, the screen covered in white snow. Brooklyn watched Porter fiddle with his fingers as he counted down the seconds and hoped his father didn't answer. That wasn't the case. Within seconds, a voice came through the static.

"My boy," Juneau rumbled. "I was hoping to hear from you much sooner."

The sight of his father took Porter off-guard, and he tripped over his words momentarily. "Dad...yeah, I uh, I didn't have any other way of getting a hold of you after we left Eleven."

"Of course you didn't. Have you got this thing out of your system yet? I've been watching my own son run around like some kind of wild animal for five days now. I hope you've had your fun."

"They aren't animals, Dad...I think you should..." Porter paused and his words faded.

Juneau stared at him. There was a pair of glasses, round and thin on the man's nose. His eyes weren't as bright as Porter's, but they were the same shape. He had a bit of scruff around his mouth speckled with stray grey hairs.

"You think I should...? Go on, Porter. I don't have much time," Juneau said.

"I think you should stop. I want you to stop.

These people are my friends, and I can't pretend like I agree with this anymore. Please, please, just let them go, and you can work on another project."

"You know that isn't going to happen," Juneau laughed. "I know what you're doing, and I know why you're doing it. I wanted to give you the chance to come back and celebrate the success we've had with this, but it looks like you've already compromised that, haven't you?"

Porter's mouth zipped shut, and his eyes narrowed.

"I have been watching you since the night you left," Juneau said through a sigh. "And it looks like these Omens are some of the strongest we have. The training will continue. I'm assuming you used the failsafe, correct?"

Porter paused and then nodded.

"And obviously your system has welcomed the virus. You know what that means, don't you, son?"

"It means I'm a part of this."

"This is an understatement, Porter. This is the future, and you haven't become a part of it. You've redefined it. Thank you for delivering the Omens to me. We'll take it from here."

Dawson straightened his back, and Brooklyn's heart leapt into her throat.

"Don't do this!" Porter blurted, eyes wide, filled with hope and love and maybe even admiration. "You're a good man, Dad. Please, don't do this!"

"It's done, Porter." Juneau sat back in his chair. He looked sad for a moment, head tilted to the side, palms pressed together. He stared at Porter and said, "Goodbye." The video on the screen cracked with static.

The sound of thrashing heartbeats was overwhelming. Brooklyn got to her feet as quickly as she could and waited for someone to speak. She wanted direction, an idea, a way out, but it sounded like no matter where they went it wasn't going to guarantee an escape.

"They're gonna find us," Porter said. His anxiety was thick like smoke; it tinged her tongue like rotten grapefruit, sour and tangy. "We either stay or we go, and we need to make that decision right now."

"We go, then," Dawson said. "Everyone? Yes? No?"

"Yeah, let's beat it," Amber said. "We'll get as far as we can, and then we'll fight."

"Looks like that's our best plan," Julian added.

Dawson nodded. "Get to the cars."

Brooklyn turned to make her way toward the exit, but she felt fingers around her hand, holding tight. It was Porter, taking even steps next to her. He gave her hand a light squeeze.

"They're gonna catch us," he whispered.

"Yeah," Brooklyn said quietly. "I think we all know that."

"Whatever happens, I want you to…"

"No," Brooklyn hissed. "Don't say anything."

"If something happens to me…"

Brooklyn stopped and turned on her heels. "Something is going to happen to all of us. And it's going to be the worst thing that we've ever been through, but I'm not in any way, shape, or form going to say goodbye to you or anyone else right

273

now."

"That's not what I was going to say," he protested angrily.

"Well whatever it is, you can save it, okay?"

Porter chewed on his bottom lip and stayed quiet, following as she hurried toward the door.

Amber, Charlie, and Rayce climbed into the large white Escalade while Porter, Julian, Dawson, and Brooklyn piled into the truck. The walkie-talkies they'd made use of when they'd left the first camp were out of juice, which meant they had no way to communicate back and forth.

"Wouldn't it make more sense for us all to get in the big white one?" Julian asked.

"No," Dawson breathed. "It'll be better for us to be in separate cars. If they get a hold of one group, it might give the others enough time to make it out."

Rayce made sure everyone in his car was situated then hopped out of the driver's seat and jogged over to the truck.

"Where we goin'?" he asked.

Dawson tried to think on his feet, but it was difficult to come up with anything. They were at a complete loss, trapped like rats in a maze.

"We go north toward Canada," Dawson said.

Rayce looked scared but he nodded. "I'm followin' you." His gaze traveled to the back seat where Julian was sitting and rested there for a moment. There was a very real possibility that none of them would see each other again.

"They've got good seafood up there, I hear," Rayce said.

Julian nodded, scared. "Yeah?"

"Yeah, I'm takin' you when we're outta this mess."

"Yeah, you are. When we make it out of this."

Rayce nodded, looking up and down Julian's face, and then he walked back to the white Escalade and slid into the driver's seat.

Brooklyn thought it was a good idea not to say goodbye because of just how permanent that goodbye could be. She turned around and looked out the back window. Amber was in the front seat, looking as tough as always. Her eyes were strong, and her back was straight. She was twirling one of her throwing knives between her fingers and winked at Brooklyn.

"Let's go," Dawson said.

The truck lurched forward. Brooklyn fumbled to find Julian's hand in the back seat. He gripped it tight and scooted closer to her. They didn't need to say anything. It'd always been the same deal with them. They don't leave without each other. In the end, whatever happened, whoever they lost, they didn't lose each other.

It was early afternoon, but the fog outside was grim, darkening the little bit of light that shined through the clouds. The docks weren't crowded and as they drove toward the end where the path merged with the main road. Brooklyn thought maybe they had a chance to escape. Maybe they'd left in enough time to bypass Juneau and his people.

The mist was thick. They made the turn on to the main road and saw a set of four black vans idling next to the sidewalk.

"That's them isn't it?" Dawson said.

Porter gnawed on his lip. "Yeah that has to be them."

"Julian, grab the bag under my seat," Dawson said over his shoulder.

Julian reached down and unzipped it. There was an array of different guns and knives.

"Where'd you get all these?" Julian said as he lifted up one of the sleek black pistols.

"Camp Fourteen," Dawson said. "Rayce has a bag in his car too."

"And you want us to do what with them?" Julian asked.

Dawson wasn't shy about speed and slammed his foot down on the gas as they drove down the road toward the highway. Brooklyn wasn't wearing a seat belt and almost toppled over into Julian. She looked behind her out the window. Rayce was keeping pace behind them. The four vans sped up and drove parallel to the truck, two on each side.

"If they get close enough, shoot them," Dawson said.

Porter immediately shook his head, "We can't risk that—there's innocent people everywhere. What if a bullet strays off and hits a kid or something?"

"That's why I said if they get close enough," Dawson repeated.

Brooklyn reached down by Julian's feet and grabbed one of the guns. She handed it to Porter, who was reluctant to take it, and then grabbed one for herself

"You think they wouldn't leave a bunch of guns with military-trained super humans," Julian mumbled as he strapped a large knife to his belt.

Brooklyn stared out the window. Her heart pounded. Adrenaline rushed into her fingertips, and her thoughts exploded from whispers into screams. Every natural part of her wanted to clam up, to give in to being out of control. That would have been the appropriate reaction, distress, tears, and belligerence. But she was balanced. Her focus was sharp, and she felt every muscle in her body poised on a trip wire, ready to fight.

It was a chilling realization to accept that she was built for this.

"They're gonna close you off," Porter hissed.

The vans pulled ahead and swooped in front of the truck as they came up on the exit toward the highway.

"I'm gonna hit them," Dawson warned.

"Maybe try not to hit them," Julian protested weakly.

"No, I'm gonna hit them," Dawson reiterated.

Dawson sped up until they were just inches from the closest van's bumper and then rammed into it.

Brooklyn clutched the top of Porter's seat to brace herself.

"Close enough?" Dawson shouted at Porter.

Porter clicked the safety off on his gun, but Brooklyn could tell that he was extremely hesitant about using it. She understood why. Not only were there other people around, but no matter how evil of a man Juneau was, he was still Porter's father, and he was in one of those vans.

Brooklyn rolled down her window and slid out to sit on the edge. Her legs were still inside the truck, but the rest of her body was propped on the frame of the door. Julian scrambled to hold her legs while she aimed the gun at the van in front of them.

The first shot ricocheted off the window.

She cursed and tried to shoot at the tires instead, but the van swerved away.

Julian pulled her back inside.

"They have bulletproof glass," Brooklyn said.

"Wonderful," Dawson groaned.

They passed the exit for the highway, and Dawson weaved around another set of cars. They were getting closer to populated parts of the city, which was something they wanted to avoid altogether.

"I'm taking the back roads," Dawson said. "There are some alleys around here where we might be able to lose them."

"That's also a good way to get caught in a dead end," Porter said.

"Don't have a choice," Dawson said. He made another sharp turn, and Brooklyn fell to the side against the window.

They turned down a road behind a gas station and then cut through a parking garage. Rayce drove around the parking garage and met them on the other side. All four vans kept accelerating steadily, staying right on their tails.

"We're not gonna get out of this," Julian said.

Brooklyn swatted him.

"I'm serious!" He gulped down some air. "We might just wanna let them take us so no one gets hurt."

"We're not doing that," Dawson said sternly.

"No, we aren't doing that," Brooklyn said as she glared at Julian. "Try and get toward the outskirts of the city. Maybe we can lose them if we take some of the trails; our cars can make it in the dirt."

"Good idea," Dawson turned the wheel and directed the truck down an alley toward the back lot of a church.

Seattle was a big place, and Brooklyn hadn't been used to the over-crowded nonsense of city life in a very long time. San Diego seemed so far away; even the memory of it was fuzzy. The constant strolls down Gaslamp district, taking a trolley to the beach, crashing pool parties at the resorts, it might as well have been an alternate universe.

The honking car horns, the screech of tires, and the sound of pelting rain made her flinch. The symphony of sounds on top of her heightened senses made her head spin and her heart pound faster. Even though she was impossibly focused, it constantly felt like she was tipping over the first drop on a rollercoaster. She felt like a muscle car, needle in the red, tires spinning, waiting to launch.

Brooklyn leaned over Julian's lap so she could see out the window where Rayce was driving next to them on the wrong side of the road. He swerved out of the way of oncoming traffic and got back behind Dawson.

"Problem is I don't know how to get out of this city," Dawson said as he turned down another road.

They'd driven past a school, a hardware store, several coffee joints, and a Ferris wheel.

"If you can get to the freeway, then we can get there," Brooklyn said.

"Yeah, been tryin' to do that!"

The vans pulled in front of them again. Dawson gasped, turned the wheel, and made another short but direct turn into an alley.

Rayce wasn't as quick. The Escalade sped past the alley, passing them. Brooklyn craned her neck, catching sight of something metallic and shiny. It slid out of the door of one of the vans, hitting the asphalt.

"They didn't make it!" Brooklyn shouted.

Dawson shoved the truck into reverse and pulled back out on to the road just in time to watch Rayce drive over a shark-mouthed spike strip.

Chapter Thirty-Five

It was over. Brooklyn was sure of it.

The tires on the Escalade shredded instantly, and the large vehicle came to a stop in the middle of the road.

"What do we do?" Brooklyn squealed.

"Hit the van," Porter said. He unbuckled his seatbelt and hopped out of the idling truck with his gun drawn.

"Wait! What?" Dawson yelled.

Sirens wailed in the distance, and car horns blared all around them.

Brooklyn wanted to chase after Porter and pull him back into the truck, but Julian had a firm grip on her leg.

"I think he actually wants you to run into one of those vans," Julian said to no one in particular.

"That's insane," Dawson said and flipped on the windshield wipers as the rain intensified.

The plan involved two cars to prevent this situation from playing out. The entire point of it was to allow an escape for the group that wasn't compromised. But as they watched the Escalade sit dormant in the middle of the street, none of them could move. Dawson could have driven away; they could have made it out of Seattle, kept running. But being separated again was a worse fate than going down fighting together.

"What the hell is he thinking?" Brooklyn whispered as she watched Porter walk slowly toward the two vans in front of the Escalade.

The other two black vans pulled up behind the truck in the middle of the road.

"He's distracting them," Dawson said thoughtfully.

The truck jolted forward when Dawson stepped on the gas, and Brooklyn yelped, falling back in the seat.

"Hold on!"

It happened so fast. First Brooklyn heard the raindrops hit the windshield, one right after the other, and then muffled cries erupted from the van they were about to hit. Lastly, it was the sound of crunching metal as the vehicles collided. Then a gunshot as the van was pushed forward. Porter's voice, prominent through the orchestra of sounds, boomed as he yelled, "Charlie! Get out! Get out of here!"

Brooklyn gasped as the back door next to her swung open. She was pushed to the side, falling into Julian, and felt Charlie topple in beside her.

Gunshots sounded like fireworks. Brooklyn sat up and looked over the center console.

Amber and Rayce jumped into the bed of the truck. Porter limped backward toward the passenger door, holding on to the top of his leg.

Soldiers emerged from the vans. Their faces were covered in shielded black helmets and black armored chest pieces. Dark grey pants were shoved into knee high leather boots and long-barreled guns were clasped in their hands. The weapons were odd; Brooklyn had never seen a gun like the ones they were carrying.

Porter finally got back in the truck, and as soon as he pulled the door shut, Dawson stepped on the gas. This time, he pointed the truck directly at the black-clad soldiers.

"What are those things that they're carrying?" Brooklyn asked.

Porter pressed both his hands over the top of his thigh.

"Rubber bullets and gas bombs," Porter said. His eyes squeezed shut—his breathing came in short, painful bursts.

"You got shot!" She scrambled over the center console to get a better look, but Porter wouldn't move his hand.

"Those rubber bullets are a bitch," he fumed. There was no blood, but she could imagine what pelted with one of those at such a close proximity would feel like. Porter had a nasty bruise to look forward to, but the mark wouldn't be there for long. Not with the virus changing his genetic makeup.

The soldiers didn't move until the very last second, finally diving out of the way after Dawson's side mirror clipped one of their helmets. They sped off with the last two vans following closely behind them.

"Why were you so stupid?" Brooklyn barked at Porter and slapped his arm.

He flinched away from her. "Don't hit me for trying to save our friends!"

"Thank you," Charlie said. She tried to catch her breath and leaned against the seat with her eyes closed. "I expected you guys to take off while you had the chance."

"Yeah, well." Dawson turned the wheel and took a sudden right turn. "We decided to stick together for once."

Rayce and Amber tried to stay steady as they sat in the bed of the truck. Dawson made turn after turn, weaving in and out of traffic, trying to shake Juneau's soldiers. Brooklyn imagined this was what it might be like during hunting season, when packs of wolves ran through their own homes, desperate to stay alive.

She imagined that last moment, when Juneau's men took her, and she imagined a frightened animal looking at the dark void of the barrel of a gun, teeth bared.

Amber's voice was muffled by the wind, but Brooklyn heard her yelling, "I think ya lost 'em! Keep going!"

The vans were gone, blocked out by rows and rows of cars that either slowed down or moved out of the way for Dawson when they caught sight of him dipping in and out of traffic.

"Did we lose them?" Dawson asked hopefully.

"I think so," Brooklyn said.

As soon as the tightness in her chest began to loosen and the anxiety knotted at the base of her spine started to unwind, everything once again came crashing down around them.

An ear-splitting howl echoed from one of the side streets they were about to pass. The tension in the car spiked. Everyone knew what it was.

"They brought Surrogates? Seriously?" Julian groaned.

The Surros sprinted out of the rain and hurtled themselves at the truck. The impact of their lithe bodies was enough to almost knock it over. Dawson slammed on the brakes when a Surro's fist plunged through the windshield, shattering it.

Charlie kicked the door open and was torn out of the car when a large Surro grabbed her arm and tossed her effortlessly from the truck. Brooklyn lifted her gun and fired. Charlie squirmed, avoiding the Surro's body when it fell toward the asphalt.

"Are you okay?" Brooklyn shouted as she jumped out of the truck.

Charlie got back on her feet. "I am now."

The Surros were everywhere, running out of the shadows, jumping on the roof of the truck, and crawling out from beneath it.

Brooklyn fired bullet after bullet, aiming for the temple, the neck, the chest, until one Surro climbed up on to the hood of the truck and leapt on to her back. She tried to brace herself, was knocked flat on the ground. The concrete tore at her cheek. The weight on her back pressed down, causing her lungs to heave, burning for air. Her ribs screamed, a pain in her chest splintering through the rest of her body. The force of two bony knees held her down against the ground.

Thick black blood leaked from its lips, dripped down onto her neck like tar. She tried to wiggle free, knuckles bleach white from excruciation. She hadn't given up, but the pain in her chest was getting exceedingly worse. She yelped, eyes stinging with tears when the Surro ground its knees into her lower back, a hand fisted in her hair, pressing her face into the concrete.

The sound of its heavy breathing and vicious growls were cut short. Brooklyn gasped, breath coming a little easier. She felt the Surro struggle as some of its weight lifted off of her. She rolled out from underneath it, gazing up at Charlie, who held the creature up by a thin silver wire, a garrote imbedded in the meat of its throat.

"Get up!" Charlie said. The body of the Surro slumped. Brooklyn pushed herself back to her feet. "Amber ran in that building!"

There was a sharp pain that burrowed in Brooklyn's left side, but she ignored it.

"Rayce ran in after her, come on! Let's get out of here!" Charlie yelled.

Brooklyn tried to run, but the pain in her ribs protested. She limped along next to Charlie until they made it to the side door.

Charlie opened the door and ran inside. Brooklyn held it open with one hand while the other moved down to clutch her side. She didn't know what the wound consisted of, whether something was broken or ruptured, but whatever it was, it wasn't good.

Porter's voice startled her. She turned around with her gun pointed right at his forehead.

"Hey, Brooklyn, get inside!" He pushed her until

she stumbled backward.

"Where's Dawson?"

"He's in here! Julian went in after Rayce, and Dawson followed," Porter said.

Brooklyn's body convulsed and quivered. Porter could feel it. She hadn't moved her hand from where it was plastered over her side and gripped it tight, hoping if she kept her palm there it would magically disappear. The pain was nearly unbearable, far worse than being shot. Her stomach dropped when her thoughts clicked into place and she realized her hand was slick with something warm and wet.

Porter held her out at arm's length in the dark room. "What's happened to you?"

"I don't know," she said. Her head started to spin from the pain.

The building was packed with people. Music thrummed from a DJ booth high up on the second floor. There was a dance floor packed with bodies moving and grinding to the high-energy beats. A bar was on the other side of it, lit up with neon lights and decorative bottles.

"What the hell is this place? It's the middle of the day," Brooklyn said.

Porter settled her against the nearest wall. She let her weight rest against it, thankful for a chance to relax.

"I think it's a one of those weird two to two clubs," he said. He reached out and found her hand. "Let me see it."

"It's just a scratch."

"Then let me see it," he repeated.

She moved her shaky hand away and saw it was caked with blood. Porter went from looking uneasy to completely aghast.

"Okay," he breathed, nodding to himself. "This is gonna hurt."

"What's wrong with me?" she asked and looked down at herself.

A piece of jagged white bone jutted through her shirt. Blood soaked all the way down her shirt, through her jacket and into her jeans. It was much worse than she'd first thought, and looking at it made it even more painful.

"Holy shit," Brooklyn gagged and turned her head away. "Is that...? What *is* that?"

"It's one of your ribs. I have to push it back into place or at least get it back under your skin."

"We don't have time for this. Just do it," she snarled.

Porter didn't give her any time to ready herself, which she was almost thankful for, and went straight for the bone. He used his thumb to slide the broken rib back into place, or get it as close as he could under the circumstances. It felt like electricity was lighting a fire to the entire left side of her body. The pain was excruciating.

She screamed, but Porter smothered the sound with his hand, shoving his palm over her mouth beneath her nostrils.

"Okay," he soothed. "It's okay. I'm done. You're okay."

Her whole body shook, but she forced life back into her legs and pushed off the wall. The pain gave her a little momentum, propelling her forward as she walked toward the crowd on the dancefloor. The club was huge, and even though she could see well in the dark, the neon lights made it hard for her to lock on to anyone she knew. She squinted, even lifted her nose to catch a scent other than the burn of alcohol or the chemical residue of recreational drugs.

Porter stayed behind her, his worry a damp floral scent. He was close enough that when she lost her footing he caught her.

"You might have punctured your lung." His lips were pressed right against her ear. She tried to stay steady, to take another step, but her chest throbbed. "Don't move. Just stay right here."

Porter was careful with her and took his time turning her around to face him.

"Where are your glasses?" Brooklyn asked.

He smiled, tired and worn. "Don't need 'em anymore."

The people moving on the dancefloor were full of energy. They twisted and turned, circled their hips, and let the music guide them. Right then, in that moment with Porter holding her up and the music vibrating their bodies, it became easy for Brooklyn to give up. She allowed herself to take a breath and rested her hand on Porter's face before she pulled him into a fierce kiss.

Their lips collided, and Brooklyn felt alive. His lips were chapped, but they molded against hers well enough. His hands dug into the bones of her hips, and she winced when he pulled her in closer. Her chest was stinging, and her head was spinning, but kissing Porter was something she'd put off for too long.

It felt just as right as she always thought it would, like sleeping in on a Sunday morning and diving off a cliff, plunging into clear water. It was easy to picture them together, barefoot on hardwood floors in an apartment by the sea. She thought of what it might be like to wake up in another life with him. She thought of what it would be like to kiss him for the hell of it and not because it might be her only chance.

Brooklyn opened her eyes when he pulled away, but the swell of her bottom lip was still snug between his teeth.

They'd both heard it, the inevitable. The screams from the people around them. The music coming to an abrupt stop. They knew what was next.

Porter drew his gun first. Brooklyn spun around and leaned against his chest with her gun aimed at the group of soldiers standing in a row by the bar.

Juneau stood in front of them, his smile smug and eyes slanted mischievously.

Dawson, Julian, and Amber were with them. Large black cuffs covered their hands like oval gloves, and each one of them had a soldier standing behind them with an electric prod poised an inch from their necks.

"I see why now!" Juneau laughed and clapped his hands. "You thought you could actually tame one enough to date? Ambitious like always, Porter."

Porter didn't lower his gun.

"I'm sure Miss Harper would rather not see her friends here get hurt, though, I presume? Isn't that right?"

Brooklyn's hand was trembling from the pain in her chest. She wanted to shoot him. It was all she could think about. But she knew that even if she did take his life, there was someone else trained and capable waiting to take his place.

"Shoot this little bitch ass!" Amber cursed when the soldier behind her jabbed the tip of the prodder against her neck and shocked her.

Porter gripped Brooklyn's waist.

"Come with me. We'll get you cleaned up and fed. You can rest, get back into training, and we can talk. I'd like to get to know all of you," Juneau said pleasantly. He had his arms open wide in some kind of mock invitation. His smile was devious, and the suit he was wearing, stitched with expensive thread, made Brooklyn want to vomit.

"We're not your belongings," Brooklyn bit.

Her arm sank, but she flinched and forced it back up, gun still aimed right at Juneau's head.

"Of course not," Juneau said. He pouted and frowned. "We're all friends here."

Brooklyn coughed. The coppery taste of blood filled her mouth. Her head spun, thoughts swimming in murky water. She resisted the feeling of Porter taking on more and more of her weight. But it was inevitable. Her eyes started to close—her lungs squeezed tight, reaching for air.

They didn't have a choice. It was really over this time.

The last thing Brooklyn heard was her gun clattering to the floor, fingertips numb when she dropped it, and Porter's voice yelling her name as the soldiers dragged him away.

Chapter Thirty-Six

Everything was blurry, distorted by white light.

The voices around her came in and out like someone was playing with the volume on a pair of speakers.

Cold hands covered in latex grabbed her arms and pulled her body this way and that, but Brooklyn couldn't will her arms or legs to move. She was stuck. She was paralyzed, completely immobile. She'd been taken.

She couldn't keep her eyes open for more than a few seconds at a time. She blinked once. Twice. Three times and then finally was able to squint. The only thing she could see besides the bright honeycomb light directly above her was the ceiling. A hand wrapped in a blue glove obscured her vision.

Her neck felt heavy as she pushed her chin and looked to the side. There was a bed, white sheets, metal cuffs, long poles...IVs filled with bags of swirling grey liquid. Someone was there, lying in it. Brooklyn opened her eyes a little more.

Dark skin. Shaved head. Rayce.

She wanted to lurch forward off of the cold slab she was lying on, but the two sets of blue gloves forced her back down. She struggled, squirmed, tried to yell for help, but there was nothing, absolute nothing. No sound left her lips—she didn't even know if her mouth had opened. Brooklyn couldn't find them. Her eyes bounced around the unfamiliar space, the empty room, the tiny windows shielded by black window covers. The seating. A plane. She was on a plane.

Her mind went to Porter first, the memory of his lips parting from hers, and then she thought of Dawson, Julian, Amber, and Charlie. She couldn't find them.

The pain in her side sparked, prompting the memory of Porter's thumb shoving her rib back underneath her skin, and she whimpered.

"Miss Harper, stay still. You broke a couple ribs, and we're draining your lung right now," a feminine voice came from behind a medical mask.

Two nurses looked down at her.

She wanted to talk, but her tongue flopped numbly and wouldn't cooperate. All she could do was whine.

"This one's strong," one of the nurses said softly. "One of the strongest we've collected."

"What about that girl that came in a few days ago? Chest wound, scar on her lip?"

Brooklyn's heart sped up, her stomach twisted, and she opened her eyes wide. She thrashed against the metal table, but the straps kept her trapped. She struggled to make her body work against whatever drugs they'd been pumping her full of, willed her mind to clear.

One of the nurses lowered a clear mask over her face.

"The other one from Eleven? Yeah, she's our most promising."

Brooklyn gasped. Oxygen, clean and cold, filled her lungs. Sleeping gas followed, its taste stale and bitter.

Gabriel was alive.

Chapter Thirty-Seven

A long hallway stretched toward a set of steel double doors. The linoleum floor that led to them was crisp and chilled. The walls were too clean, a blanket of pearl that made the space never-ending and ominous. There was nothing to listen to, no music, and no people, just absolute stillness. Tall white doors lined each wall, and small oval windows allowed the outside to peer in.

Muffled voices spoke freely behind the set of steels doors. Two weathered hands pushed them open.

"Ladies!"

Juneau Malloy's shoes clicked against the smooth floor. His smile was filled with emptiness, but an aura of excitement beamed around him. His glasses were folded up and hung from the collar of his onyx dress shirt. He tapped his fingers against the table in the center of the room and chuckled to himself, looking at the women sitting on the other side of it.

"I haven't seen potential like you two in quite

some time. We've had help developing a program that will give your minds a good push. You'll get the chance to build up a proper tolerance to any extraction you might face in the field. I'm sure I can count on you both to comply? I would hope more than anything that you would be excited! Opportunities like these don't come around often, do they?"

Stephanie's back straightened. Her hair was groomed into long red ringlets. Her tiny pointed chin bobbed in a nod, pale hands folded neatly in her lap. "I don't see a problem. I'm available for training immediately."

Juneau grinned and sat down in a metal chair. He looked across, just to the right of Stephanie and raised his brows. "And you, Miss Serisky?"

Gabriel's mouth twitched. She pulled at the cuffs of the navy blue blazer she wore. Her lips were lined and coated in deep red lipstick; black eyeliner, thick and sharp, swept across her eyelids.

"You know my terms," Gabriel said through a bored sigh, running her hand through her hair.

Juneau slid a tall stack of papers toward her. "Of course, and as I told you, ISO will do its best to accommodate those terms."

He held his hand out to her, but she ignored him and focused on the bland, distorted reflection of herself in the chrome table.

"This is what you were born for," Juneau added. "This is your destiny."

Gabriel smirked.

"I don't have a destiny," she said. Her nails clicked against the table, long and perfectly manicured.

She lifted them up and eyed them carefully, fingers stretched out in the light.

"Pretty color," Stephanie mused, gesturing to Gabriel's fingernail polish.

Gabriel shook her head. "I don't like it."

Juneau clasped his hands together. "They'll be ready for simulation training soon, by the way. Miss Harper's time in the medical bay is almost up."

Gabriel continued to ignore him. Instead, she focused on the light dancing across the shine of her nails, painted a bright canary yellow.

Acknowledgments

I'd like to thank a multitude of people who helped me produce Omen Operation. This book would not have been possible without the team at Limitless Publishing, thank you for taking on The Isolation Series and giving my dreams a voice. I'd also like to mention my editors Matthew Devine and Darryl Cook, who took a lumpy piece of coal and helped me transform it into a diamond. I'd like to give a special shout out to Deranged Doctor Designs for the beautiful cover art work. Last but not least, to my family, friends, and readers, the overwhelming support I have received from all of you is what kept me writing when I was convinced giving up would be easier, and your continuous support is what will keep me writing from this day forward.

About the Author

Taylor Brooke is the author of the upcoming sci-fi adventure trilogy The Isolation Series. She started out as a freelance makeup artist, and quickly discovered her love of elves, zombies, mermaids, kaiju, and monsters of all kinds. After receiving eight professional certifications in special effects makeup, working on countless projects, and fleshing out a multitude of fantastical creatures, she turned her imagination back to her one true love-books. Taylor has had a knack for writing since she was a little girl, and received recognition for her skills throughout grade school and junior college. When she's not nestled in a blanket typing away on her laptop, she can be found haunting the local bookstore with a cup of steaming hot tea in her hands, scanning the shelves for new reads, or hiking one of the many mountains that surround her home of Bend Oregon.

Twitter:
https://twitter.com/taysalion

Website:
http://lion--ness.tumblr.com/